# The Farm

Randy O'Brien

# The Farm

Addison & Highsmith

# Addison & Highsmith Publishers

Las Vegas ◊ Chicago ◊ Palm Beach

Published in the United States of America by
Histria Books
7181 N. Hualapai Way, Ste. 130-86
Las Vegas, NV 89166 USA
HistriaBooks.com

Addison & Highsmith is an imprint of Histria Books. Titles published under the imprints of Histria Books are distributed worldwide.

Library of Congress Control Number: 2023939585


ISBN 978-1-59211-323-1 (hardcover)
ISBN 978-1-59211-335-4 (eBook)

# Dedication

Thanks to my editor Dr. Kurt Brackob for his support and professionalism. Thanks to Diana Livesay for being thoughtful and for her intellect. Thanks to Dr. Elizabeth Taylor for her insight into Camp Forrest. Thank you to my grandmother and my aunts for their love and guidance. Thanks to my mother and father for their belief in me and to my sister Cindy for her continued support and love. Thanks to Deb Scally for her photographic skills. Thanks to my daughter Molly for bringing light and happiness and to my darling wife, Beth, who brings joy and laughter into my life.

# Chapter 1

Olaf made the slightest movement with his hand as it rested on the blanket. He had turned it over so the palm pointed to his cot. He moved it back and forth, parallel to the floor. It was a gesture he hoped the medic standing near him would take as a sign of surrender.

The SS soldier had been in pain for hours and was ready to die. He had sworn an oath to the Fatherland and believed in his heart that it was his duty to serve until death took him to "Himmel," the German word that translated to both Heaven and sky.

But there was too much noise and commotion in the makeshift hospital, and he could barely speak. The doctor, the nurses, and Stanley, the medic that had tended to Olaf on his journey from the battlefield to this makeshift hospital, all failed to notice Olaf's gesture.

Stanley pointed the triage doctor toward the boy's open wound, likely caused by a bayonet. The young medic watched the doctor pull his scarf tighter around his neck against the temperature that had hovered well below freezing for the last five days. While the cold caused severe trench foot and frostbite cases for some men, Stanley knew from his experience in the field that the below-freezing temperatures had likely saved this boy's life. His blood had left his extremities and slowed the flow to his wounded thigh. Dirt and blood covered the boy's uniform, and Stanley could smell sweat, vomit, and the coppery aroma of blood.

Stanley saw a tattoo on the inside of the soldier's right forearm. Black ink and his pale skin made the three interlocking triangles of the Valknut appear in stark contrast with the brown blanket.

The medic had no idea that wearing this symbol on Olaf's body was a family tradition. German pragmatism and Olaf, sometimes called Ollie by his friends, believed in family honor and wisdom gained through experience.

Olaf was an uncommon German first name. He'd been called Olaf after his Swedish mother's grandfather. This caused him to be teased at school, but he knew he was German, through and through, no matter the origin of his name.

Earlier, Stanley was one of the stretcher-bearers who had carried him from the bomb-pocked field. Stanley's job involved dodging bullets and bombs as he and his friend, John, dashed around battlefields and through foxholes.

He wore the red cross on a white square on his helmet and armband, but no bullet respected that symbol. He'd felt the 'whizz' of rounds overhead and once fell and dropped a man as an aerial bomb landed thirty feet to his left. John temporarily lost his hearing in his right ear during that run. The boys tried to perform the 'worst job' in the Army with skill and precision, but it wasn't easy and, most times, impossible.

Olaf had felt every bump and turn but wouldn't let his enemy know he was in pain as his rescuers ran through the rough terrain. Later, Stanley and John strapped the soldier to the back of a jeep and drove to the abandoned church that had been commandeered as a field hospital.

The church initially had four spires. A few days ago, Stanley crouched near the altar, head covered, when a Luftwaffe bombing run took down the steeple on the south side. Today, the remaining spires on the north side waited for the early morning sun to melt off the night's latest snowfall.

Stanley knew cold weather from growing up in Tennessee, but he'd had a warm coat, hat, and gloves there. Unfortunately, the Army failed to provide such materials for soldiers during what was eventually determined to be one of the coldest winters on record in Europe.

John and Stanley took the soldier from the jeep through the tall, open door and deposited him in front of the altar. Stanley saw wounded men covering much of the floor, many wrapped in thin, gray blankets. He watched a doctor go from man to man, diagnose each soldier's condition, and determine his place in line.

On the jeep, Stanley had watched Olaf's sandy blond hair flutter in the icy breeze. His high cheekbones and blue eyes made him an example of the personification of the Aryan race advocated by the Fuhrer. He had been severely wounded and captured just miles from here. What was the name of the town? Malmedy. Stanley had no idea where the township was or was familiar with the name, only that it was in Belgium.

Olaf considered Belgium captured territory and believed in protecting the Fatherland and its assets with his last breath. He knew what he was fighting for was pure and true. He challenged the notion that the Nazi attempt to conquer the world was ending and the war would likely be over soon with Germany's victory. He wanted to lay down his life for his Fuhrer. He hoped the gesture he'd made to the doctor, his movement indicating surrender to his fate, would allow this to happen.

Stanley had never seen such a signal where a patient wanted to refuse treatment. Still, he'd seen so many strange and unexplainable things during his service as a medic that he knew this refusal of treatment wasn't an option. Stanley had taken an oath to help relieve suffering and to aid in natural healing whenever and wherever he could, without regard to race, color, or an enemy of America.

Stanley Comer saw the gesture even though the surgeon didn't. Still, he was serious about his commitment to saving lives less than ten miles from what would later be deemed the Battle of the Bulge, and he wasn't about to break that commitment now. But the action shocked him, and Stanley thought he'd seen just about everything in his time as an Army medic.

The medic knew he would never be able to clear that from his memory. He began to work on his patient, motioning to the nurse that it was time to put the prisoner under anesthesia.

"What is your name?" Stanley asked. A puzzled look crossed Olaf's face. He had picked up a few English phrases during the war, but this question had somehow never come up. The medic pointed to his chest and said, "I'm Stanley."

He saw the soldier frown with comprehension. "Olaf Weber," he said slowly between tight lips, "Ollie."

"All righty then," Stanley said. He motioned to the nurse, and she poured ether over the cotton mask.

Stanley caught a glance from the surgeon two tables over. He tipped his chin toward the vaulted ceiling as if indicating that death had claimed another soul to Heaven. The gesture had become the signal that he was about to move to his next patient. He raised his chin, and Stanley saw the disappointment in the surgeon's eyes, indicating that he'd lost another patient.

Stanley's gaze moved from the doctor to the nurse at the head of the table. She was tall, slim, and attractive, with shiny black hair. Just weeks before, she had lived in England as an Italian refugee, and now she was using her nursing skills to help save lives. She was frightened by the assignment but wanted to assist in the war effort, and she knew nurses were needed. Everyone, no matter their talent or skill, wanted to help. Moreover, she believed she was being sent to a 'safe' place, given the terrain and the fact that the German army was unlikely to move through the Ardennes Forest. She was wrong.

The triage doctor had assured Olaf in German that the wound in his leg would likely require amputation. Still, he would live and return home someday after the war.

"Beginnen sie mit zehn neun acht sieben," Stanley said to the soldier as the nurse approached with the ether. He was using one of the few phrases in German he'd picked up in his time at the hospital, "begin with ten, nine, eight..." but patients rarely needed to count down past seven.

Dr. Harold Jones was one of a handful of Black surgeons in the medical corp. He'd worked with Stanley, a brave young man with a soft Tennessee accent, for several weeks. Unfortunately, Harold's efforts were occasionally met with sneers by his fellow soldiers. You might think that someone trying to save your life might help keep your prejudice in check, but on more than one occasion, a wounded man would rebel against a 'nigger' doctor working on them.

This was Harold's first German soldier, and he expected a representative of the master race would reject his efforts to aid him. Ollie wanted to die for his country, and any doctor would be met with the same rejection as Harold. Meanwhile, Harold just took the glare as Ollie looked up at him from his cot as something akin to the hatred he'd fielded from the American soldiers. "*This boy's feelings don't matter,*" Harold thought, "*my job is to fix what's put in front of me.*"

The surgeon remembered he had read an article in a journal a year ago. Yes, he had that kind of memory. It was about a new surgery technique that might save the boy's leg. But, of course, it would probably be something he should run by his superior. Still, he remembered a saying from his favorite biology teacher at Howard, "It's better to beg forgiveness than to seek denial."

Stanley worked alongside the team of three nurses and the surgeon deep into the night. In the distance, he heard muffled explosions as tanks rumbled through cobblestone streets just outside the ancient stone building.

It was moments when the action seemed closest that Stanley would think of home. He remembered the strong chin and large, brown eyes of the wife he'd left in Tennessee. The beautiful Millie had promised she'd be waiting for him and that when he returned, they'd start the family they both had talked about with enthusiasm and hope.

Harold looked at the gaping wound in the boy's leg. Given the field conditions, he wondered if the surgeon could pull off this medical miracle. Dr. Jones took a bit of blood vessel from the uninjured left leg and sewed it to the sheared-off piece of artery currently clamped and throbbing. Stanley knew Harold would save the leg if he could stretch the tissue.

Throughout history, battlefield medical marvels born of necessity created new techniques for the surgeon's repertoire. Harold liked the idea that his name might become synonymous with the new procedure. He had been inspired by his father, a plumber. He'd worked summers with the old man and had seen him create wonders when the materials were either the wrong size or wouldn't fit. For example, he saw his father use 'C' clamps, rubber tubes, and welding to fix seemingly impossible leaks.

Would that translate to his son working as an Army doctor? Time would tell, and in the case of this German soldier, probably in two or three days. Harold looked down into the opening and marveled at the intricate stitching and the delicate connections. Then, he would let Stanley sew up the leg.

Stanley stood, hands steady and eyes fixed on the wound. He had impressed the surgeon. Harold would suggest over chow that night that the young man pursue medicine as a profession after the war. He might even write a letter of recommendation if Stanley thought it might help.

As to the patient, once his condition stabilized, he'd be processed and eventually end up in a prisoner of war camp, likely in England or possibly America. Then, if all went well, Olaf would be shipped off for healing and rehabilitation in forty-eight hours.

Of course, there wasn't a holding facility for that kind of help here on the front, so, ironically, the German would get a ticket to America. It wasn't fair, and, in Stanley's mind, it was ironic that the one person that likely didn't want to go to America was the one who would be first on the boat.

# Chapter 2

Snaps stood in front of the full-length mirror in the upstairs hallway and sang softly into her hairbrush. She had already finished her morning ritual of one hundred strokes through her coal-black hair. It was something she'd seen her mother do every night, and the practice was passed down to the next generation.

She didn't want to wake up her sisters, who slept in the next room or the rest of the house, but she knew that her mother was likely already awake and preparing for the day. So she put the hairbrush on top of her dresser.

Snaps, a loving nickname given to her by her father, had a magnetic personality. Her real name was Ginger, and she was a spicy young woman who radiated her own kind of light when she was on stage. Whenever the spotlight hit her, she felt like she'd finally found her place in the world.

She placed her feet a bit wider than her shoulders and stared at her reflection. She had big, expressive brown eyes and arched brows. Her cheekbones accentuated her wide smile and bright, white teeth. She would jut her chin out on stage, believing it elongated her face and projected her features to the back row of the theater.

She had played various parts as an actress and singer in the past, and tonight, she'd lead the cast through a dress rehearsal. Her mother and sisters would be there to support her on Saturday, but she knew they wouldn't be there on stage with her, and it was up to her to tell the story, sing the songs, and entertain the crowd.

The stage was her calling, her reason for living. She'd performed for the family since she was a small child. Laughing, joking, singing, dancing, doing impressions of family members and voices she'd heard on the radio. She taught herself tap dancing after reading a book. She memorized poetry and, with help from a loving freshman English teacher, Mrs. Northcutt, soliloquies from Shakespeare's famous plays.

Snaps knew Hamlet's speech asking the most crucial question in life and performed it frequently. She'd found the perfect natural proscenium near a meadow on the farm and often practiced to the stream and trees on the back property.

"To be or not to be," she asked the resident rabbits and squirrels. "Whether 'tis nobler in the mind to suffer the slings and arrows of outrageous fortune, or take arms against a sea of troubles and by opposing end them."

She would stand on the limestone outcropping that was her place of solitude and reflection. Birds would leave the sky and look for a limb to sit on so they might enjoy the show. Crickets quieted and rested on blades of grass, guaranteeing they, too, would have a front-row seat.

"To die," she said with a sly and envious smile, "—to sleep, no more; and by sleep to say we end the heartache and the thousand natural shocks that flesh…"

She turned and plucked at the skin of her forearm.

"is heir to 'tis a consummation devoutly to be wish'd."

She closed her eyes and let the dying sun wash over the contours of her face. "To die, to sleep;" with no dramatic pause this time. "To sleep, perchance to dream," her large eyes flew open and darted around the small grassy meadow leading to the water's edge and said with a sly smile, "—ay, there's the rub:"

She slowed her approach even more, allowing a dirge-like cadence to pace her delivery as she said, "For in that sleep of death, what dreams may come?"

It was the question she knew there was no answer to yet. She had asked it in Sunday school, and the teacher fell into the standard Southern Baptist line of sitting at the right hand of God in Heaven forever. But that answer had never been enough for Snaps.

She continued, "When we have shuffled off this mortal coil, must give us pause—there's the respect that makes calamity of so long life."

Her elocution studies, again from a book she'd found in the school library, told her to open her mouth and enunciate. "For who would bear the whips and scorns of time?" she asked. "The oppressor's wrong, the proud man's contumely, the pangs of dispriz'd love, the law's delay, the insolence of office, and the spurns that patient merit of the unworthy takes."

She slowed again and turned as if imploring an adoring crowd of listeners. "When he himself might his quietus make with a bare bodkin? Who would fardels bear, to grunt and sweat under a weary life, but that the dread of something after death, the undiscovered country, from whose bourn no traveler returns?"

She allowed an upward lilt in her voice to encapsulate her delivery as she said, "Puzzles the will and makes us rather bear those ills we have than fly to others that we know not of?"

A small laugh as she recited, "Thus conscience does make cowards of us all, and thus the native hue of resolution is sickled," she mispronounced, "o'er with the pale cast of thought, and enterprises of great pitch and moment with this regard their currents turn away and lose the name of action."

She took a bow, ended the soliloquy, and removed an invisible hat. In her imagination, it was most likely adorned with long, colorful peacock feathers, and she let it sweep the top of her perch.

She listened to the water gurgling and a light wind rustling the trees. Was there another sound? She turned, squinted her eyes, and let her gaze sweep the small meadow and the gurgling waters below her. Was it a bobcat? There had been sightings in the neighborhood. Was it a bear? Too far from the Smoky Mountains for that. She chuckled and leaped from the rock.

It had been three days since her performance, and her tender, twisted ankle reminded her that she shouldn't take a leap like that again.

She stared at her image in the mirror and turned, her ears straining. "To be, or not to be?"

She heard her mother as she gathered the milk buckets just a floor below her. The clanging was muffled as much as possible because Mary Lou was a good mother who wanted to let her girls sleep. "Momma," Snaps whispered.

# Chapter 3

Millie lay in her bed and listened as the noise of the milk barrels faded toward the barn. Anne snored in the bed next to the door. She had read her new book from the library deep into the night, and Millie knew it would be some time before she was up and ready to perform her daily duties.

The eldest girl and the only married one wasn't fond of the chores on the farm, and she really didn't like cows. She'd help when it was her turn, and the other girls were too busy, but she had grown tired of farm life. She had the bright lights of the city in her eyes, and, in her mind, she was just months, maybe weeks, away from her husband coming home from the war. She believed he'd take her away from all this, and she'd never cut hay, weed the garden, or milk cows again.

As the oldest of the three girls, it would seem she would be the leader of the next generation, but that role had somehow fallen to Snaps. She made plans, delegated tasks, and expressed the sisters' needs in times of trouble. Anne was the negotiator and expressed outrage and support when the situation called for it.

But Millie married her high school sweetheart, Stanley Comer, just before he shipped off to Europe. She was the first to walk down the aisle, just weeks before Daddy passed away. She felt lucky he'd seen at least one of his girls marry, and to a young man he liked and respected.

Daddy was an infantryman in the Great War. While he had plenty of stories to tell, the girls had asked many times, he constantly checked with Mary Lou first, and she always shook her head no. Now that father was gone, Millie wished she'd insisted on hearing about his life in the trenches and how that had shaped his world view. Sometimes he exploded at the slightest little upset, an odd sound, or an unexplained shadow. Still, Brother was usually there, and Daddy calmed down.

Millie turned over, pushed the sheet and quilt from her body, and forced herself out of bed. She knew time was wasting, and chores like house cleaning, cooking, and laundry, had to be done. Today, she would shoulder much of the burden of the truck garden in the morning and feeding the cows in the afternoon.

The garden, nearly an acre and a half behind the house, was the neighborhood's most productive and well-regarded plot. The family incorporated a variety of vegetables into the mix, rotating the crops. The process ensured the rich, black earth would not be depleted and would continue to provide nutrients to the plants. They specialized in tomatoes and corn, with green beans and butter beans second in the population. In addition, cucumbers, peas, squash, watermelons, and cantaloupes grew in carefully measured and cultivated rows.

This morning, as soon as the dew burned off the grass and soil, Millie would haul out the push plow and break up the ground between the rows. The rain from two days before dampened the ground, so some areas would be more mud than dirt, but Millie was strong, and while she might feel the effects of the task later in her shoulders and back, she knew it had to be done.

She sighed as she moved the big wheel up and down the rows. Bugs flew around her legs, and she swatted at them but kept pushing. She knew how important it was to keep the soil around the plants aerated and weed-free. Her family depended on the sale of the harvest, and while that was weeks away, she knew diligence now would pay off later.

As she pushed, she gritted her teeth and thought of Stanley. She had known him for years in school and watched him emerge from his awkward years into the handsome and caring man he was today. She remembered their wedding and their wedding night. She was glad they'd waited until then to learn together how to love each other. She had been shy that night, insisting he turn off the lights in their little honeymoon bungalow. He had gotten into bed first while she took off her clothes in the bathroom. She groped her way through the dark, fingers searching for the bed. She was surprised he still had his boxer shorts on—and she was naked.

She touched his stomach and felt the waistband. "Why are you still wearin' those?" she asked.

"I don't know. Do you know why you do everythin' you do?"

She didn't want to be too forward, so she pulled her hand back.

"It's alright now. I mean, we can do whatever we want now," Stanley said. Millie touched his cheek and felt the heat. She was glad the lights were off. She didn't want to embarrass him.

"Yes," she said. "We can do whatever we want."

Millie grew up on a farm and knew from the randy animals what sex was at an early age, but had saved herself for him because that's what the preacher said to do. Not in so many words, as such, but she was a good girl, and all the long walks with Stanley that ended in kissing and nothing else cemented her belief that she had done the right thing by waiting.

Stanley moved to her, his boxers on the floor next to the bed. She felt his fingertips on her hot, silky skin. He moved them over her stomach and her hips as he kissed her. She moaned at his touch. "Stanley," she whispered, "slow and easy."

"Slow and easy," he agreed.

Millie bit the inside of her cheek as he slowly entered her. She knew sex might hurt, but she had no idea how much pain there would be. She breathed in and out as slowly as possible, but the pain was almost too much. Finally, she gripped the edge of the mattress and clamped her eyes shut.

She thought, "*Be over soon, be over soon, be over soon,*" but held her tongue.

After a minute, he stopped. He kissed her neck and moved to his side of the bed.

"I wish I didn't have to go over there," he said. A tone of resignation crept through his voice.

She knew immediately what he was referring to. It was a subject they'd discussed endlessly. "I wish you didn't have to either," she agreed. She raised herself up on one elbow and looked at Stanley.

"I'll be back soon," he said, hope in his voice now.

"And I'll be here waitin' for you."

She kissed his cheek. She felt the sticky liquid on her thigh and moved away from him. She used a warm, wet washcloth in the bathroom to clean the mess they'd made.

She was no longer a girl; a woman now and a wife. He was a married soldier who would soon end his training to be a medic and be shipped to Europe. She would sometimes run her finger over the surface of the world map she'd bought when she found out where he would be deployed.

"Belgium," she sighed. To her ear, it sounded like the name of another planet.

# Chapter 4

Stanley thought of his beautiful Millie as he sat there waiting for orders about where he would be shipped next. He'd heard about the German prisoner-of-war camps but never thought he'd be captured and imprisoned in one.

He knew from his training that the Geneva Convention covered the humane treatment of soldiers apprehended in war. He looked at his armband and the red cross that made his skills valuable to both sides of the conflict. It would be challenging, but he believed he'd survive until the war's end. Now, the front lines were close, but he felt his odds of living until it ended were still good.

He sat on the ground and poked at a rock with a stick. Bored and hungry. When was the last time he ate? He waited for orders.

He knew these orders would be different in a foreign language than he was used to. He was waiting in a fenced-in area behind a small barn. His fellow soldiers waited there too. He estimated that there were several hundred. The day had turned dark and dreary. The temperature had dropped into the thirties, and while the weather made him think of Christmas at home, he sighed, knowing there was no way he'd be there this year.

His red cross armband hadn't stopped him from being captured by the SS soldiers. They didn't shoot him, but they did rough him up as he tried to administer to a fallen allied fighter. From the man's uniform, Stanley knew he was a member of the British Army. The soldiers shoved him to the ground, forcing Stanley to watch. While held to the ground, the life drained from the wounded man's eyes.

Harold had tried to help also. He'd been captured at the same time as Stanley, and they raised their chins to the sky, their agreed-upon gesture, as they watched the man pass away.

Harold was the only Black soldier captured, and Stanley hoped his red cross armband might also keep him alive. Still, Stanley knew the German's hatred of anyone without Aryan blood. He worried that Harold would be singled out and killed before they were rescued.

Stanley didn't know if there was anything he could have done for the British soldier, but he was glad he was there to hold that man's last gaze upon another human face as he died. The soldier wouldn't leave this earth alone.

The young medic wasn't exactly sure where he was. He'd seen a map earlier in the day, and a sergeant had pointed to the small town's name. Malmedy meant nothing to him at that time. It was just another foreign word that fell into his ear with a painful clang.

Now, he wanted to hear the sounds of home, like the pealing of the bell in the church tower downtown. He wished he could listen to his cow's mooing and his pig's grunts. He wanted to hear bees buzzing around the flowers in the family yard. And most of all, he wanted to hear the voice of his beautiful Millie, saying his name and telling him how much she loved him.

It seemed decades since they'd seen each other. Stanley carried a small snapshot from their wedding day, but it wasn't enough. He rubbed his chest and felt the thin cardboard that held the image. He wanted to feel her arms around him and nestle in her bosom again.

The SS soldier guarding the prisoners sneered at the men sitting on the ground. He stood tall and stiff in his gray uniform. His boots might have been shined to perfection at one time, but now they were crusted with mud. He shifted his rifle from one shoulder to the other as he pulled a cigarette from his jacket.

Stanley sat on the cold ground and glanced up at his captor. He had tried to quit smoking. He knew it was bad for his lungs, but at this moment, he would have given the man a week's pay for just one puff.

The SS soldier somehow sensed or saw the desire in Stanley's eyes as the smoke wafted around his stern, granite face. Stanley took a chance.

He moved his hand in front of his face and motioned with his fingers the movement that should have been interpreted as smoking. The SS soldier grinned down at Stanley and shook his head no. Their shared addiction would not allow them to bond. From the beginning of his service, the soldier had been taught that the allies, especially the Americans, were weak and easily defeated. This poor medic trying to bum a cigarette from him proved to him his instructors were right. These men were not fighters or even real men. To this soldier, they were little more than ants underfoot that needed to be exterminated. Also, even though the war had been going poorly recently, he trusted the Fuhrer would soon lead them to victory.

Stanley looked down at his boot and fiddled with his shoelace. He needed to tie it, but the SS sergeant barked out an order. Harold stood next to Stanley and lowered his hand to help Stanley to his feet.

The Nazi commander's underlings moved quickly and rousted the prisoners. Stanley, Harold, and all the other men lined up as best they could in the rough terrain of the field. Many of them slouched under the emotional weight of their detention. They were all cold, hungry, and thirsty and wanted to return to their platoons. And most of all, they were afraid. They feigned bravery in front of their captors, but deep down, they felt alone and desperate.

A line of SS soldiers appeared to the left of the small group. Harold looked at the men. Stanley stood next to the doctor and turned his head to see Harold raise his chin to the sky.

Stanley didn't want to believe it; he couldn't accept that this was his fate. He had too much to live for. Yet, Harold somehow knew what might happen next and had steeled himself.

The line of men all held machine guns, and with a bark of words from the sergeant, they opened fire.

Stanley stood in awe for a moment. He couldn't believe what was happening. It was against the law. There were rules of war that all parties agreed had to be followed.

The sound of the machine guns rattled through the chilled air. Stanley didn't see Harold fall, but he knew his friend was dead. He turned and ran.

Stanley heard the men standing next to him turn and run, too. They huffed and slung their arms out to try and get as much speed as possible in their escape.

They knew barbed wire surrounded the field and believed they might get enough momentum to push through or leap over the barriers.

Stanley heard one soldier pass him and then saw him cut down as bullets slammed into his back. The man stumbled and fell face-first into the frozen ground.

Another came shoulder-to-shoulder with Stanley. He glanced over, saw the red cross armband, and smiled as if to say, "Being this close to you will save me." It was Harold. His armband flashed, and for a moment, Stanley believed they both would make it.

Stanley continued, feeling more confident now that he could run across the field, leap over a flat portion of the barbed wire, and escape. Still, he felt a tug on his left foot and saw his shoelace was tangled. He jerked his arm down but couldn't grab the end of it. A bullet whizzed over his head.

"Oh, Lord," he wheezed.

The shoelace flew under his shoe, and he tripped.

It was something so simple, so essential. He hadn't taken the opportunity to tie his shoe when he had the time; now, it would save his life. He stumbled another step before falling face-first to the ground. He was lucky.

Stanley lay there, trying to control his breathing. He knew what the SS soldiers were doing was against the rules of war. What was that called? His mind was blank, and he didn't think it would matter at this time. He wanted to appear as dead as possible so they would leave him behind and move on without putting him in a prison camp. He would 'play possum,' and the SS soldiers would leave him behind.

He wanted to be back with his troop. He wanted to be back in his country. He wanted to be back with Millie. His mind slowed, and he called up an image of her. He smiled. He rubbed the thin cardboard with Millie's picture in his shirt pocket. Lost in that moment with Millie, he didn't hear the soldier approaching.

He was almost free, almost back home.

It was the same soldier who wouldn't share a cigarette with Stanley who cocked his pistol and took aim at the back of the medic's head. He had received orders, and it was his job to execute them to the best of his ability. He knew there were rules against treating prisoners this way, but an order was an order. In his mind, he was just following orders from a superior officer.

Stanley gripped the earth with his right hand. His left arm moved away from his body. For a moment, he believed he could leap to his feet and fight the man with the gun. He would fight for his life and live to be with Millie again.

The SS soldier's eyes opened wide, and he took a deep breath. This was the first time he'd killed a man lying on the ground, unable to defend himself. Somewhere deep in his soul, he knew it was wrong, and for an instant, he considered defying orders and letting the poor man live.

Stanley sensed he'd have a split second to make a fight of this, and as he pushed himself up to his knees, the soldier pulled the trigger and ended Stanley's dreams, hopes, and life.

The soldier stood over the dying body and turned him over. As the life left Stanley's eyes, the soldier slowly put his fingers to his lips in a 'V' and sucked in his breath.

# Chapter 5

Mary Lou had named the calf 'Fibber McGee' after the radio comedian. The show followed a married couple and their mundane daily problems. Molly was the level-headed one, and Fibber was slipshod and disorganized. Each show's highlight was the closet opening, where a cacophony of objects would rain down on Fibber. He almost always ended the bit by saying he would have to clean out that closet some-day. That day never came.

Mary Lou watched as Fibber McGee matured into a cow with a bad attitude. Even though milking relieved the pressure she felt in her bag, Mary Lou's hands were never welcome on the cow's teats.

She would lift her leg to kick as Mary Lou approached. "No," Mary Lou would say as softly as possible, "don't you kick me, girl."

She had painfully learned all the cow's tricks. She'd been butted, pushed, snorted at, bitten, and kicked. No broken bones, thank goodness, but the cow had an attitude.

Mary Lou had heard of cows, primarily bulls, who had seriously injured farm-ers. She knew dealing with domesticated animals sometimes put her well-being in danger. Unfortunately, it was just part of the job.

"Fibber," she cooed, "this is goin' to happen, so let's get it over with."

She'd sometimes quote her poems to the cows as she milked them. For most, this soothed them, and some even swayed to the rhythm of the words.

"With distant rain comes the farmer's hope."

She grasped a hind teat and squeezed. Fibber switched her tail but refrained from trying to kick Mary Lou or overturn the milk bucket.

"The dry, brown earth of the northern slope."

The cow snorted and let out a deep bass bellow as if calling for help from her friends.

"A drought has held the land in tow."

Mary Lou put her right hand on the cow's haunch. The cow's hide twitched, and she lifted her leg. She tried to step on Mary Lou's foot, but the woman had seen that trick before and moved before she suffered bruised toes.

"The seeds sit idle instead of sown."

"That one still needs some work," Snaps said. She was dressed for farm work in her overalls, long-sleeved white shirt, boots, and straw hat. She smiled at her mother with bright, white teeth and the dimples she'd inherited from her father.

"They all need work," Mary Lou said. She glanced back at the girl. In that light, with the sun rising behind her, she could see why the boys sometimes called her Mae West. She had filled out nicely, and while there were boys at school and church who took a fancy to her, Mary Lou knew she was a good, hard-working girl. She was sure she'd wait for her husband to have sex, whomever that young man of the future might be.

"What you got goin' on today?" Mary Lou asked.

Surprised, Snaps let a slight twinge of anger cross her lips before she said, "I've got final rehearsal for the show this afternoon."

"Oh, of course, sorry," Mary Lou said, "how could I forget that?"

She knew the folly of the girl's desires but allowed the daydream to continue a while longer.

"What do you want me to do?" Snaps asked.

"Take a fork and pull down some of that hay. Cows gotta eat when there ain't no grass."

"I know," Snaps sighed. She wasn't a fan of farm work but knew it was necessary. So she picked up a pitchfork from a rack in the barn hall.

"And no singin' into the handle. Work!" Mary Lou yelled. She liked to tease the girl about her ambitions, hoping to maybe soften the blow when she would have to put away her foolishness, get married, and raise babies.

"Yes, ma'am," Snaps said. She opened the door to the manger, where the loose hay was stored. She stabbed a pile and carried it out into the hallway.

The barn door at the north end of the hall was open. The crisp, chilled air reddened Snap's cheeks and hands. A drop of snot formed at the end of her nose. She pitched the hay into the feed trough and wiped her nose with the back of her hand.

"Ma!" she screeched.

"Yes, dear," Mary Lou replied. The milk bucket was almost full, and she shifted her weight on the stool.

"How much for each cow?"

"Two forkfuls for everyone."

"Right," Snaps whispered to herself.

"She already knows that. Her head is always in the clouds," Mary Lou muttered. All the girls were good helpers, but she knew that since her husband's death over a decade ago, they needed continued discipline and structure.

The cow let out a low moo and moved back toward Mary Lou. She somehow knew the bucket would be cumbersome, and the woman might not have time to grab the handle. Even distracted, Mary Lou seemed to read the cow's mind. She grabbed the bucket and stood. The cow kicked the stool and pushed against Mary Lou with her hindquarters.

"Why I never had you made into steaks will always be a puzzle to me," Mary Lou said.

She opened the door, grabbed her three-legged stool, and pushed the cow into the hallway. The cow looked left and then right. She saw the open door at the end of the hall and lumbered toward the corral. She kicked at Mary Lou as she left the manger.

"She's a bitch," Snaps said. She caught her breath as she saw her mother's face. She tried to hold in her grin, but it was too hard.

"Language," Mary Lou sniffed. Then, she pointed toward Snap's nose and made a wiping motion.

"I know, sorry," Snaps said.

Mary Lou removed the milk barrel lid and poured the liquid through a filter. As the bucket neared empty, she turned and watched the cow lope out the door.

Snaps leaned on the pitchfork handle and said, "Maybe it's time for Brother to put a headgate on those troughs."

Mary Lou looked up at her. She was growing up so fast—her baby.

"That's probably a good idea," Mary Lou said.

"Yeah, you're not getting any younger," Snaps said without realizing the statement might offend her mother.

Mary Lou tapped the edge of the milk bucket on the top of the barrel. The last few drops fell into the filter. At that moment, she knew Snaps and all the other girls would make excellent farmers, either here or on their husbands' lands. She had done her job well, and a feeling of pride and accomplishment welled up in her.

A single tear formed at the corner of Mary Lou's eye. She wiped it away, but not before Snaps caught a glimpse of the silver liquid.

Mary Lou felt something break inside, and all her concerns about her daughter's future tumbled. She knew while she could guide and advise her girls, they would have to make hard choices. Sometimes they would listen, but most times, they wouldn't. She picked up the empty bucket and moved to the next stable.

Mary Lou croaked, "Put that lid on the barrel for me, would 'cha?"

Snaps watched her mother open the slide lock on the door and slip inside. She pulled the door closed, and the cow inside moved from one side of the stable to the other. Mary Lou said, "Snaps, baby, you got nothing to worry about. Momma will handle this."

Snaps whispered, "Just like you've handled everything else."

# Chapter 6

On December 17th, 1944, "the Malmedy Massacre," as it was called by a war crimes trial and eventually the media, found that 84 American prisoners were machine-gunned or executed up close by soldiers. SS Colonel Joachim Peiper led the German soldiers involved. The men were killed at a road intersection near Malmedy, Belgium, during the offensive soon to be named the Battle of the Bulge.

The bulge was a thrust of German forces into Belgium in an attempt to capture Antwerp, an essential supply hub for the Allied effort. Hitler thought that if he had this port under his control, it would open a door for a bid to sue for peace.

The slaughter was only one of several incidents where German soldiers took Allied prisoners and executed them. Word of the Malmedy Massacre and other killings spread through the ranks of the Allied soldiers. The atrocity strengthened their determination to block the German offensive through the rocky terrain, thick trees, and underbrush of the Ardennes Forest. The death of Stanley Comer and the others inspired a new urgency and intensity to the Allied efforts. He and the others might have thought they'd died in vain, but they were wrong.

War crimes investigators began collecting evidence soon after the event took place. Still, many victims lay on the ground for nearly two weeks because the area was under German control. Over one hundred men, women, and non-combatants were also killed during the offensive led by Peiper.

All seventy-three of the accused SS soldiers who participated in the massacre were found guilty on July 16th, 1946. They were sentenced to death by a general military government court of seven U.S. Army officers. Of the SS soldiers convicted, forty-three were sentenced to death by hanging, including Peiper; twenty-two were sentenced to life imprisonment, two were sentenced to 20 years imprisonment, one was sentenced to fifteen years in prison, and five were sentenced to ten years imprisonment.

News of the deaths eventually reached America shortly after the area was recaptured by American troops. The list of victims represented men from almost every area of the country. Many were from large cities, and others were from small towns and were simple farmers, laborers, and clerks. They likely couldn't have found Belgium on a map just months earlier.

While the girls and Mary Lou and Brother listened to the news on their second-hand radio every night, they had little idea that Stanley had been murdered. They believed, hoped, that his role as a medic would keep him from being killed. They thought the red cross on a white patch would save him.

They heard Edward R. Murrow rattle off statistics of the dead and injured, the movements of the Allied troops, and the German response every night. They prayed that Stanley would be safe and would return home soon.

But, when the chaplain approached the front door with another soldier and their beloved pastor in tow, the family knew their hopes, dreams, and prayers had been dashed.

Mary Lou answered the door with Brother standing behind her. His face twisted into a painful grimace. He had come home from World War One in time to see a similar scene following his younger brother's death.

The chaplain removed his hat and tucked it under his arm. "I'm Chaplain Dalloway with the 101st Airborne."

Mary Lou took a deep breath, and Brother laid his hand on her shoulder. He said, "Come in. Please," when it seemed Mary Lou couldn't form the words.

Millie hid behind the dining room door as the family welcomed the soldiers and Preacher Kemper into their home. The fire in the living room's fireplace had dimmed, and Brother was considering putting another lump of coal behind the screen. There were three chairs, a sofa, a china cabinet, and a coffee table in the middle of the room. A daybed sat in the east corner, and Millie sat on the edge. Snaps perched next to her and held her hand.

"This is a letter," Chaplain Dalloway said as he unfolded the paper he pulled from his inside pocket. "It's from General Omar Bradley."

The temperature in the room dipped, and Mary Lou pulled her shawl closer to her shoulders. Brother felt the chill in the air and stopped his rocking chair.

"It is with the deepest regret that I have to inform you that Corporal Stanley Comer was killed on December 17$^{th}$ while in the custody of German troops near the small Belgium town of Malmedy."

Anne's eyes flashed as the realization struck her mind. "But there are rules of war. The Geneva Convention says prisoners must be treated with…. " She stopped when she heard a gurgling sound behind her right shoulder. She turned.

Millie sat with her head down and her shoulders slumped. Snaps held her and rocked her as if she were a baby. "There, there," she said.

Millie cleared her throat, and the gurgling, whining sound began again. Snaps had heard this before when Millie's puppy had to be put to sleep. She'd listened to the same whimper when Daddy died. It was Millie's effort to keep from crying.

Anne was thin, dressed in a skirt and sweater. She had just washed her hair, and the ends were still wet. She held Millie's hand. A drop of water fell on Millie's index finger.

Millie remembered how she had touched Stanley's cheek when he was on the Nashville train. She'd already kissed him and savored the warmth of his hand on her back as he hugged her.

"I'm so sorry to have to bring you this news," Chaplain Dalloway said.

Preacher Kemper considered offering a Bible verse of wisdom and comfort but decided he'd wait for another opportunity later. Brother and Mary Lou looked at each other and then at the floor. They both knew the sting of loss and the emotions stirred by death.

"I'm sorry," the chaplain repeated. "This isn't the first time I've had to tell people bad news, and it never gets any easier."

"I'm sure you are," Mary Lou said. "Can I get somethin' for you, gentlemen? I've got fresh milk from tonight's milkin'."

Chaplain Dalloway had just ripped this family's world apart, yet they offered him neighborly kindness. Maybe they shared the sorrow he felt while doing his duty. He had seen it repeatedly, but the simple act of forgiveness for bringing the bad news touched his heart.

"No, thank you very kindly," he said. He took the letter and handed it to Brother.

For him, the letter was a symbol of the evil and unfairness of the world. Brother considered throwing it in the fire but realized Millie might want to keep it.

"Is there anything we can do, anyone we can call on to help?" The chaplain asked.

Mary Lou shook her head. Her plans, her vision for Millie's future, dimmed.

Preacher Kemper asked. "Maybe a prayer," he said, reaching for his hat and preparing to stand.

"Ain't the Lord done enough?" Mary Lou asked. It was a rare rebuke, and she blurted out the words before she had a chance to edit herself. She quickly corrected, "No, that's all right," Mary Lou said, changing her mind. She pivoted to a different subject, saying, "The boy only has his papa left, and we ain't had contact with him since the wedding."

"We'll find him, don't you worry," the chaplain said and stood. He offered his hand for Brother to shake. Brother adjusted his overalls and stood.

"I was in the Great War," he said. "I know this kind of thing don't never get any easier."

The chaplain and preacher nodded in unison and helped themselves out.

Before the chaplain left, he turned and said, "You can find some solace in the fact that the news of the massacre encouraged the men still in the field to fight."

"I don't find any solace in that," Millie said.

"You may someday," the chaplain said and closed the door.

Mary Lou moved across the room and touched the top of Millie's sobbing head. The girl's face was streaked with tears, and she drew ragged breaths.

"Stanley and me talked about this, Momma," Millie said, "but I didn't think it would happen. We prayed."

"No," Mary Lou said, an angry tone that belied her usual faith in the will of the All-Mighty, "God keeps these little secrets to hisself."

# Chapter 7

Mary Lou pulled the envelopes from the cabinet. Of course, the smudged names of the vegetables and spices could be read, but after all these years, she knew precisely which seeds were in which envelope just by opening the flap.

There were two kinds of tomatoes, yellow and white corn, a variety of root vegetables, and several envelopes with spices. Mary Lou had picked the healthiest and best-looking from last year's harvest to cull the seeds and dry them on flour sacks. The children had learned early on to give a wide berth to the linen cabinet in the dining room where seeds were drying. Those seeds and the milk they sold to the local dairy were their primary income source. Then, of course, Brother's handyman income augmented that, but the main source of money to pay taxes and keep the family afloat was the cows and those seeds.

Mary Lou knew the recent rains would subside soon, and the garden would need tilling. There was a time when she, Brother, and her husband, Ben, would take shovels and pitchforks to bring fresh soil to the surface. Mary Lou had a deal with Farmer White to get his tractor from across the railroad track to turn over the garden as soon as the ground dried.

Planting involved several days of using the push plow and long strings that stretched from one side of the garden to the other. This ensured that the rows were straight, that there would be room for all the plants, and that there would be no overlapping of taller plants over plants closer to the ground.

While Mary Lou believed wholeheartedly in God, she planted according to the signs of the zodiac she found in a copy of the Farmer's Almanac. It wasn't logical or based on science, but routine had dug a groove into Mary Lou's mind that caused her to think that success at the truck farm depended on how the stars aligned.

This effort involved all the family with as much cooperation as possible, even from Snaps, who usually grumbled that she had better things to do. Mary Lou always reminded her that all hands would be needed, given the family's financial status. Planting the seeds would keep them in the black for the following year.

Mary Lou handed out the envelopes, and the girls sprinkled the seeds into the deep, black ditches. Brother would use his rake to pull the earth over the seeds, flattening the recently turned ground. Finally, a coal bucket filled with dried chicken manure was scattered over the newly planted seeds.

For the root plants, some made from cuttings and others from seeds, they copied the same process. Finally, Mary Lou made a hole with a long, sharp stick creating a new home for potatoes, sweet potatoes, and beets.

Snaps looked up at the sound of the mail truck as it paused at the front gate, idled for a moment, and then rushed away. She tossed her large-brimmed hat toward a fence post and ran through the front yard. She passed the huge maple tree that gave her a perspective on life from high above. She opened the gate that Brother and Farmer White had constructed so long ago, opened the mailbox, pulled out two envelopes, and read the return addresses.

"It's here!" she yelled.

"What's here?" Mary Lou said and then remembered what the long-awaited letter might read. Their lives would change significantly if the letter said what they'd hoped.

"It's for me," Millie said as she tossed her hat at the same fencepost Snaps had aimed at and missed. Unfortunately, Millie's aim was no better.

"I need to open it!" she yelled at Snaps.

Snaps respected her sister and knew from the return address that Millie needed to be the one who opened the letter. It was addressed to Mrs. Millie Comer.

Millie snatched the envelope from Snaps' hand. She ripped open the end, not waiting to read the return address and the official U.S. Government stamp.

"Dear Mrs. Comer," the letter from Congressman John Ridley Mitchell began. Millie read the contents and handed it back to Snaps. She read the same but didn't display the sad face of Millie's lost hope. Snaps was angry.

"They can't do this," she began, her voice more than loud enough for the rest of the family still in the garden could hear.

Mary Lou tipped the edge of her hat up and wiped the sweat from her cheek with her shirt sleeve. She had hoped for good news but knew Snaps' reaction meant it was terrible. Brother looked up too, but his face registered more a grimace of expected pain as if he were removing an adhesive bandage.

Anne ran to the front gate where Snaps stood, still holding the letter. She passed Millie as the widow stumbled to the porch swing. "He said he…," she mumbled.

Anne took the letter from Snaps and read the first two paragraphs. "That ain't right."

"Isn't right," Snaps corrected her but felt awful about it almost instantly.

"She needs that money," Anne insisted. "It would help all of us, but she really needs it."

Mary Lou walked past Millie as she gently moved the porch swing with her foot. The girl looked like she'd suffered an electric shock.

Mary Lou took the letter from Anne and read the same sad words.

"Our investigation into the matter hasn't yielded the result you may have hoped. When Stanley Comer enlisted in the Army, he filed the legal paperwork listing his next of kin and family contacts. Then, when he married Mildred Wright, he changed some names on his personal contact form. Still, he neglected to change the beneficiary of his Army-issued life insurance policy. The good news is you will receive a spousal benefit until you remarry. We regret that this happened and wish you well." The congressman's signature was scrawled across the bottom of the page. "I guess we better hang on to this for a while," Mary Lou said.

"We could get a lawyer," Anne said. She had learned a good deal in administration classes while attending Rucker High School. "We could appeal to the Army."

"What if she'd had a baby?" Brother asked. He'd sauntered past the porch and now stood next to Mary Lou and the sisters.

"We know where Jess Comer lives, where he hangs out," Anne said.

"We can appeal to his better nature," Snaps said.

Mary Lou took a deep breath, "I guess there's no harm in tryin'."

Brother placed his hand on the top of the gate post. "If'n I know anythin' about Jess Comer, it's that his better nature is well hidden."

Anne looked over at Millie as she rocked on the porch swing. "Maybe if he don't want to give her all the life insurance money, he'll be willin' to share."

Snaps pushed down her urge to correct Anne's grammar again and said, "We have to try for her."

# Chapter 8

Nurses and aides took good care of Olaf in his transfer from the field hospital to the pier, where he would be shipped out. They were called Liberty ships and held nearly thirty thousand soldiers. Olaf had never seen such a large vessel and wondered if he might get lost in the crowd. However, he hoped there would be enough people on board to help him. Later, he realized that the women and men who cared for him, gave him injections of morphine to ease his pain, brought him food, and emptied his bedpan did an excellent job of nursing him back to health.

On the ship, Ollie had time to contemplate the battle he'd fought and was wounded. "*Was there something I could have done differently?*" he asked himself.

There were three of them in the bunker looking down a slight slope. Ollie sat next to his best friend, Gunther, as they surveyed the ground in front of them. They knew Allied soldiers were in the area but had received no intelligence about their location.

Ollie pulled the sides of his coat closer to his chest. The temperature was well below freezing that afternoon, and his boots and socks were wet from the snow.

The sun sat low in a gray and hazy sky. Ollie stared down the hill and poked his friend in the side, assuring him they were ready.

They weren't ready for a troop of Americans who had fixed bayonets and decided to charge down the hill, surprising the Nazi soldiers. Given the advantage of long-range rifles, there were few opportunities for hand-to-hand combat. The lieutenant surmised a quiet assault would be more effective. With his soldiers trembling with fear behind him, he motioned for them to follow him down the embankment.

The whoops and hollers of the charging Americans filled the air, and the German soldiers were genuinely surprised by the assault. They tried to turn and fire, but it was too late. Most German soldiers in the foxholes were killed or severely wounded. Ollie sustained a leg wound and was captured. He wept in pain from his injury and the loss of his friend. He vowed revenge but didn't know how he'd attain it.

The successful operation to close the wound on his leg meant he'd be processed as a prisoner of war. He wondered what would be done with him when he arrived in America. He'd heard horror stories of prison camps and forced labor. He asked if he'd be free to move around the institution and get fresh food and clean air. He didn't know where the camp was located, but he believed he'd find a way to endure and maybe even fight back for the glory of the Fatherland.

He saw the piers in Boston harbor, a few streets and buildings, and the train station. He had healed enough while on board that he was on crutches now, and while his leg still hurt, he would endure. The morphine injections ended when he touched land.

The nurses on the truck and the train gave him aspirin, which did help some, but not like the morphine. There were times he gritted his teeth so much that his jaw hurt. A soldier guarding the prisoners saw this and offered Olaf a few sticks of gum. While this didn't help with his leg pain, the gum did keep him from grinding his teeth. "*Chewing gum,*" he thought, "*a horrible practice, outlawed in his ranks, but accepted and easily found in America.*"

Ollie never got used to the shackles and being tethered to the other prisoners with his chains. He knew from visiting German camps while on duty that prisoners had to become accustomed to a shortened range of motion. He never thought he'd have to experience anything like that.

The luxury and comfort of the Pullman cars flabbergasted him. And, while he'd seen Negro soldiers in the field, there were ticket takers, waiters, and even Black men as managers overseeing the other workers. "*What a strange country,*" Olaf thought.

He saw long stretches of the landscape as the train took him across the country. It was early spring, and he felt he was back home where some of the same trees and flowers would be budding. Olaf liked the look, the space, and the lack of destruction of America, even if the country represented everything he hated.

At the train station in Nashville, he asked one of the other prisoners who had more expertise in reading English what it was called. He translated it to 'Union Station.' Olaf misunderstood, wondering why the people of Nashville would name their train station after the victorious Union army of the Civil War. In Olaf's mind, it would be like a German city naming a park after George Patton.

The train station bustled with hundreds of men and women, some in uniform, and children. Olaf hadn't seen many children recently, and he marveled at how their world seemed so free of pain and anxiety. He wished he were as light and happy as them.

His guard helped him onto the bus labeled 'Department of Defense.' It was white with black lettering that Olaf couldn't read. He knew where they were taking him, and his understanding of written English lagged. At the same time, he'd practiced conversational English on the ship and the train.

Talk on the ship between the prisoners fueled speculation that the camps forced men to work on war materials and cook and clean for the Americans. Olaf didn't like this, and many said they planned to protest. For example, they would throw their 'Sieg Heil' salutes to the American officers and when the American flag was raised in the morning and lowered at night.

Olaf stumbled as he moved his crutches to the ground and stepped off the bus's bottom step. His chain connected to the soldier behind him tripped him, and he grimaced in pain.

The guard standing there grabbed his shoulder and steadied him. He said, "Welcome to America."

Olaf wasn't sure how he was supposed to respond. Was the comment sincere or a jab at his being captured?

"Danke," Olaf said with a flat tone in his voice. He didn't want to sound as if he might acquiesce to his imprisonment, but he also knew that getting along with his captors might hasten his release. Olaf knew how to play the game and wanted to win for himself and the Fatherland.

Camp Forrest, named for the notorious Confederate general Nathan Bedford Forrest, originally was part of a massive Army base where eleven infantry divisions, two battalions of Rangers, numerous medical and supply units, and many Army Air Corps personnel were stationed for training.

In fact, Stanley Comer received his training as a medic at the facility. Camp Forrest, which covered over seventy-five thousand acres, cost over thirty-six million dollars. The camp housed so-called alien civilians, mostly of German and Italian ancestry, from January until November 1942. It was the first [1]civilian internment camp in the country.

The base was repurposed as a prisoner-of-war camp and training facility as the war intensified.

Dozens of quickly-constructed buildings housed draftees and employed over twelve thousand civilians at the height of its mission. Ultimately, over twenty-four thousand prisoners of war were held there.

Olaf entered his tent carrying his kit bag and moved toward the open bunk. His crutches clattered to the floor, and he stretched out his still-healing leg. He would make do with this challenging situation. He would follow orders, do his chores, and get stronger in case the war took a turn, and he might find a way to serve again.

In his bunk late at night, he prayed for his family and the Fuhrer. For Olaf, Hitler became a strong father figure. His mother and father said they couldn't have children, so they adopted Olaf from an orphanage. Deep inside, he believed that Hitler might be his 'real' father. He smiled at the thought. His arm shot out from under the blanket, and he silently mouthed 'Sieg Heil' three times. Then, he folded his arms across his chest, rubbed his leg once more, and placed his chewing gum on the corner of the bunk.

---

[1] Nathan Bedford Forrest rose quickly from private to the rank of lieutenant colonel, bypassing any professional military training. Nicknamed the 'Wizard of the Saddle,' Forrest conducted successful Confederate cavalry raids during the conclusion of the Civil War. He led the massacre of over two hundred surrendering Black Union soldiers at a battle near Fort Pillow. This act of butchery emboldened Union soldiers, who rallied with the slogan "Remember Fort Pillow," motivating them to victory. After the war ended, Forrest created the Ku Klux Klan to right what he felt were the injustices of reconstruction. Forrest would later denounce the organization, but it was too late. The KKK and its philosophy became popular and effective for decades.

# Chapter 9

Snaps walked to center stage and stood, feet shoulder-width apart and her hands at her side. It was the same posture she took when she practiced on her limestone proscenium in the meadow behind the house. Her teacher, Mrs. Northcutt, had taught her that stance. She'd taught Snaps about controlling her breathing and projecting her voice to the back row of the auditorium. And now, Mrs. Northcutt sat in the center row with the text on her lap.

"Snaps, let's hear it from the top," she directed.

Mrs. Brenda Northcutt had taken her swings in the majors when she left her small town in Missouri for the bright lights of New York City. She'd given herself a year to break through; after that, she'd make another plan, maybe Los Angeles.

She was tall and thin, with wavy red hair and bright blue eyes. Her black-and-white headshots emphasized her high cheekbones and arched eyebrows. Her most significant selling point was her lips, pouty on the bottom and raised just a bit over bright, white teeth on the top. Most male casting directors noted in their evaluations, 'very kissable.' Jason Northcutt was one of them. He'd interviewed and booked Brenda Bookenhauser for three different auditions but no acting jobs.

Nevertheless, he believed in Brenda's talent and fought an urge deep down inside to stare into those eyes with as much love and lust as he could feel. He'd also tried making it in New York as an actor, but after pounding the boards for too many years, he shifted to playing a role backstage. He liked working with the young people who crossed his office threshold and more than once bit off a piece of the forbidden fruit of dating some of the actresses. With Brenda, though, his interest involved all aspects of her—looks, personality, intellect, and body. They dated, fell in love, and were married within months of their first meeting.

Brenda soon became pregnant, and Jason was called to war. She returned to his hometown in Tennessee and had the baby. She got a teaching job in the local high school and was soon replicating what her husband had found so fulfilling, helping young people develop raw talent.

"Whenever you're ready," Brenda said as she watched Snaps take the stance she'd taught her.

Snaps began the soliloquy she'd practiced the day before, and when she finished with a frown and her chin tipped to the front of the stage, she felt she'd done well. She'd gotten all the words pronounced correctly and liked the emphasis she brought to Hamlet's questions and observations.

"Most women choose Ophelia's speech in Act Three, Scene One, for auditions," Mrs. Northcutt said. She recited, "O, what a noble mind is here o'erthrown!" She stood and stared at Snaps as she performed the lines. "The courtier's, soldier's, scholar's, eye, tongue, sword, Th' expectancy and rose of the fair state, The glass of fashion and the mould of form, Th' observ'd of all observers, quite, quite down! And I, of ladies most deject and wretched, suck'd the honey of his music vows. Now see that noble and most sovereign reason Like sweet bells jangled out of tune and harsh, That unmatch'd form and feature of blown youth Blasted with ecstasy. O, woe is me T' have seen what I have seen, see what I see."

Snaps' mouth hung open for a moment as Mrs. Northcutt finished. She had no idea of her talent and range.

"Why did you choose Hamlet over Ophelia?"

"It spoke to me," Snaps said.

"Well, I'm not feeling the emotions in Hamlet's soliloquy. I hear the words. I see your face and hand movements. I see your eyes, but you're not connecting with what is really going on in his mind. I hear *your* words but not *his* words," Brenda said. She'd sat down after finishing her soliloquy. She leaned forward in her chair for a moment. Her hands dangled over the back of the red cushion of the seat in front of her.

"I'm sorry," Snaps said. "I'm not sure what you mean?" Her words echoed through the empty auditorium. Three hundred empty seats stared back at her. Maybe because there was no audience, she wasn't feeling it.

"Singing, dancing, light comedy, musical comedy, Snaps, you've got all those covered. A lightness reflects into the audience when you open your mouth. But for drama, and even some comedies, you must draw out emotions from yourself and the other actors. The audience can tell when it's real."

Snaps put her left hand on her hip. She wasn't used to negative criticism from Mrs. Northcutt; deep down, she felt she needed to fight back.

"How can I feel the emotions of a suicidal Prince of Denmark?"

Mrs. Northcutt smiled. "That's it. That's what you're looking for. You've got it when you understand the character, what's happened to them, and how they express that."

Snaps took a step forward. She wanted to leap off the stage and get in Mrs. Northcutt's face, but she decided she'd think about what the teacher had said. Maybe there was something to her critique that she could use. "*Probably not,*" she thought. But she said, "Yes, Mrs. Northcutt."

Brenda could feel Snaps edging toward being defensive about her performance notes and knew that while she was right, it might take a while for her words to sink through Snaps' ego and into a place where she could use them.

"You need all the tools in your toolbox to be as sharp as possible," the teacher said.

"Yes, Mrs. Northcutt," Snaps said, but this time an almost imperceptible sneer flashed at the corner of her mouth.

# Chapter 10

"Raise up that there beam, and I'll put her in place," Brother said as Farmer White and his son stood on the floor of the second level of the loft of the storage building. The ultimate purpose of the building hadn't been determined, so much of the downstairs floorplan was still open. Asphalt tile panels would cover the roof once the arches were secured. At that point, Farmer White would have flexibility on how many rooms the building would have and where everything would go.

Brother stood in the bright sunlight, hammer in hand, wearing an apron filled with different sizes of nails. His overdeveloped forearms glistened with sweat, and the blood from a small, unnoticed cut had dried into the shape of a cross. His shoulders and chest swelled against the confines of his white, long-sleeve shirt. His overalls were dirty, and a small hole had formed over the right knee.

"It's heavy, Brother," the White boy said.

"Yes, boy," Farmer White said. "Don't you drop it."

The boy and his father held the arch beam in place with two long two-by-fours. Brother nailed the bottom of the planks and pulled out a level. He knew nailing this frame into place would be permanent, and now was the time to make sure he didn't have to tear it all down because it leaned or wasn't stable.

He looked over the edge of the floor as he nailed the roof arch. It was twelve feet to the ground, and Brother had lost count of the number of times he'd dropped a tool or material or fallen himself from a project. Experience had taught him to use the loops on his overalls and apron to hang on to tools and to be extra careful near the edges. Ladders were another danger he'd experienced over the years. While it had been some time since he'd dropped anything from one of them, he knew there would be a task where he'd have to climb one again. Of all the times he'd fallen, he'd only injured himself twice. A sprained right knee still bothered him when rain approached. Today it told him a shower would be here in the next day or two. He had no idea how much rain or for how long, but he knew the moisture would be harmful to the wood frame of the project. His opposing ankle was broken when he'd fallen into a rock pile near a house he was constructing. Lastly, he'd dropped about five feet less than six months ago and landed on his right shoulder. He'd heard a crunch, and while it wasn't broken, it did sustain some joint and ligament damage. He'd had to stop working for two weeks. Experience had taught him that landing on his feet or shoulder first would always be better than falling on his back or head.

Brother didn't care for heights, but given his profession, he knew there would be times he'd have to swallow hard and do what was necessary. Today would be easy. Farmer White and his son (*what was the boy's name?*) were helping.

"Jody," finally remembering his name, "you be careful there," Brother said as he watched the boy's foot creep close to the edge of the loft floor.

Brother hadn't cared much for children until he'd moved in with Mary Lou and her girls. He'd watched them grow into graceful sprites with long, thin arms and legs and big, inquisitive eyes. But, on the other hand, he believed boys were gawky, uncoordinated, and gross in their hygiene and demeanors.

Brother walked to the side where Farmer White held the tall wooden arch. A pained expression covered the man's face. He was younger than Brother but not in as good condition. White had beef cattle, and his chores involved horses and trucks instead of push-plows and hand tools.

"I got it," Brother said. He started the nail and slammed it into place with three sharp blows.

"Damn," Farmer White said.

"Only takes a lifetime to learn how to do that," Brother said, smiling.

The brace for the arch creaked as Jody took a deep breath. Brother could see from thirty feet away that the boy's strength was waning.

"I'm comin', boy," Brother said as he touched Farmer White's shoulder, signaling he could let go.

"I got it," Jody said. Sweat trickled down his cheek, dipping his head to catch it on his sleeve. A splinter slid into his hand, and he jerked in pain.

Brother moved swiftly across the loft floor. He leaped over the hole leading to the stairs to the first floor and caught the arch above Jody's hand. He bumped the boy, what he perceived ever so slightly, but given the boy's weight and slender build, it was enough to push him toward the outer edge of the floor.

Brother saw how the boy would fall and let go of the arch. He took his hand off the wooden brace, dropped his hammer over the edge, and grabbed for the boy.

Jody wore overalls and no shirt underneath. His arms were slick with sweat, and his boots had holes in the toes. One of the toes caught on the edge of the roof arch, and he was falling backward.

"No!" Farmer White yelled.

"I got you," Brother said, but he didn't have the boy at that moment. He steadied himself with the roof brace and grabbed for the back of the boy's overalls. Brother snagged him and grimaced at the weight as it tugged at his previously injured shoulder.

Farmer White had raced across the loft floor with hands outstretched. He grabbed for the boy and missed.

Brother held fast to the boy's overalls as his father tried again, pulling Jody to safety. Finally, the boy looked up from sitting on the wooden floor. "That could'a hurt," he said with no understatement in his voice.

Brother stretched his arm and rubbed his shoulder. He didn't realize until that moment that it was still healing. "Yeah, that could'a been bad."

The boy took a deep breath, sprang to his feet, and looked at his father.

"You be more careful," the older man said.

"I got a splinter," the boy said and started digging out the sliver of wood with his teeth.

Brother pulled his knife from his pocket. "Let me look at that." He scraped the blade across the splinter, realized which direction the wood was angled, and pulled it out. "Like new," Brother said.

An Angus mooed in the distance, and Farmer White's head turned toward the sound. "Maybe we should take a break." He wanted to go look at his cattle and catch his breath. Staring at beef on the hoof reminded him of how much money he'd likely make on sale day. Attending the auction was one of his favorite things.

"Too early for lunch, but ain't no reason we can't take a water break," Brother said. He could see the boy was still shaken up and probably needed to get his bearings.

"Gotta go down and get your hammer," Jody said.

Nineteen more arches would need to be pulled up and nailed into place. Brother didn't have a schedule to finish the job. Still, he knew that rain would warp the wood, and a roof was the only answer to keeping his work from becoming a public eyesore or magnet for ridicule. A twinge of pain in his knee forecast the downpour.

"Go get the hammer and toss it up," Brother instructed.

The boy scampered down the stairs behind his father and appeared below Brother on the loft floor.

"Here she comes," Jody said, looking away as John the bull bellowed.

The night before, the radio announcer detailed the recent bombings of Hiroshima and Nagasaki. Brother didn't recognize the names of either of the towns, and he had no idea of the destructive nature of the atomic bomb, but he knew about *surprise*. Success in war sometimes meant surprising the enemy with a new tactic, an innovative weapon, or an unanticipated location. Brother learned this through his experience in World War I, but there were times when he still reacted reflexively. He'd found that he didn't like surprises in his life.

The hammer tumbled end over end, making the task of grabbing the tool out of thin air extremely hard. Brother stretched out his right hand, holding the arch with his other hand. He missed catching it, and the hammer smacked the boy in the face as he turned back to look at Brother.

The force of the blow broke his nose, and Brother rushed down the steps to find Farmer White holding the boy in his arms.

"Looks like his nose is broken," Brother said. There was a small gash on Jody's cheek that would heal quickly.

"I can fix it," Brother said as he looked at Farmer White. He knew what a visit to the doctor would cost, and it was weeks before the man would be taking his beef cattle to market.

"Do your best," Farmer White said. He held the boy's head as Brother moved his hands onto Jody's face.

"No!" the boy yelled, struggling against his father's grasp.

"Now, Jody, it's got to be done."

"But Daddy!" the boy continued his protests.

Brother's hands moved quickly on each side of the boy's nose. He jerked the cartilage back into place as the boy cried.

"I'll go to the house and get some aspirin and some tape to hold it in place," Farmer White said. "Jody, you're done for the day."

Brother looked at the father and son as they sat on the ground. Jody's shoulders were relaxing, and his breathing was getting deeper. He saw the scene of the father soothing his son and wondered what kind of father he would have made if he'd been given a chance.

Brother knew Jody's nose would likely have a bit of a bend to it now, but it couldn't be helped. When the swelling went down, it might serve him well in school. He'd have a story, and people always loved stories.

# Chapter 11

Snaps stomped past the full-length mirror, glancing at herself, still in her costume. She ran into her room and threw herself on the bed. She'd been crying since Mary Lou had picked her up at the stage door.

She knew she couldn't complain to her mother. Snaps believed the woman wouldn't understand her mistakes and their importance to the play.

Anne heard Snap's footsteps and the slamming of the bedroom door. She tapped once and asked, "Hey, what happened?

"Go away," Snaps said, her words muffled by the closed door and the bed covers that buried her face. She had made sure her costume was still straight and unwrinkled as she continued her protests.

"Okay, I'll leave, but I'm not happy," Anne said. She turned and took two steps down the hall before the door cracked open.

"Come in," Snaps said, turned, and flung herself on the bed again.

"Was it a speech or a dance step?"

Anne sat on the end of the bed and stroked Snaps' back.

"Both," she sniffed.

"So, the show wasn't perfect."

"It was a complete disaster," Snaps mumbled. "I'll never go on stage again."

"Now, now, sister," Anne said. She looked up as Mary Lou moved across the open door.

"It was in the second act, just before the big dance number and the ballad. I just lost my mind," Snaps said. She turned and looked up at Anne with wet eyes, and her mouth twisted into a trembling frown.

Anne loved her sister but knew she could be a handful at times. "Do you think anyone in the audience noticed?"

"I, maybe, I covered it pretty well. The other kids, they knew. I got some weird looks," Snaps said, "and Mrs. Northcutt, she knew, of course."

"Did she say anything?" Anne asked.

"No," Snaps said, "but I knew." With the word 'knew' turning into an elongated 'boo hoo hoo.'

The moon cast light through the windowpane making the shadow look like a cross on the floor. There was a sewing mannequin still wearing Snaps' backup costume. A mirror topped the dresser across from the bed. Snaps caught the reflection of Anne as she frowned behind Snaps' back. It was hard. Anne tried to think of sad things, like when a calf dies or someone else or something dies. It wasn't working.

"You're tryin' to keep from laughing," Snaps sputtered.

Anne stifled a smile and turned her head away from the mirror. "I am not."

Snaps turned quickly and glared at her sister. "You didn't even come to the performance."

"I'd already seen it twice, once in dress rehearsal and again on opening night."

Snaps huffed and threw herself back into her pillow.

"If'n I'd known you were goin' to mess up this big, I would have gone." It was a good joke, but Anne wished she hadn't said it. Sometimes her witticisms just popped out before she could control them.

Snaps tried not to laugh out loud, but she had to admit Anne was funny. She had always seen the world from a different point of view.

"I'm ruined!"

Anne shook her head. "Do you think Ethel Merman ever had a bad night?"

"No," Snaps snapped.

Anne thought a second, "Well, you might be right on that one. How about Teresa Wright?"

Snaps raised herself up on one elbow. "Maybe." She thought for a moment. "I love her. She is the cutest thing. So yeah, that could happen."

Anne put as much seriousness as she could into her voice. "Did that stop her from goin' out the next night, the night after that, and the night after that?" she asked. She pulled the edge of her nightgown down past her knees. The temperature in the room had dropped, and the light from the moon turned from white to yellow.

"That's no excus…" Snaps started, "I mean, we practiced like crazy." She smirked and said, "*Pal Joey* is a lot."

"It's a lot of singin' and dancin' and sometimes doin' both at the same time," Anne said. "That ain't easy."

"You're darn tootin' it ain't easy." Snaps shot up in bed and twisted herself to look in the mirror. She smoothed the front of her costume so the wrinkles wouldn't set in.

"So, you're goin' to be okay?" Anne already knew the answer to that question. Snaps had experienced setbacks before, but she always bounced back. The theater was in her blood, though no one knew where it might have come from, and Snaps was a star.

"We've got one more show, and then we close," Snaps said.

"That means you've got a chance to get it right again tomorrow night."

"Last show. Curtain down, lights out, no second chances," Snaps said, determination filtering into her voice.

"Last show," Anne said, "and I'll be there."

"You will," Snaps said with enthusiasm.

"I wouldn't miss it for the world," Anne assured her.

"What about that boy?" Snaps asked. "Do you think you could get him to come, too?"

"Well, I could ask him tomorrow at school."

"All you can do is ask," Snaps said.

Anne scooted off the bed and walked to the still-open bedroom door. She looked back and watched Snaps bound off her bed. Her sister was picking up her hairbrush and was about to start singing.

She knew Snaps would be all right now. No bad review or poor performance would keep that girl off the stage. "No way," Anne whispered.

"What did you say?" Snaps asked. Her eyes were still bright from the tears she'd shed, but her smile reached from ear to ear.

"I said you'll be great," Anne said as she closed the door. She heard the tapping of happy feet and vocal exercises.

"Yes, nothin's gonna stop that girl," she said to herself, turned, and saw Mary Lou standing at the end of the hall in front of the full-length mirror. Mother put her finger to her lips and shushed.

# Chapter 12

Olaf, now called Ollie by many of the guards, led the others in the Nazi salute or 'Sieg Heil' as the American flag rose over the prison camp. He was not an officer but big and robust, embodying the Aryan ideal. The guards frowned but knew the Geneva Convention's rules involving prisoners' care. Although the display of German pride around the flagpole was disgusting, at the same time, it wasn't something that needed punishment.

Olaf still walked with a limp as he sauntered through the wet grass and loose gravel in the middle of the camp. His duties today included peeling potatoes and making a birthday cake for the American commander. It would have been an ideal time to slip something into the recipe. Still, guards in the kitchen kept a close eye on food preparation, especially involving their beloved base commander.

The circuit doctor, a general practitioner assigned to four different camps, had deemed Olaf fit for full duty. He could now be assigned to yard work, fence repair, or any task requiring heavy lifting. But Olaf's newly-discovered talent was cooking. He had a deft touch with the spices necessary to turn a mundane plate of eggs into a masterpiece of consistency and taste. He knew, instinctively, without measuring the exact amount of sugar, lard, flour, and other ingredients to add to the big mixing bowls scattered around the kitchen.

Prisoners attended to the mess tent adjacent to the kitchen with grumbling and resistance. Many men were ranked above the guards overlooking them and felt their responsibilities were beneath their status. Some initially refused but soon found the tedium of waiting to be evaluated for deportation without anything to do was worse than picking up dirty plates and cleaning tables and chairs.

Olaf had made friends with several guards, although 'acquaintances' was more accurate, and called them by name. Since he was one of the prisoners who had learned to speak English, he was occasionally called on to translate.

He knew how important it was that communication between his SS superiors and the camp administration be as accurate as possible. He also knew there might be opportunities to twist the English translation to his advantage. He realized this would allow him to enjoy secret, special privileges that others were denied because of short supplies or long-term tasks.

Olaf liked his responsibilities at the camp and learned how to make the best of his time. However, he knew he'd likely be deported soon. When he returned home, if Olaf were found innocent of any crimes during the war, he'd join what he assumed would be a resistance to the Allied occupation. Olaf had read newspaper stories of how Roosevelt, Stalin, and Churchill had met in Yalta, Crimea, and divided up the spoils of their victory. Olaf vowed that while his beloved homeland suffered greatly during the war, he'd continue to fight for the cause.

He was standing next to a former SS captain when Snaps first entered the back of the kitchen. Her dress clung tightly to her thighs and knees. It was not a work dress, but she knew how wearing it made her feel, and she needed an ego boost. While there had been one bad performance, she basked in the adulation of the others, but she couldn't get that horrible night out of her mind.

There was a guard there she had made eyes at, and she knew if she shrugged her shoulders just the right way, she resembled the movie star whose name she'd been tagged with in high school.

"Hello, Mae West," Olaf said. His accent twisted the pronunciation of the words a bit, but Snaps knew what he was inferring.

She had seen this blond god before. She'd taken over driving the truck to the camp from Brother a month ago. While most prisoners looked like hardened criminals, this one appeared soft and vulnerable. While she knew he had likely killed American soldiers during the war, there were times she felt sympathy for him as he worked for his captors.

"You shouldn't call her that," said Sweeney, the kitchen guard who stood next to Snaps as she helped unload the milk cans, eggs, and vegetables from the back of Farmer White's truck. Snaps had a driver's license and made weekly deliveries to the prison camp.

Sweeney's dark eyes flashed, fingering the baton holstered on his belt. He was shorter than Olaf, with black hair instead of blonde, thinner, and not as handsome.

"I was merely complimenting her on her dress. It's a beautiful one. What did you say your name was?" Olaf feigned stupidity. He remembered the girl's name as if it were his own, but he knew how to flirt and manipulate girls into doing what he wanted. He had moves, and he knew how to use them.

"Snaps," she said. She could feel the heat rising into her cheeks. She couldn't help it. This boy was so big and beautiful.

"You don't have to talk to him if you don't want to, Ma'am," Sweeney said. He had picked up a basket of eggs from the back of the truck and walked them slowly through the back flap of the kitchen tent.

The captain working next to Ollie in the kitchen stopped stirring the big bowl filled with cake batter and said, "Dieses dumme Mädchen könnte unser Weg hier raus sein."

Sweeney asked, "Ollie, what's he sayin'?"

What Olaf heard was, "That silly girl could be our way out of here," but what he told Sweeney was, "How much longer must I stir this batter?"

Sweeney nodded and picked up another basket of eggs from the back of the truck. Snaps grabbed a box filled with tomatoes. It must have weighed thirty pounds, but she wasn't going to let the Germans see she was weak. Her knees buckled under the task.

"Here," Olaf said, "let me."

He rushed to the back of the truck, past Sweeney, who was carefully negotiating the egg basket under the tent flap and to Snaps' side.

Olaf grabbed the edge of the wooden basket. He felt a sliver of wood break off and splinter into his hand, but he didn't flinch. Instead, he put his other, uninjured hand under the basket and brushed the back of Snaps' hand with the other.

She felt it. Like a small electric shock, the touch of his skin, the tiny hairs that bristled near Olaf's wrist, made her jump.

If he hadn't been there, she would have dropped the tomatoes. But she didn't. Of course, if he hadn't touched her, she would have balanced the box on her knee to get a better grip.

"Thank you," she gasped.

"Danke," he said reflexively. He was tall, and his deep blue eyes bore a hole into her soul. He was close enough for her to feel his breath on her bare shoulder.

"Okay, that's enough," Sweeney said. He shifted his weight from his heels to the balls of his feet. He'd been itching for a fight since he'd enlisted. The war was almost over by the time he finished boot camp, and he needed to feel some blood on his hands.

"I'm going," Olaf said.

He turned and carried the box to the tent. He looked over his shoulder and smiled at Snaps.

The girl's hands hung limply at her side, and her eyes grew even larger. None of the boys at school or who came by to sit with her on the front porch swing had produced a feeling like that in her chest.

She leaned against the tailgate and counted to three, just like she always did as she stood in the wings before the curtain went up.

"*Showtime*," she thought.

# Chapter 13

The Wright family gathered around the radio and listened as the news reporter delivered the circumstances surrounding the death of President Roosevelt. They all revered him and believed that the lives they enjoyed now had happened because of his leadership.

The day had begun as most did on the farm, with the usual chores being performed, and ended with a dinner of vegetables and fresh milk. The day's talk centered on finishing the spring planting and plans for attending church that Sunday.

Brother had proposed taking a short drive after the service to look at a new stud to help grow the herd. The bull in question was one county over, and while Mary Lou showed interest, the girls expressed their need to do anything else. It was rare for them to refuse a trip off the farm, but even this task failed to garner enough interest for them to sign on to the journey.

At the end of the day, the light illuminating the radio dial cast a yellow glow over the faces as they listened to the announcer give the who, what, when, and where of the day's events. The president had been sitting for a portrait and suffered a stroke. He died instantly. The new president, Harry Truman, took office almost immediately.

Millie, Mary Lou, and Brother remembered the name from their voting sheets but didn't know much about the man, except that FDR had chosen him in case something happened. So they trusted the president's judgment, and if he was good enough for Roosevelt, Harry was good enough for them.

FDR provided hope and courage for the family during the Depression. In their hearts, they believed the country they loved and had fought for would not have survived without his stewardship. He wasn't perfect, but they knew he loved America and its people.

Mary Lou said, "We should pray for Eleanor and Mr. Truman."

They all dutifully dipped their heads, even Snaps, who often didn't like to pray when other people were around. However, she harbored a deep secret and would take it to her grave. The only reason she attended church was so she could sing.

Snaps wasn't sure there was a God, and she had no idea what happened to people when they died. She considered what awaited Mr. Roosevelt and Mr. Hitler after their lives ended. What followed their last breaths? For them, was it Heaven or Hell? She'd read all there was in the Sunday School books and the Bible, but the answers didn't satisfy her questions. So, in church, she just sang her heart out and believed in the power of a song.

What kind of tribute would she perform for Mr. Roosevelt if given a chance? She thought about it later that night as she lay in her bed. What would his family appreciate? Maybe it was silly to think about, but what would she sing for a president?

A few weeks later, she'd consider the same question as the reporter told the news of the death of Adolph Hitler. The man's voice seemed less fragile and on the edge of emotion this time. A tone of satisfaction and knowing seeped into his delivery as he reported the leader of the Nazis had committed suicide rather than face justice before a court and twelve of his peers.

Weeks after that, the announcer reported the news of the death camps and that millions of people had been killed for little more than the way they looked, who they loved, their family heritage, and the God they worshiped. That night, Snaps returned to her questioning what death meant and whether God knew and did nothing about it. How could a just God let something so horrible happen? She continued to sing in church, and there might have been more emphasis in her voice as she held the notes that people complimented her on after the service.

Snaps would nod and accept their words of encouragement, but deep down, she continued to question, is there a God?

# Chapter 14

Millie rocked as she snapped the ends off the green beans. Her mouth clenched as the soap opera on the radio, *As the World Turns*, dramatized the final meeting between Jess Carter and his soon-to-be estranged wife, Lisa. He told her he had enlisted in the Navy, and the story was getting too close to her reality for Millie.

The radio sat next to the fireplace. The light of the tuning dial didn't show the station frequencies at this time of day. At night, Mary Lou would watch the backs of the girl's heads as they listened to the adventures of the Lone Ranger or the music of the Grand Ole Opry. "*Stories*," Mary Lou thought, "*how could something as simple as stories make that big a difference in people's lives?*"

She knew the answer to the question, of course. Stories helped people survive the unfortunate events of their lives by dramatizing how people cope and overcome them. Stories also created fantasies of the way people wish things might be. The Bible and the preachers told stories that helped people suffering trials and tribulations feel better.

Mary Lou saw Millie's hands clench as the story of a husband leaving his wife affected her daughter. Could Millie find solace or insight from the drama unfolding in her ears? Mary Lou was unsure but hoped it helped heal Millie's heart—she knew her poetry helped her.

For Mary Lou, poetry fueled by a burst of emotion or an observation was her salvation. Poetry helped her make sense of things. When the house was quiet, she would pull out her journal almost every night and write down her thoughts and feelings of the day, usually in rhyming couplets. But, of course, she had no idea what couplets were. She'd dropped out of school in the fifth grade to work on her family's farm. Still, Mary Lou knew what felt suitable for her, and the "a" and "b" rhyme scheme matched the melody she heard in her head.

A stab of music from an organ split the radio speaker. Millie flinched and dropped one of the beans. She leaned over and picked it up. She noticed her mother's shoe had a hole in the side. The thought of her mother needing new shoes made her angry. The money from her husband's life insurance policy could do so much for her family and her future. She didn't want to think about her personal failure to provide. She hoped Stanley's father could be convinced that she should be the beneficiary, not him.

"Fibber McGee's probably gonna be good tonight," Mary Lou said. She was rocking, too. Unfortunately, her pan of green beans was not as full as Millie's because the story had captivated her, slowing her production.

"I know. I'm lookin' forward to that one, too," Millie said. But, again, her mouth clamped tight, and her mother could see her jaw grinding.

"You know, we could use some tea," Mary Lou said.

Millie didn't look up from her work. She focused on the beans and the radio dialogue between the two characters. "Maybe later," she muttered.

"Next commercial," Mary Lou said.

Ever the obedient daughter, even at her age, Millie said, "Yes, ma'am."

The women rocked almost in unison for a moment or two more, and then the announcer implored them to "stay tuned, *As the World Turns* will be right back."

Millie rose from her chair and gathered the bean leaves and scraps in her apron. She shuffled to the front door, opened it, walked to the edge of the porch, and flapped the cloth in the wind. Looking up, she shielded her eyes from the sun as she gazed at the gravel road in front of the house. She thought she saw a figure in the distance. It was moving slowly, almost dragging along the ruts made by the wagons and other vehicles. She'd seen this before, imagined what it would be like if the Army had been mistaken, that Stanley was still alive, and he was walking down that road back to her.

Millie had never seen Stanley's grave and didn't know where she might find it if she tried. Instead, she wanted to believe in the story she'd told herself repeatedly.

She didn't notice when Mary Lou walked to the door and stood right behind her. "I seen Frank comin' up the road right after he passed," she said in Millie's ear. The girl didn't turn and kept looking at the dark patch of shadow as it disappeared with the sun's movement.

"I know, Momma."

"I must'a jumped off this porch and started runnin' through the yard a dozen times, maybe more," Mary Lou said. She moved her hands toward Millie's waist.

Millie neared the edge of the porch, and Mary Lou caught her, holding her from behind.

"Let me go, Momma," she said.

"I will, I will," Mary Lou said. She tightened her grip on the girl's waist and buried her face in the back of her shoulder.

She felt the sobs coming through Millie's body, and a tear fell on her bare arm. "We'll get by, don't you worry," Mary Lou said.

"I know," Millie said, "let go."

"I will."

"I said, 'Let go.'"

She released her grip on her daughter and stepped back. The girl looked at the road. She moved again toward the edge of the porch but stopped. She looked down at her feet and then again at Mary Lou. A white sock poked through the side of Mary Lou's shoe.

Millie turned and looked at her mother. "Let me get that tea for ya," she said, her voice a raspy croak.

"I'd like that. It's hot as fire today," Mary Lou said as she touched Millie's shoulder.

The screen door slammed. "Brother should look at that. Spring's too tight," Millie said as Mary Lou jumped at the sound.

"Fibber McGee better be awfully good tonight," she whispered.

# Chapter 15

Ollie always talked with the guards. They soon tired of his relentless yammering, but they knew a complaint to the camp administrator would likely gain nothing. So they would endure and ignore Ollie's questions about their families and what their lives were like before the war. They thought Ollie was just curious about the camp, the guards, and America. But he was gathering intelligence he believed he could use on a mission.

He'd studied several languages in school, and teachers soon recognized he had a talent for composition. With diligent practice and study, his conversational English improved to the point where his German accent didn't keep him from being misunderstood by the guards.

Ollie continued translating his superior's requests to the camp administrators, allowing him to see documents and listen to sensitive negotiations. With this information, a plan formed in Ollie's mind. He'd find a way out of the camp and travel back to Germany. He'd lead a resistance to the foreign soldiers who'd stayed behind to help rebuild his destroyed homeland. He'd be part of the greatest revolution and return the Third Reich to world domination.

Ollie heard stories from the high-ranking officers of how they were recruited into the cause by the Fuhrer. He had difficulty hiding his envy as they related personal encounters with the great man.

His adoptive parents had attended a 'Brown-Shirt' rally in Nuremberg in 1929. They talked about how even though Ollie was young, it was his idea for him to go with them. They were packed into a courtyard, looking up at Hitler as he stood on a stone balcony and spoke about how Germany would soon rise. They told Ollie, who was too young to remember what was said, about how the Jews, the gypsies, and the queers were enemies to all Germans. They felt so proud as they reminded him that, while he was still only a youngster, Ollie had raised his tiny hand in the same 'Sieg Heil' as everyone around him.

Of course, the acceptance of these societal norms took years. Death to the enemies, conveniently recognized by Hitler, infused a banal evil into the culture.

The church continued to lecture that suicide was a mortal sin, damning the participant to Hell. Still, the war's end brought the acceptance of this final act versus life under occupation. The religious commandment of 'Thou shalt not kill' became 'Thou shalt kill' without discrimination or punishment during the war. A society built on the latter idea readily accepted the Nazi charge to kill again if only turned inward for one final time.

News from Germany continued to dominate the media until the death of Franklin Roosevelt. At that point, the world's attention shifted to the new president and the continuing war in the Pacific. Letters from the Fatherland became the most reliable form of reporting, and much of what was being said disturbed the camp residents.

As Berlin fell and the Russian army approached, many Nazi sympathizers decided that a political ideology begun with the deaths of identified scapegoats would obviously need to end in more killing. But the destruction that advanced across country borders turned inward, and thoughts of suicide dominated the minds of survivors in the war's wake. Ironically, maybe it was the prospect of living under the control of another foreign power that caused thousands of Germans to take their own lives. Domination by Russia became the most feared by those left living. The Red Army losses totaled in the millions. Germans knew well there would be a taste for revenge because of all the losses. Many believed that the same emotion would dominate rule over them from their communist conquerors.

Ollie read discarded letters from imprisoned soldiers' relatives, telling stories of how people back home were left with despondency and dishonor. They knew that if the gruesome tales of Red Army soldiers' evil were true, life in the Fatherland would be filled with anguish and misery, so tens of thousands decided to follow their Fuhrer one last time into their graves. There were stories of how fathers would shoot their children, their wives, and themselves. Elderly couples hung themselves holding hands. Widowed mothers would march into freezing rivers, dragging their children behind them.

Finally, one fateful day, Ollie received a letter from a distant cousin with the news that Ollie's parents had died. They had lain on their bed and embraced as their home burned around them. Ollie read the letter with so many tears in his eyes that he couldn't see the benediction.

He sat back in his chair in the mess tent and looked out the flap that pointed west. The setting sun's light reminded him of the day that seemed so long ago in the courtyard where he'd heard the Fuhrer speak and felt his father's hand resting on his shoulder.

Allied troops had destroyed his home and his homeland, and he vowed he'd soon have a plan to right the wrongs of the past and move Germany to a future that was as bright and powerful as the sun.

# Chapter 16

Making moonshine was an art. The large metal pot held the boiling mix of corn squeezins and pure stream water. The copper tubing on top condensed the steam as it rose and cooled, eventually captured in brown jugs. Jess Comer liked to add flavors and spices to his brews, and his products were well-received by his patrons.

As owner and operator, he enjoyed testing new concoctions to make sure they were 'just right' before he decided to make his work available. At times, the heat and smells distressed him, but the sampling always took away his discomfort.

He was at a hollow on his property when he heard the truck approaching. He liked to move his equipment so that law enforcement would have a more challenging time keeping up with his operation's location.

He always kept a shotgun close by in a tent. He listened to determine if the vehicle was a police car, a federal revenue vehicle, or a customer. The approaching truck likely held a customer or two by the engine's sound. So Jess decided the shotgun could stay in its place.

He squatted near the fire, heating the corn mash and waiting as the customers approached. He could tell there was more than one person in the vehicle, and experience taught him that the more people, the more money.

"Jess," Brother shouted, "don't shoot. It's us."

Without looking up from the fire, Jess said, " I know it wasn't federals."

The trio broke through the underbrush to the north of the camp. They slid down the side of the hill, grasping tree branches to steady themselves. Mary Lou led, followed by Brother and Millie. They had dressed in their Sunday best to meet with Millie's father-in-law in hopes of impressing him.

Mary Lou asked, "Did ya' get a good crop to pick from this year?"

"Sweet corn, fullest kernels I've seen in ten years," Jess said. He tugged at the strap on his overalls, it was too hot to wear a shirt, and he crossed his muddy boots as he sat on a stool.

"You usin' hickory for your fire?" Brother asked.

"Sometimes hickory, sometimes oak," Jess said, not looking up from the fire. "Guess it's time to add another stick."

He turned to his left and reached toward his woodpile. Millie stood next to the half-cord of wood. She'd picked out her red print dress and wore low heels so she wouldn't be too tall as she talked with Jess.

"Be careful there, little lady, wouldn't want you to get snake bit," Jess said. A sly grin played with the corners of his mouth. He knew he'd already chased all the snakes away from the camp, but he also knew Millie didn't know that. Millie stood firm.

"I ain't 'fraid of snakes, Father Comer," she said. She moved her feet to the width of her shoulders and put her hands on her hips.

"I didn't think you'd be."

A whippoorwill called in the distance. A slight wind rustled the leaves at the tops of the trees. Jess pulled the log from the pile and pushed it into the fire.

"We come to talk…." Brother began, but Jess cut him off.

"I know what ya' come to talk about, and I ain't got nothin' to say 'bout it."

"But Father Comer…," Millie began, and again Jess interrupted.

"I got the letter tellin' me 'bout the check comin' just the other day. It's a fair amount, don't get me wrong, but 'cordin' to the letter, it's comin' to me."

Mary Lou squatted down in front of Jess so she could talk with him eye-to-eye. "Jess Comer, I'm sorry 'bout your son. He was a good boy, and what happened to him was a God-awful shame. No doubt about it."

"Let me stop ya' right there," Jess said, looking at Mary Lou.

Brother moved behind the still and opened the collar of his shirt. He was growing uncomfortable from the heat of the day and the added steam from the still.

"Cut your shit, Jess," Brother said. His gravelly voice was a bit louder than he'd intended, and his words echoed through the small amphitheater.

"I don't have to do nothin', Brother," Jess said. He took a deep breath and looked at the black earth in front of his fire. "I lost my boy, and the government says they'll send me money to compensate for that. There ain't no money can make up for that. I'm sorry you lost your husband of, what, two months, maybe. I had him for twenty years."

"It ain't right, and it ain't fair," Millie said. She sniffed as the wind shifted, and a puff of smoke clouded her face.

"No, little girl, life ain't fair. That's in the good book, somewheres," Jess said, looking up at Millie. "Ain't nothin' more we got to talk about."

"You're doin' okay, Jess," Brother argued. "You don't need the money. For Millie, that could make a big difference for her. She could go to school, maybe even get her own place."

"I said, we ain't got nothin' more to talk about," Jess said. He stood and looked Millie in the eye. The old man shook his head and moved toward the tent. He knew this meeting would likely happen but didn't know when. He also knew that ten thousand dollars was enough for people to make moves they might not otherwise consider. He stood next to the shotgun leaning against the main tent pole.

"You're on my property, and I need you to leave," Jess said.

"This ain't over," Mary Lou said.

Jess pulled his shotgun, turned, and pointed it at the ground.

"You're gonna have to live with treatin' this girl like this the rest of your life," Mary Lou said, glancing over at Millie. She hiked up her skirt, marched up the hill, and, without turning her head, said, "Come along, family."

Brother sighed. He knew better than to challenge Mary Lou right now, and while he wished he could trounce Jess then and there, he also knew it wouldn't do any good.

Brother snapped to attention, looked Jess in the eye, and saluted him as if he were still the ranking officer he was in the First World War. Jess returned the salute. They were still brothers in arms, and deep down, Brother hoped he could someday appeal to that comradery.

Millie turned and kicked a rock free from the side of the hill. It rolled into the side of the tent.

Jess knew her intent. He could feel her anger like the heat coming from the still. He loved his boy. He was sure Stanley probably loved Millie, too, but what's right is right, and what's legal is legal.

He watched the three of them as they topped the hill and disappeared. A few moments later, he heard the truck engine turn over and the crunch of the rocks under the rubber tires. *They'll likely be back*, he surmised. And he'd be ready for them. Or, they might not. He might not see them again. Either way, that would be fine with him.

He put the shotgun back next to the tent flap and saw the brown jug sitting beside it. He pulled the jug to his shoulder, held the bottle on top of the crook of his elbow, pulled out the corn cob stopper, and took a swig. This batch tasted bitter. He knew some of his customers liked that, but he was never a fan. He'd have to call it something. Customers loved the names he'd come up with for his brews. "Bitter tears," he mumbled.

He took another swig. "Sounds 'bout right."

# Chapter 17

Ollie could feel an odd vibe in the camp. He noticed it first in the guards. They smiled in a way he hadn't seen before, and it unnerved him. He wanted to ask them what was going on, but he knew better than to jump rank and talk out of turn. He'd wait until his camp commander explained what was happening.

The next day, May ninth, 1945, Commander Switzer told his lieutenants, who then dispersed the news to the rest of the men in the camp. The war ended yesterday with the surrender of Germany the day before. Ollie put his hands over his face and wept.

He knew the battle he'd been wounded in was a last-ditch attempt to win. He didn't see the name of the fight, but he believed his divine Fuhrer had a plan to bring victory to the Rhineland. Unfortunately, he'd been at sea when the campaign failed. Given the remoteness of Camp Forrest, the news took days, sometimes weeks, to arrive.

Ollie's duties continued, and as he regained his strength, expanded. He became a trusted worker for the camp commander and did everything he asked. For example, when a vital message needed to be relayed across the camp, Ollie would carry the small square of paper even with his still-healing leg wound. There were times when he'd write the message in the palm of his hand and hold his arm away from his body so that the words wouldn't smudge as he walked.

Ollie heard the news of the Fuhrer's death in April but refused to believe it since there were no recognizable remains. He knew Hitler's men in the bunker possessed great loyalty and would move heaven and earth to keep their leader and the hope of continued conquest alive. Ollie decided he wanted to help.

He grew angry and then sad at the notion that the war was over, and while he'd done all he could in the theater of battle, the outcome was still a failure. He ate his dinner from a tin plate with wooden utensils believing the conflict wasn't over. Finally, he looked up from the plate and, with tears in his eyes, asked God, could he be an instrument of revenge on those who continued to walk the Earth and oppose Germany? He said this in German so the men around him could understand but keep the guards in the dark.

When his gaze returned to his plate, he saw the dish filled with red, ripe tomatoes and sliced cucumber. He saw pure, white milk in his cup, and he gripped the side of it until his knuckles paled. "Ich lehne ab," he whispered to himself.

Other prisoners around the table quieted and looked at Ollie. Their faces registered the same shock and sorrow as Ollie's. Their minds raced, just as Ollie's did, trying to compute the facts of the day's news. The man sitting next to Ollie looked at his cup of milk and said, "ich lehne ab." The rest of the men around the table picked up the chant and raised their voices from whispers to shouts, "ich lehne ab."

Ollie stood. He raised his wooden fork to the roof of the mess tent and said, "ich lehne ab." He looked around the room and down at the dirt floor.

He stepped onto his rickety wooden chair and raised his fork, "ich lehne ab," although he knew that given the weakness in his leg from the still-healing bayonet wound, he was taking a chance that he'd fall and become the laughingstock of the entire troop.

A guard heard Ollie and the others. He watched for a moment as Ollie stepped up on the chair and led the others in his chant. He had no idea what they were saying, but he quickly realized from the tone and Ollie's flashing eyes it wasn't good. The boy was sweating, and his voice carried throughout the tent.

"Take your seat," the guard yelled over the growing din. "I said, get back in your chair."

Ollie ignored the guard and continued chanting, leading the men with words and an occasional 'Sieg Heil' to the Eastern corner of the tent. The war wasn't over until Ollie said it was, and a nub of an idea grew in the back of his mind. He stood in the homeland of his enemy. He was still a soldier and believed the war wouldn't end until he said so. "Ich lehne ab!" he screamed, raising his arm and grinning maniacally at the others in the tent.

The prisoners grew louder with their screams of support. Then, many stood and threw Nazi salutes at each other, encouraging even more raucous behavior.

The guard flashed by Ollie, swept his baton against the chair legs, and pushed him to the ground. Ollie looked up, the breath forced out of him and his eyes watering.

"You lost! Stay down!" the guard yelled.

While Ollie was clearly down, he wasn't out. He had a new plan and knew just the 'mädchen' that could help make it happen.

# Chapter 18

Olaf knew the 'Mae West' delivery occurred every two weeks, usually on a Tuesday. He told his captain about his plan, and they devised a diversion so he could easily slip into the truck when the guards weren't looking. If the plan worked, it would likely be several hours before they discovered Olaf was missing.

Ollie had charmed her for almost two months, and they had bumped into each other several times but never touched on purpose. Instead, Sweeney, the guard that seemed most attached to Snaps, hovered over every delivery. Olaf knew he'd have to find a way to distract Sweeney from his appointed duties.

The fight began between the captain and another soldier just as Snaps and Olaf finished unloading the truck. Sweeney unsnapped the strap on his baton as if showing her he had the situation under control. "You need to get out of here, Snaps!" he yelled. She jumped into the truck cab and cranked the engine.

The fight near the center of the camp grew even more violent. The players had prepared the crowd, telling them who they should root for in the contest. They even agreed on how long the altercation should last. They believed Olaf would only need a few minutes, but they wanted to make sure. They turned on the guards, ensuring the fighters and many others in the crowd would find themselves in solitary confinement once the diversion was over.

Olaf pulled the wooden boxes and baskets to the front of the truck bed. He covered himself with the black tarpaulin Snaps and Brother used to secure the load and keep sunlight off the produce.

The guard at the gate also found Snaps attractive and tried to flirt with her. Today, he watched the ruckus at the center of the camp and, with the other eye, quickly processed Snaps through the gate. The escalating situation near the flagpole grew louder.

"See ya' next time, Miss," the guard said. He absentmindedly saluted Snaps as his gaze turned to the fight.

Snaps pressed the accelerator. As she pulled onto the road in front of the facility, the old truck backfired.

The guard jerked, looked around for guidance, fumbled with a ring of keys, and lurched toward a cabinet holding rifles and handguns.

Snaps said, "Come on now, Bessie. We gotta get home."

Snaps liked the delivery run. It provided time away from the family and allowed her to practice singing at the top of her lungs, something she couldn't do in the house. Sure, she could sing in the barn and the field behind the house where her makeshift rock stage still stood but the open road, the hum of the tires on the asphalt, and the breeze in her hair inspired Snaps.

"Way down upon the Swanee River," she sang. She started the song in her lowest range to finish big and strong. She knew from practice that while it seemed a simple melody to most people, finding the right tone and pacing was the key to an excellent performance. She began again. "Way down upon the Swanee River, far, far away."

Olaf pulled back a corner of the tarp and moved his head closer to the open driver's side window. He hadn't heard Snaps sing before, and he was impressed. Most of the time he'd spent in beer halls in Berlin featured singers only half as talented as 'Mae West.'

"That's where my heart is yearning ever," Snaps crooned, "home where the old folks stay."

Snaps realized the tires, as they whined, created a rhythm that accompanied her singing. It was as if the universe was telling her, "Sing, girl, sing."

Snaps worked up a good head of steam as she approached the song's ending. Her stage experience gave her confidence, and her belief that only she could hear the music helped her find the emotion of the last phrases.

"I'm still a'longin' for the old plantation, oh, for the old folks at home."

She held the last note and pounded the heel of her hand on the steering wheel as she finished. She smiled as a police car approached. She hoped they wouldn't pull her over and write her a ticket for singing too loudly.

She chuckled at her little joke and waved to the black and white car as they passed. She was loud but not enough to disturb the peace.

Olaf smiled as Snaps finished her performance. She was beautiful and talented. And he knew from talking with her all these weeks she was smart, too. He believed he could turn her from an enemy to an ally with a smile and a twinkle in his eye.

Snaps pointed the nose of the truck at the entrance to the driveway in front of the house. It was a well-worn path and would likely need more gravel after last night's rain. That was Brother's responsibility, and she was glad she didn't have to help him push that wheelbarrow full of rocks across the yard. She had stupidly volunteered once when bored and learned that once was enough.

She parked the truck in the usual spot, turned off the engine, and raced to the front porch. Mary Lou stood at the edge of the porch and looked at the road north of the farm.

"What'cha lookin' at, Ma?" Snaps asked. She walked up behind the old woman and touched her arm.

Children sometimes fail to realize what adults are doing as they peer far into the distance. It's only when they have hundreds of days to remember and relive that the practice makes sense. Mary Lou appeared in a trance, and it was only as she shook her head and looked at Snaps that she returned to Earth.

"What 'cha lookin' at?"

"Nothin'. You didn't stop on the way, did ya'?"

"No, ma'am," Snaps said as she reached into her pocket and pulled out a small manila envelope. The agreed-upon amount from the Army was thirty-seven dollars and fifty cents per load. Mary Lou figured just what that would buy and how far she could stretch it.

"No troubles?" Mary Lou asked as she slipped the envelope into her apron pocket.

Snaps thought about telling Momma about the fight and her singing performance. She decided to downplay the events of the trip.

"Nothin' goin' on," Snaps said. She snapped off a salute to her mother, mimicking the soldier at the camp's exit gate, turned, and opened the screen door. It closed with a slap.

The family visit with Jess Comer yesterday made Mary Lou's blood boil. She read the second letter from the congressman's office advising Millie that her widow's benefit from Social Security would begin in a month. It wasn't much, just over two hundred dollars, but it might help Millie a bit.

Mary Lou heard a sound. It could have been the wind. She trained her gaze on the road and at the truck. She shook her head and was just about to open the screen door.

Snaps hummed the tune to *Swanee River* and burst into song at the second verse.

"Honey," Mary Lou said, "please, I've got a headache."

Snaps smiled, knowing it was the right idea to sing on the way back from the camp. Now, she'd have to go down to the creek and sing.

*"I'll be glad when I'm gone from here, and I can do whatever I want,"* she thought.

# Chapter 19

Olaf should have come up with a better plan after he escaped. He wore the prison-issue white shirt and pants with the black belt and black shoes he'd been given when he first arrived in America. The boy knew if he kept the same clothes on, he'd stand out against the bright greens of the surrounding landscape. He needed to change.

He crept around the truck's rear fender and stayed low as he approached the chicken coop and barn. Clothes hung on the line running from the house's back door to the garden. He touched a pair of overalls and frowned when he found them still wet. He pulled them down from the line and turned toward the barn.

There were flower beds and fruit trees along the path to the barn. He rushed from behind a rose bush, to behind a peach tree, to behind an azalea bush. He moved with as much stealth as he could muster, given it was noon and anyone could see him. He opened the fence gate, slipped through, and hid behind the wooden slats.

Olaf saw her coming out the back door with a basket loaded with more wet laundry. It was 'Mae West.' She had mentioned living with her sisters, mother, and uncle, but he was surprised she was the first person he saw. "*Lucky,*" he thought.

She was still wearing the same summer dress she'd worn when she made the delivery to the camp. He liked that dress; he couldn't find anything wrong with the girl.

He even liked her attitude. She was whistling and smiling now. Olaf liked that most about her. She seemed such a happy girl.

He turned and ran fifty yards to the barn's front door as quietly as possible. He slipped open the slide lock and dipped his shoulder as he slithered inside.

He changed quickly. He left the white shirt on, balled up the white pants, and shoved them behind a mound of hay. There was a small nest, and he scooped up the two eggs the hen had left, held them up over his face, cracked one and the other, and gobbled them down.

Ollie took a deep breath and considered where he might do the most good for the cause. If he could make his way to Washington, he could get to Truman and make him pay for what was done to his homeland. He'd read that Roosevelt had died, and Truman was sworn in just last week. He'd be an easy target with all the confusion of his taking office. The objective was to kill Truman, but the new president was six hundred miles away. He hoped he could make his way to the train tracks and maybe hitch a ride east.

Olaf had heard a train whistle as the girl drove through the small town. He'd have to make his way back there and find connections. The soldier also believed that some people didn't believe in the war against Germany and might help him. All he had to do was find them.

Hours later, he heard the barn door clasp slide open, and the large door screeched on its hinges. An older woman held a milk bucket. She wore a plaid bonnet, men's jeans, a shirt, boots, and a bandanna. Olaf guessed this was Mary Lou from the descriptions Snaps had shared. He knew she was a widow and that it had been a struggle for the family through the Depression, but they had made it with her leadership.

"Come along, kitty," she said. Her voice was soft and low. He could hear a tone that she shared with Snaps. Olaf detected a distinct accent when Mary Lou spoke, something Snaps had excised from her speech.

The kitten scooted through the big door, and Mary Lou closed it behind them. The cat knew milking time meant there may be some spillover that she could have, so she got as close to Mary Lou's boots as possible.

"Don't you try and trip me."

The cat meowed and cooed as Mary Lou stopped and looked at the back door. It was open. She had told Millie to close it that morning after the milking, but that poor girl's mind was still wandering about.

"Lord, help us," Mary Lou prayed. It comforted her to talk with God, and since she was rarely alone, it was times like these that she found a moment to look up and ask for help. She liked to believe the Lord had a plan.

Olaf moved closer to the stack of hay in the corner of the room. He could see Mary Lou through the slats and felt easily exposed if she turned her head.

The kitten bounded down the barn hallway toward the open door. She stopped and turned as the cows moved from the corral into the barn hall. She turned and scampered back to Mary Lou.

"Them cows are a bit bigger than you, aren't they?"

The kitten meowed as if answering the question.

Olaf moved. His boot scraped a tiny knothole in a plank. He held his breath as the cat turned her gaze toward him.

Mary Lou walked to the door and closed it just as one of the cows approached. It wasn't milking time, and Mary Lou had a strict schedule. She found being a few hours early or late could affect the yield.

The cat didn't have a plan but lived in the moment. She heard something stirring in one of the rooms where feed and hay were stored, which meant that a mouse might need catching. The cat liked milk but loved a good, warm mouse. She darted toward the door, squeezed through a crack, and scanned the room. She fully extended her ears and sniffed the air. She was still young, but her instincts made her a natural predator.

Olaf pushed deeper into the hay, pulling some over his feet and body. He knew it wasn't a good hiding place, but he'd have to make the best of it.

The cat saw Olaf's hands move through the hay and pounced, claws and teeth fully extended. He pushed her away and put both hands in front of himself as if to say, "Stay, don't come any closer."

She didn't understand or care, so she bit Olaf's thumb and drew blood. He chewed his bottom lip to keep from crying out. When the cat tasted human blood, she knew she'd made a mistake and retreated through the crack around the door.

"What'cha got goin' on there, Kitten?"

The cat looked over her shoulder and then back at Mary Lou. She surmised an absence of prey existed in the feed room. She'd return to her original plan of lapping some excess milk from a bowl as Mary Lou cleaned the buckets and milk cans.

It was not unusual for the cat to act this way. Kitten was always finding new ways to get into trouble.

Mary Lou hummed a hymn as she worked the brush and fanned the clean filters through the mushroom tops of the milk cans.

Olaf moved his left leg. A cramp caught in his calf muscle, and he rubbed it.

The cat homed in on the sound. Mary Lou turned her head.

"You got a mouse in there, cat?"

Mary Lou finished cleaning the buckets and cans and hung them on wooden posts to dry. The afternoon soap opera would likely be a doozie since it was Friday, and they always came up with a cliffhanger to get you to tune in on Monday.

"I betcha Grant's gonna ask Lisa to get married," she said to the cat as they walked to the front barn door, opened it, and sauntered back to the house.

Olaf took a deep breath. He knew he'd almost gotten caught with help from the cat. He had to get out of there now, and he would need some help.

# Chapter 20

Anne remembered when she was young, and the family survived on the garden's bounty and what little money they could earn from selling milk and eggs. It was at that time she honed her skills as a baker.

Most of her deliveries were within walking distance of the farm. Still, when Brother found an old bicycle in a ditch and refurbished it, her radius of opportunity increased. She would take off early this Saturday morning with two baskets, one filled with raisin cinnamon muffins and another with corn muffins.

Her route through the neighborhood brought her to fifteen different farms. While Anne was always successful, baking and distributing her wares made for a long day. She would rise early those days, prepare the batter, and be ready to make her rounds by ten a.m.

She knew her appearance was important on those days, so she ensured her dress was clean and pressed. Her hair would be drawn into a bow behind her head, and she would clean her shoes, though they would be dusty soon after she left home, given the state of the gravel roads in the neighborhood. She was doing well in school, so taking a day off for enterprise was not only accepted but encouraged. She had a deal with Mary Lou to share profits with the family. Property taxes would be due soon. While many opportunities for barter services like Brother's talent with a hammer and nail were easily obtained, hard currency was sometimes challenging to come by.

She coasted down a small hill and slowed as she approached the front gate of the Wilson home. She rang the bell on her bicycle and pulled the baskets from the handlebars.

"Hello," she called out. She knew they were likely home, but it was always best to approach a house in the country making some noise. There were too many people afraid of the tax collector, sheriff, or loan collector to take a chance of getting shot at.

"Hello," she called again as she climbed the rock stairs leading to the porch.

"Hey there," Jody White said. It had been some time since she'd seen him. She was three years behind him in school, and the social strata deemed that grade difference meant little acknowledgment from the higher-ups.

"I was makin' the rounds and wanted to know if your folks might be interested in some baked goods. Fresh out of the oven," Anne said. She tucked a stray sprig of hair behind her ear and smiled at Jody.

The two-story house was a Sears package home like several others in the neighborhood. A catalog allowed people to browse the plans available, the prices, and the estimated time it would take to construct the building.

The two-story shed Brother, Jody, and his father had built earlier that year stood behind and to the right of the main house. Cows ambled around the open doors, and a stack of hay bales peeked from slats in the door. They'd painted the shed the same shade of white as the main house.

About the same time as the White's Sears home construction, Brother had built Mary Lou's house after the original home across the creek caught fire and burned to the ground. He'd also helped other neighbors with putting similar homes together. They would be delivered in boxes, and the plans were detailed. Brother liked to laugh that he hoped they had at least one nail more than the plan called for in case he dropped one and couldn't find it in the grass.

Jody had grown five inches, and muscles covered his once bony frame. He wore a T-shirt and jeans, and he was barefoot. He walked across the porch and leaned against a white pillar.

There was something strange about his face she hadn't noticed before. There was a slight crook in his nose. It wasn't that she didn't like it. She thought it gave him character and a lop-sidedness that made his brown eyes more soulful.

"I've got corn muffins," she said, but she couldn't take her eyes off his face, "and I made raisin cinnamon. They seem to be the most popular today."

"How much you want for 'em?"

He looked down on her as she rested one foot on the stone step that led to the porch. He hadn't kept up with her in school, but he should have. She had turned into a natural beauty and looked cute in her Saturday outfit.

"They're two for a quarter," she said with an upbeat tone as if to say the price was right.

"Whoo wee, ain't that a bit high?" he asked. He flashed a grin at her, and she frowned. She'd used the ploy before making a sale to a young man who might be vulnerable to a bright smile.

"Well, they are awfully good," she said, flashing her pearly whites again.

"Oh, all right," he said, reaching into his pocket. "I think I've got two bits."

He handed her the coin, and his fingers touched her palm. She felt her cheeks flush, so she dipped her head so he wouldn't notice. Too late.

"Hey, you all right?" he asked.

She pulled a cloth from the basket, wrapped up two raisin cinnamon, and handed them to him. Again, his hand touched hers. She felt another rush. "*What's wrong with me,*" she thought. "*He's just a silly old boy.*"

"Great," he said. He pulled the cloth from the muffin, picked one up, and took a bite. "Hey, how'd you know I'd pick this one?"

"I just took a guess. Fifty-fifty chance I'd be right."

She turned and put the basket back on her handlebars.

"You're livin' on the edge," he said, chuckling at his joke.

He was right and didn't know it. Anne was the one everyone looked to if there was a question of chance. Luckily, she was right most times, even if many of her decisions were based on a guess.

"You just seemed like a cinnamon raisin kind of man," she said. Her back was turned, but she knew he could hear her.

"Say, Anne, you goin' to church tomorrow?"

"Not sure about tomorrow." She really didn't know. They were infrequent visitors to the Lord's house, mostly too tired to get ready Sundays. "We usually go to Stone Creek Baptist."

"Ah, we're Methodist," he said, a tone of genuine disappointment in his voice.

"I don't think there's that much difference between the two," she remarked. She was astride the bike now and looking at Jody with large, round eyes.

"*What's happened to her?*" he thought. "*How has she become so attractive without my noticing?*"

These were common questions as adolescents grew into adulthood. The rapid maturation during those years turned many an ugly duckling into a beautiful swan.

"Oh, yeah, r-r-right," he stammered, "I was wonderin' if you might like to go with me tomorrow? Me and my family," he quickly corrected himself.

"Let me think," she pondered for a moment, what her answer might mean. What if he was only interested in increasing the attendance to the morning service and saw her as a stray lamb? "I guess that'd be all right."

He smiled, "Great, I'll come by and pick you up around nine. Is that okay? *We'll* come and pick you up, I mean."

She flushed again. "I'll be ready." She turned quickly and pedaled toward the gate in the fence that encircled the yard. She hoped she'd have a chance to ask him what happened to his nose tomorrow, but it might have to wait. Questions about personal appearance during a church service might be inappropriate.

The better question might be, why didn't Brother tell the family about the incident during the shed construction? Was it embarrassment, or did it just slip the man's mind?

She turned and waved as she rode through the gate. She saw Jody was eating his muffin and that he tipped his chin to her as he chewed.

# Chapter 21

Olaf's third day on the farm included finding five eggs and two cups of milk only a few hours from turning sour. The family had little food waste, and he was starting to feel the same hunger pangs he'd grown so familiar with while growing up in war-torn Berlin.

He scavenged some of the land around the farm and found a rusty tin of tuna fish in a scrap heap. He knew the danger of eating possibly tainted food, but he was on a mission and couldn't kill President Truman if he starved to death.

He ate the fish, and as expected, his stomach ached until he finally threw up the contents in the corner of the barn's hall. He rested in the feed room that had become his bedroom and didn't notice when Snaps slid the clasp on the barn door.

She wore blue jeans and a long-sleeved white shirt. Her hair was pulled back, and her sneakers were black. She carried a basket under her arm and scanned the barn hall.

"Stupid chickens," she said. "Why can't you lay eggs in the hen house like you're supposed to?"

Olaf knew it was a rhetorical question, but he wondered what would happen if he answered? Would she turn him over to the authorities or keep quiet about hiding there? So he burrowed deeper into his hiding place.

She began her search along the sides of the walls with two-inch gaps between the slats. First, she looked in the feed troughs. Hens had laid eggs there in the past. She even searched around some of the bags of grain Brother stored on elevated platforms with the idea that mice wouldn't bother them there.

"Not one," Snaps mumbled.

She looked at the hall's back door and marveled at how the slanting sunlight illuminated the dust particles as they drifted through the air. She chuckled to herself that she'd probably miss country life when she left home.

She moved toward the entrance door, swinging the empty basket. She was sliding the bolt on the door when she heard it. It was a scraping noise with a sharp squeak at the end. She first thought it was the cat lying in wait for a mouse and that the mouse was now part of an afternoon snack. Next, she considered that the cat might be moving through Brother's tools in the feed room, and the movement had caused a hoe or a rake to shift against the wall where they hung.

She opened the feed room door and looked inside. The yellow sunlight invaded each corner of the small space. Stacks of grain and hay lined the walls. The tools sat motionless, undisturbed by a cat or mouse. She was about to turn and leave when she caught the smell of Olaf's regurgitated tuna.

Olaf had washed out his mouth as best he could after throwing up the fish, but at that moment, he realized a tiny spot of the dried vomit clung to the cuff of his shirt. He considered rubbing it but feared the noise would be a more significant attraction than the smell.

Barns were filled with strange and awful aromas. Olaf was a city kid, but even he knew the fishy smell currently sticking to him was different.

"Is there someone there?" Snaps asked as she scanned the room. She didn't know what she was looking for but was sure she'd know something was amiss when she saw it.

"Mae West," Olaf whispered.

She turned. Her gaze locked onto Olaf's icy blue eyes. She shivered.

"What are you…"

"I had to get out," he said, emerging from behind the stack of hay bales. "It was killing me there." His accent seemed thicker now than when they'd talked in the camp.

She could see he was wearing Brother's overalls and shirt. She also now knew where the odd fish smell was coming from.

"How did you…" she began.

He interrupted her again. "Mae West, I'm sorry. I hid in the back of the truck, and I've been here."

"Since Tuesday?"

"I'm not sure what day it is," he began. He tried to appear as weak and helpless as possible. He believed she was someone who might help him make his way out of town. He knew he couldn't tell her of his plan.

"You stay right here," she ordered.

"I'm not alone," he lied. "If you turn me in now, he'll track down and kill all your family. This, I know."

She thought for a moment. Could she take a chance he and another prisoner had escaped in the back of her truck? Now, it was up to her to save her family.

"Prove it," she demanded.

"Why would you want to take that chance?" He responded. He let a harsh tone enter his voice and slowly drew his index finger across the base of his neck. "Just like that."

Snaps didn't want to take that chance. The war in Europe had only been over for a few weeks, and she had no idea what a German prisoner might do if pushed.

"You'll stay here," Snaps said. She shifted her basket from her left hand to her right. She was prepared to use it as a weapon and run.

He looked up at the corner of the loft. He believed he could convince Snaps there was someone else up there and that her family was in danger. At that moment, a rat scampered across the wooden slats of the floor. It was perfect timing enough to convince Snaps he was telling the truth.

"I'll meet you at the truck," he said with force and authority.

"I can't..." she started, but he cut her off again.

"You will, and if you don't, well, could you live with knowing that your family died because of you?"

She slowly shook her head and backed away from him.

"Get the keys, and I'll meet you at the end of the road," he said. He pointed to a corner of the lot where the road disappeared around a bend.

"You were always so nice to me," she said. Unfortunately, there was a 'little girl lost' quality to her protestation, which caused a stab of pain to enter his chest. He remembered how Stanley, the medic was so kind and caring there at the field hospital. He felt terrible that he was taking advantage of this poor country girl. Still, Olaf had decided to do whatever it took to complete his self-assigned mission, and he wouldn't let anyone or anything stand in the way.

# Chapter 22

"How much money can you get?" Olaf asked.

Snaps put her finger to her bottom lip as she reviewed how much she had in a box under her bed. She had to guess how much was in the coffee jar in the kitchen.

"Maybe fifteen dollars," she said. She looked at him. His blue eyes pierced her heart, just as they had when they first met, but now she saw a coldness there.

"That will have to do," Olaf said. He shifted his weight away from his wounded leg. The boy felt pain when his knee turned the wrong way or the sky was filled with storm clouds. Through the slats in the feed room wall, he could see the bright, white sun and not a cloud in the sky. Today would be a good day.

"I'll go in with you," he said. His usually muted German accent rose in his voice.

The trace of the enemy's voice Snaps had heard portrayed on the radio scared her. She'd listened to the news reports where German voices in plain English leaped from the speakers. This was the voice of the men who killed Millie's husband, Stanley, and murdered countless more. Snaps shivered and walked toward the feed room door.

Just then, Mary Lou opened the slide lock on the barn door.

"Snaps!" she bellowed, "where are you, girl?"

Snaps looked at Olaf and answered before he could stop her.

"I'm right in here," she said.

Olaf put his finger to his lips and shooshed her away. "Remember, I can kill all your family."

Mary Lou stuck her head through the door. From that angle, it would be impossible for her to see through the slats that made up the walls of the feed room.

"Come to the house as soon as you can. *As the World Turns* starts in a couple of minutes, and we have snap peas." She closed the slide lock and walked back toward the house.

As they listened to Mary Lou leaving, Snaps and Olaf held their breath.

Olaf knew from experience that there were ways to control people, especially women, with great success. He was not above using his looks and body to make them comply.

He stepped toward her and grabbed a handful of her shirt. Snaps eyes grew large, and she grimaced. She had been on dates and even had to shove away some 'hungry hands' sometimes, but she was saving herself for her wedding night. Before that, she believed she could do whatever was necessary to fight off any man.

Olaf wasn't just any man. He knew what he was doing, and soon he had Snaps up against the slats of the feed room wall. He tried kissing her, but she kept turning her head. She swung her egg basket and luckily hit him in the still-healing wound on his leg. She saw him buckle in pain and fall to his knees.

"You bitch," he said through clenched teeth.

She stumbled toward the door to the left, but Olaf caught her ankle, and she tumbled to the floor. He had regained his breath and was on her in an instant. He covered her mouth, yanked down her pants, and reached inside her underwear.

Snaps tried to scream, but Olaf's hand gripped her mouth. In fact, his fingers came dangerously close to covering her mouth and nose, cutting off her air. She tried biting him, but his strength overcame her. She cried, and tears streamed down her cheeks.

He wished he didn't have to be so forceful, but she put up such a fight. He opened the clasps on his overalls and put his knee between her legs. "Stop this instant," he whispered.

She felt weak, and her head started hurting. She wanted to scream out, but she had no air. The room was spinning, and suddenly there was a sharp pain between her legs. That pain subsided and transformed into a dull throb. She felt warm liquid dripping down the side of her inner thigh. She felt his weight against her chest and stomach. He was too big, too heavy, and she wanted him off. She pushed her hips up against his as he moved against her. It was no use.

She couldn't look down, but she could close her eyes. She prayed, believing God would stop the attack. With seconds feeling like hours, she asked simply that the pain go away and that if it was her time to die, she be taken to heaven right now.

Snaps opened her eyes and saw Olaf smiling down at her. Shock crossed her mind like a lightning bolt as she realized he was enjoying himself. *"How could I have fooled myself into thinking he was a good man?"* she asked herself. She didn't understand that he had taken his hand from her nose, and she could breathe easily again.

"You surprise me, Mae West," he said in a lecherous tone. "No bra."

She felt him reach inside her torn blouse and fondle her. She wiggled her shoulders, thinking the gesture of resistance might distract him. She was right.

She freed one hand and punched him in the leg. He bellowed as she struck the place where he'd been injured all those months ago. How could she have known just the right place to hit him?

"Help!" Snaps screamed through his fingers.

Olaf took a deep breath, closed his eyes, and shuddered against her. He removed his hand.

"Stop!" Snaps yelled, "Get offa me, you son-of-a-bitch!"

Olaf smiled at her and said, "You will now do as I say." Just as he rose to his knees, Brother hit him in the head with a shovel.

# Chapter 23

The sheriff studied the corpse for a moment, looked at Brother, and asked to look at the shovel. He turned the tool over and over in his hands. Then, he held it before himself and swung it like a baseball bat.

"Too bad you didn't just knock him out," the old man said, switching his toothpick from one side of his mouth to the other. "I wish I'd had a chance to get him behind the jail for a few minutes."

Brother knew what the man was talking about, and he agreed. There were times the justice system worked, and there were instances when it was most satisfying to practice 'frontier' justice. An escaped German prisoner who attacks and rapes a young, virgin American woman would be an opportunity for the latter.

"I'll leave out that part where Ginger, well, you know," the sheriff said, trying to be as delicate as he could about the sexual assault.

Brother nodded and said, "Ain't no reason the rest of the girl's life gotta be ruined by the likes of this bastard."

The salty language wasn't shocking to the sheriff. He'd served in the Army and fought in France about the same time as Brother, but he was a good Christian and didn't believe in cursing. He didn't feel the need to correct Brother right now, but there might come a time when he would witness to him the saving grace of the Lord.

"Please tell her I'm sorry 'bout what happened. I'd give her a hug if'n I could," he said.

The sheriff knew that wouldn't be appropriate in this instance. Still, there were times when something as simple as a gentle hug for a wayward boy who'd broken into a barn would turn the lad away from his wickedness. Or have a talk with his fist to a drunk and abusive husband as the man's wife lay in a bloody pile on the floor. He always made a point of being extra attentive to people with physical and emotional wounds whenever he could. He would have to run for reelection soon, and word got around, both the positive and the negative.

"For now," the sheriff said, "I'll just pray for her."

The sheriff took the shovel, put it in the back of his car, and promised to return it once all the paperwork had been filed. Brother stood next to the barn door and looked at the boy's body, wrapped in a sheet, as it lay on an Army surplus stretcher. Blood still oozed from the boy's head and stained the sheet.

Bodies on stretchers were a common sight for Brother. He'd seen plenty of wounded in the First World War, even killed Germans then, but this boy seemed much younger than the ones he'd faced on the battlefield.

Brother remembered standing in a trench filled with knee-deep mud as he waited for the order to advance. His foot rested on the rung of a ladder. He shifted his rifle from his shoulder to his hand. But, no, that wouldn't work. He'd need both hands to climb. "*As long as I've been on the line, you'd think I'd have learned something by now*," he thought.

His most recent bunkmate had caught the flu, so he felt more alone as he stood there. He had faced the possibility of death so many times in the past. He listened to the machine gun rattling in the distance. He knew that it would likely be his time when they stopped to reload.

Brother swallowed hard and took a deep breath. Facing the machine gun nest and the accompanying cannon fire made the muddy field in front of him an obstacle course with few good options. He'd have to run to a bomb crater and hunker down until he could move forward. Sometimes, he wished he had a shovel to make the hole even deeper.

Standing there, watching the car pull away with the boy's body, a slight grin tickled Brother's lip. He didn't have a shovel that day in the bunker, but the one he had today sure came in handy.

Mary Lou and, eventually, all the girls had run to the barn when Brother started yelling. They ran, jerked open the door, and found poor Snaps huddled in the corner of the feed room.

Her eyes were large, and she kept gulping air like a fish out of water. Mary Lou patted the girl's hair as Millie hugged her.

"I didn't want to. He r-r-raped me," Snaps stammered. Looking at the feed room floor, she felt her face grow red in shame.

"You're alive now," Mary Lou assured her.

"And he ain't," Anne said. She glanced over at the body of the blonde boy, fighting the urge to stomp across the room and kick him in the ribs several times.

Mary Lou and the girls picked up Snaps under the arms and guided her, feet scraping the ground, to the house. Mary Lou put Snaps in a bath and tucked her into bed before the doctor arrived. Still in deep shock and pain, the girl cried herself to sleep. Mary Lou sat next to her bed and watched her lying there. She considered all her mistakes over the years and how much she loved her girls. She vowed she'd never let anything else bad happen to them.

# Chapter 24

Snaps awoke from her recurring nightmare, drenched in sweat and nauseated. She sat up in bed and looked for the nightlight her mother had left in the hallway. It was always there.

The nightmare involved her being chased through the woods. There was a creature making terrible howling noises echoing behind her. She wore her nightgown and no shoes. Her feet were torn and bloody from running through the underbrush. She stopped, gasping for breath as she hugged a tree. She wondered what was chasing her and what it wanted.

She looked over her shoulder at a clump of bushes as she stood there. She was still, but her breath was rapid and ragged. "W-w-w-who's there?" she would always ask.

As the creature emerged from the bushes, she opened her eyes and found the mattress's edge with her fingers. Gravity seemed to fail her at that moment. She felt light and heavy energy waves until she swung her feet over the edge of the bed and looked at the dark panels of the painted pine flooring.

Mary Lou would hear the girl's screams and rush to her bedside. It had happened so often that she considered just sleeping there on the floor as when Snaps had some childhood illness, but she hoped there would be peace one night.

Millie and Anne, whose bedroom was next door, had grown accustomed to the nightly ritual. Putting a pillow over their heads usually shut out the commotion.

This night, five weeks after the attack and the death of escaped prisoner of war Olaf Weber, much of the necessary paperwork had been filed. The guards at the POW camp were reprimanded, and Corporal Sweeney, who felt responsible for the escape and the attack, was demoted. There was talk of him possibly being discharged because of his negligence. However, there was still a need for help at the camp, and one less-experienced guard right now would maybe put other Americans at risk.

Sweeney wrote a letter to Snaps, hoping she would someday forgive him. Instead, he read what he had written, balled it up, and threw the paper in the trash. He knew she wouldn't have the heart to accept his apology, nor should she.

Mary Lou brought a wet towel to Snaps' room. Unfortunately, the routine of the aftermath of the nightmare called for a change in bedclothes and a sponge bath before the girl could attempt to go back to sleep.

"Here we go," Mary Lou said, "let's get this wet shirt off."

Snaps stood, shoulders slumped, with her back to her mother.

"Do you think this will ever end?" the girl asked.

"The doctor said it might take a while for you to get back to normal," Mary Lou said. And she thought about raising Snaps, singing a song, or reciting a poem to help ease her mind. Still, she knew deep down that the girl was no longer a child and would take a lot more than a song to bring her back to herself.

"Yeah," Snaps said. She wiped her face, arms, and stomach with the towel.

"It'll take some time," Mary Lou said as she pulled a clean, white nightgown from a dresser drawer.

"I know," Snaps said with her head hung low. Her white panties glowed in the slanting moonlight.

Mary Lou gathered up the nightgown, and as she slipped it over her head, Snaps said, "I didn't have my period."

This was Mary Lou's nightmare. She knew Snaps was a good girl and that while she was popular, she had the good sense to remain a virgin. That was all ruined now.

"That don't mean nothin'. Well, you're likely gonna be late what you been through."

"I've never been late before," she said. A forlorn, helpless tone crept into her voice, and her shoulders shook. Mary Lou stood behind her daughter, but she knew she was crying.

"We'll go to the doctor tomorrow and get you checked out. You ain't got nothin' to worry about," Mary Lou said.

"What will people say?" the girl whispered.

Mary Lou turned Snaps around and took her chin between her index finger and thumb. "You don't worry about a thing. You hear me. It's probably nothin'."

She wanted to believe her daughter wasn't with child. Mary Lou needed to believe that the damage that had been done by that German son-of-a-bitch was over. She hoped her precious baby could get on with her life.

Millie stood in the hallway. She could see Snaps and Mary Lou hugging and that they were crying. She hugged her pillow to her stomach and bit her bottom lip. She looked through the gap where the door hinges glowed yellow in the moonlight.

"Good Lord, please," Millie whispered, "too much, too much."

# Chapter 25

Just as Anne predicted, Methodists were Baptists-lite. While the Baptists had to dunk you fully in the water so your sins could be forgiven, Methodists sprinkled. She was okay with that, and when she told Jody that she might join his church soon, he could not hide his joy.

"Really, Anne?" he said, his voice pitched an octave higher.

"I like the people here. They're so nice. And the music is good. Good piano player," she added.

They stood on the front steps of the small church. The Sunday morning sun shone yellow high in the sky, and a breeze moved the leaves in the trees. A rabbit dashed across the road near the entrance to the parking lot.

Their dates had included several walks along the riverbank, a few trips to town to sit in Jody's car and watch traffic circle the town square, and one sumptuous dinner at the City Café. In addition, their three church dates over three months included the early morning Easter service and two others with more mundane intent.

Of course, Anne's interest in a church meant more now than it did before she started seeing Jody. The attack on Snaps initially prompted rage in Anne, anger at God for letting this happen to her sister, and a deep depression with a sour outlook on the world. Only Jody, with his cute grin and crooked nose, pulled her back to her former self.

Anne and Millie had taken similar walks by the creek, where Anne expressed her anger at the U.S. Army, the president, and God about what happened to Snaps. A couple of times, Anne shook her fist at the sky and almost cursed as they walked. Millie stayed silent for much of their ramblings. She had problems with God, too, with her husband being killed in action and his promise to care for her thwarted by Stanley's father.

"We ought to throw some rocks," Anne said. She stood by the rushing water, watching the sun glance off the ripples.

For Millie, nature meant peace and understanding. Her walks, sometimes by herself, allowed her to breathe easily and not get caught in endless loops of what might have been if only Stanley had lived.

Anne expressed interest in a nice boy several farms away, and Millie found solace in that. They discussed how he liked working with his father and that their assets meant Anne would have a chance to build on her ambitions. The word of her delicious baked goods had spread throughout the community, and with the right equipment, her hobby might become a profession. People always needed cakes for weddings and birthdays and pies for Thanksgiving and Christmas. Anne could ramp up production and fill that need.

"We don't have to be mad at God," Millie said. She picked up a rock and skipped it across a calm part of the creek.

"It don't hurt nothin' to be angry every once in a while," Anne said without looking at her sister.

"No, you might feel better for a while, no doubt, but," Millie took a deep breath, "you gotta move on and let go."

"I remember a preacher sayin' somethin' like that once, let go and let God."

"Yes," the eldest sister said. "I remember that, too."

"And I remember a preacher sayin' you can't have a rainbow without the rain."

Millie chuckled, "I think that's a song."

They both laughed for a moment. Millie led the way as they ambled down the creekside.

"If it ain't a song, it oughta be," Anne said, snickering.

The wind picked up, and Millie stumbled as her foot struck a rock. Anne caught her arm before she could fall.

"Thanks," Millie said.

"Nothin' to it," Anne said, nodding. She felt Millie's strong hand in hers, knowing their anger would eventually subside.

Anne raced ahead and picked up a rock. The bank slanted toward the water, her shoes caught in the mud, and she lost her balance. Millie tried to catch her, but Anne fell face-first into the slow-moving clear water in a split second.

"Shoot," she said as she struggled to her feet. Unfortunately, her shoes were caught in the mud again.

"You be careful," Millie said, tugging Anne's sleeve as she found her feet.

"Baptized," Anne laughed.

"Not sprinkled at all," Millie said, joining in on the funny observation.

"Yep," Anne said.

"Does that mean you're gonna set your cap for that boy, Jody?"

"Water dries," she said, brushing mud from her hands where she'd tried to catch herself before she fell into the water.

"Yes, it does," Millie said.

This brought Anne to the church steps the next day, talking with Jody. She liked him. Maybe someday soon, she might even love him.

Anne and Jody heard the beginning chords of a hymn from the open front door as the piano player warmed up the crowd.

"Are you ready to go in?" Jody asked. He offered her his hand.

She looked up at him from where she stood a step below. The sun shadowed the hollows of his face and made his teeth dazzle.

Anne reached up and took his hand. She could feel the strength and assurance in his touch. "Yes, I'm ready," she said.

# Chapter 26

Morning sickness forced three changes to Snaps' daily routine. She would forego her reading from the *Complete Works of William Shakespeare*. She would instead find herself listening to the morning news on the radio and eating oatmeal, something she detested before being with child. Thirdly, she would walk to her impromptu stage, sit on the outcropping, and watch the sunrise.

One morning, she imagined what William S. would make of her situation. What would he have to say if Juliet and Romeo were preparing to have a child?

Emoting now, "Dear friar, has thou hearest of this unless thou tell me how I may prevent it. If in thy wisdom thou canst give no help, do thou but call my resolution west, and with this knife, I'll find it presently."

She picked up an invisible knife and turned it in her hand.

"The blade, so sharp, the handle feels just right." She showed the invisible friar her knife. "God joined my heart and Romeo's, thou our hands; And ere this hand, by thee to Romeo's sealed."

She extended her right hand as if giving it to her groom. "Shall be the label to another deed, or my true heart with treacherous revolt."

Snaps considered Juliet's thoughts at this point in her life. Juliet's father had declared war on the family of her husband. What should have been an opportunity for a truce escalated into a fiery declaration. The answer seemed obvious to Juliet; take herself and Romeo out of the equation, and the conflict would be averted.

The friar, God's messenger, pleaded for her not to take her own life.

"Therefore," she orated to the distant stream, the rocks, trees, rabbits, and voles that made the forest home, "out of thy long-experienced time, give me some present counsel, or, behold, 'twixt my extremes and me this bloody knife Shall play the umpire,"

Again, Snaps twisted the invisible tool in her hand as if catching the sun's rays on the blade. Finally, she turned as if looking into the eyes of the friar. "arbitrating that which the commission of thy years and art could bring to no issue of true honor. Be not so long to speak. I long to die if what thou speak'st speak not of remedy."

She wore new jeans, a blue work shirt, white socks, and heavy boots. The clothes she'd worn during the attack had long since been dumped into a pile and burned by Mary Lou and Snaps. It was an attempt, an old ritual practiced by the hill people from which Mary Lou had come, that symbolized cleansing and a new beginning. They had gathered the clothes after her nightmare that had upset the whole family.

The two of them had snuck out of the house and gone past the barn to a small indention in a field. Mary Lou sprinkled kerosene over the pile, and Snaps scratched a kitchen match over the sandpaper outside the box.

The fire spread quickly and moved from the clothes to the dry grass around the hollow. Mary Lou took one step but hesitated and allowed Snaps to stomp out the fire before it could set the entire lot ablaze.

It also was an attempt by the mother to show the girl she wasn't bound by the vicious act of another person. She wanted to show Snaps she didn't have to hold on to the past.

And then Snaps found out she was pregnant.

Mary Lou knew motherhood caused strange changes in a woman's body and mind. She also knew that while she wanted to help Snaps, there was likely little more she could do than just be supportive. Mary Lou wondered what that would mean to her youngest daughter.

Snaps shifted her weight forward as she sat on the limestone precipice that was her stage. She pulled the invisible folds of a velvet robe to her body and told the invisible friar, "Go, get thee hence, for I will not away." As if making a promise to him that she would not take her own life.

The friar left.

Snaps bent down and contemplated the body of her Romeo. "What's here? A cup closed in my true love's hand?" She picked up the invisible cup and raised it to her nose.

"'tis poison."

She nodded and said again to the corpse, "I see, hath been his timeless end."

Over the top now, the emotion in her delivery increased in volume. "O churl, drunk all, and left no friendly drop to help me after!"

Still contemplating whether to take her own life, the pendulum swings to and fro for Juliet.

"I will kiss thy lips." She paused and remembered Olaf's sweating face above hers and how he smelled. She licked her lips and tasted the salt from his perspiration. How could that be? That happened weeks ago.

"Haply some poison yet doth hang on them," she whispered. Now contemplating as Juliet had at that moment. "To make die with a restorative."

She bent over, clutching the edges of her invisible robe. She kissed the phantom actor.

"Thy lips are warm!"

And with that, the melding of Snaps' imaginary world and reality became too much. Her lips twisted into a cruel grin. The correct decision became clear. Tonight, the answer to the question.

# Chapter 27

Mary Lou rolled the aluminum milk can into the little cart Brother had made for her three years ago. It had become apparent that carrying them had become too much of a struggle for her. He'd even painted the cart to match the color of the cans with the tight-fitting mushroom tops. The large, silver-painted, four-spoked wheels wore a groove in the grass, making transport easy.

She pushed the little wagon to the end of the driveway that connected the barn entrance to the road. She'd timed it precisely as the delivery truck rounded the curve, sped to the gate, and skidded to a stop, creating a cloud of dust from the dry, gravel road.

Pete opened the door and hopped down from the cab. His cap rested far back on his head, showing the brilliant morning sun on his broad, brown forehead. He drove this route twice a day and always had something nice to say to Mary Lou as he checked her delivery off the list on his clipboard.

"Mornin' Missy," he said. His hand moved as if he might doff his cap, but he thought better of it. He was a veteran who had served in Italy. While he and the other Black soldiers were heartily welcomed as liberators there, he still met with some resistance back home. Mary Lou wasn't like that. Her reputation for treating everyone equally was well known, and her views were respected throughout the county.

"Pete, are you doin' all right?" she asked as she rolled the little cart with the three milk cans filled with the morning and evening work.

He had injured his back in a skirmish just outside Palermo, and from time to time, he'd have to take a sick day. His replacement wasn't near as personable, so Mary Lou missed him. Pete had been off the route for over a month.

"Yes, ma'am, doing fine. Thanks for asking."

"It ain't the same when you're off."

Her compliment made the next part of his day's assignment even harder. "I got a letter for you," he said, wincing as he hefted the can on the front of the cart into the refrigerated truck and retrieved the paper from his shirt pocket.

"Good news or bad news?" Mary Lou asked as she read the letter. "*The health department requires new equipment and sanitation practices to be followed by milk producers.*" He picked up the second can, not looking at Mary Lou as she read. He didn't think he could stand it if she started crying.

She continued reading, "*Concrete floors, milking machines, and refrigeration units.*" "I can do the concrete floors and a new cooler, but milking machines, that's real money." Mary Lou said, ending the sentence with a big sigh.

"The creamery has a program where you can get a low-interest loan to make the changes. Study on it and let them know what you want to do."

Pete picked up the last milk can and hefted it into the truck. He slammed the door shut and turned with his pen. He held out the clipboard for her signature.

"It's a big change, I know that, but they want to make sure the supply is clean," he said.

She took the pen and signed her name. "I'm clean. I filter every bucket."

"I know that," he replied, turning and resting his foot on the running board of the truck's cab. It was a response he'd already heard several times on this morning's route. Of course, the farmers kept their equipment clean. Still, dedicated milk barns meant reducing pathogens that could sicken consumers. The dairy Co-op didn't need the bad publicity of a milk-borne, bacterial outbreak.

Pete carefully considered what he would say next. Other Black drivers had lost their jobs by speaking out of turn to white women. Any comment that could be taken cross-eyed meant trouble. He trusted Mary Lou was different.

"I heard what went on in the barn there," he said, glancing over her shoulder, "terrible thing."

"Yes, terrible thing," Mary Lou said, "Snaps will be all right, given time."

As promised by the sheriff, the sexual details of the attack were left out of any public record. Snaps would be spared people's knowledge of the horror and shame of the rape.

Nodding, Pete pushed his cap even farther back on his forehead. "I know she will. She's a strong, good girl. You know I was in Italy fightin' those bastards?" He paused, "Sorry."

She gave him a look that he interpreted to mean he could continue. She knew that Pete had attended church all his life, even been invited to participate in the all-white Baptist church when an afternoon of singing filled the small cathedral with groups and soloists, some with drums and guitars and the church's piano and organ. But, of course, the drums and guitars were only allowed for special services, not the Sunday morning or night gatherings.

"Them Nazis was some of the meanest, dirty-fightin'-est, well, it was bad. I only mean to say, there weren't nothin' Snaps could'a done any different. She done good."

"Uh, huh," Mary Lou mumbled.

"And Brother done even better."

He hoped she would take his comment as a joke or an encouragement, but Mary Lou's bottom lip quivered, and she turned the cart around and headed back to the barn.

There were moments when she wished she could tell someone that Snaps was in a 'family way' because of the attack. In the past, a new baby would have been a cause for celebration. In the past, there would likely have been a quick wedding. The best option now was to tuck her away for the duration so people couldn't do the math of her pregnancy.

Mary Lou didn't know what people would think if she told them, but she sure wanted to tell someone. Maybe Pete would understand.

"Say, Pete," she said without turning.

"Yes, 'am."

She again considered telling him. He was a friend. He'd understand, maybe even be helpful. She turned. She knew what he'd been through and seen in the war. Why put one more piece of wood in his overstuffed bag?

"See ya'," she said, turning back to her cart and pushing it toward the barn.

"I'll see ya' tomorrow mornin'!" he shouted. He sighed and climbed into the driver's seat. He started the engine and wiped a tear from the corner of his eye. He had seen so much destruction, pain, death, and misery while overseas. He had wished that darkness had stayed there, but somehow, it had reached this faraway place.

# Chapter 28

The dairy cooperative's letter dominated the dinner table conversation that night. Mary Lou read the entire body of the requirements as the girls and Brother passed around bowls of creamed corn, collard greens, biscuits, gravy, and a meatloaf. She stumbled as she read the word 'requirement' as if it were a rock outcropping on a pathway.

"We could build a new milk barn next to the old one," Brother said. He pinched off a bit of biscuit and popped it in his mouth.

"I bet Sears has a kit for that, too," Anne said.

"Probably," Brother said around a bite of meatloaf. Mary Lou frowned at him, and he swallowed. He wouldn't be talking with his mouth full again.

"And we could get some beef cattle," Brother said. He looked at Anne, "Maybe your boyfriend and his father could lend us a bull every once in a while."

Anne blushed and said, "He's not my boyfriend."

"I'm pretty sure he has to be since I bashed his nose with a hammer," Brother said. This time he finished up with a forkful of corn.

"What'a ya' think it's gonna cost?" Millie asked. She had received her third widow's pension check. She wanted to help but wasn't sure how much she could contribute.

"The letter says the Co-op will help as much as they can with the paperwork," Mary Lou said. "Any income we can show will help."

"And we'll put a lien on the house?" Snaps asked. She had sat quietly and was not really following the conversation. Still, she wanted to be part of the discussion to ensure the others viewed her as attentive. It might come in handy later.

"No, that won't likely be necessary. Probably only need to put up the back forty acres for collateral," Brother replied.

"Right," Mary Lou said. She nodded and tucked back into her dinner. She laid the letter on the china cupboard to the right of the dinner table.

"Anybody need more tea?" Anne asked. She stood and walked to the kitchen. There was a time she felt embarrassed when the family teased her about Jody being her boyfriend, just as they had knocked Millie about Stanley before they got married. Now, she didn't mind the comments but didn't want Snaps to feel bad about her situation. Anne couldn't imagine what Snaps was feeling and didn't want to add to her misery.

"I'll have more iced tea," Snaps said. She already felt full and didn't want too much on her stomach if she had morning sickness again.

"*What if I starved myself?*" she thought. She wondered if there might be some purgative that could cause her to miscarry. She should have asked the doctor during her second visit the day he told her the rabbit had died.

There were old wives' tales about how to induce an abortion, and Snaps considered one of them for a few minutes. One method involved a woman sitting in a steaming bath and drinking gin. Snaps had never had gin. She'd sipped a beer several times but was new to drinking hard liquor.

She had also considered talking to the pharmacist about her 'situation.' She soon realized that if the word got around the area, it might harm her reputation. She decided there had to be a better way. She remembered Juliet's knife and wondered if that would solve her problem.

"To make me die with a restorative," she mumbled, quoting Juliet.

She was sitting at the end of the long table next to Mary Lou. The light fixture hung over the middle of the table and cast shadows over Snaps' face. Mary Lou looked at her and said, "What did you say?"

"Nothin'," Snaps said. "Nothin' at all."

Mary Lou looked at the girl. She wasn't showing yet, but she knew Snaps' body would undergo significant modifications soon, and some of those changes could affect her mind.

# Chapter 29

The nightly routine involved the girls sitting around the radio listening to the news, a comedy or drama, and going to bed around ten o'clock. Snaps usually read, Shakespeare still a favorite, while the radio played. Most times, Millie stared straight ahead, lost in thought. The sounds and voices on the radio captured Anne's imagination, and she relished each moment of escapism. Mary Lou read, usually the Bible, or wrote in her journal, piecing her thoughts into rhyme schemes or occasionally into short essays.

The Friday night wrestling matches engrossed Brother to the point that there were times when he would mimic the movements described by the announcers. He would egg on the athletes with low murmurings of "Get'em Jackie" or sneer and utter "Kill the Tojo."

On Saturday night, the family listened to the *Grand Ole Opry*. Toe-tapping music and sing-alongs filled the speaker of the large table radio.

Years before, the family listened on a crystal radio. This device involved a 'cat's hair' searching a crystal for the right frequency on the amplitude-modulated spectrum. Before Rural Electrification, this 'no electricity' device was the only way the girls could follow their favorite artists. They would pass the headphones from one to the other or share if two of the three found a singer or band they had to listen to.

Mary Lou's favorite was Uncle Dave Macon. He was from the region and had talents in several areas. He was known as 'The Dixie Dewdrop' and played banjo as he sang tunes he'd written himself. He was also a comedian, and this toolbox of talent made him a beloved artist on WSM, the home station of the Opry. Macon had gold teeth, wore a plug hat which had a short brim and a tall cylindrical flat top, and shirts with a gates-ajar collar.

Around ten o'clock every night, except Sunday when bedtime seemed to come earlier, Brother would slowly rise from his chair. Each family member had their designated place in the room, with no exceptions.

He would move toward the clock resting on the mantel. Brother had built the fireplace enclosure with leftover oak lumber from furniture he'd created over the years. He'd assembled it, carved the decorative wings and flourishes, varnished, and polished it with loving care.

The clock was an inheritance from Mary Lou's husband, Frank, and Brother kept it well-oiled, cleaned, and wound to the proper tension. He could feel the resistance grow in the spring as the 'tick, tick, tick' measured the mechanism's stored energy.

The white face and black Roman numerals kept the farm apace with the rest of the world. It had kept perfect time for over three decades, proving that Brother knew how to maintain tools and equipment.

The clock ticked rhythmically and loudly with a small 'bong' at the top of every hour. The sound could be turned on and off, and Brother made a point of quieting the bell before he wandered off to bed.

"Night all," he said as he opened the door leading to the hallway up the stairs.

Most nights, one or more girls would acknowledge his leaving, but everyone seemed lost in their thoughts tonight. Brother didn't force the issue but did notice the minor slight. He might mention it in the morning and inquire about the origin of their ignoring him.

As the door closed, "He's talking about a huge amount of money," Anne whispered. She had found the Sears catalog in a magazine stack, where she had researched the cost of erecting and outfitting the new milk barn. She pulled it from under her chair and opened the page to the least expensive but most likely style of a barn the Co-op would approve. "With shipping and handling, probably over five thousand dollars."

"And that's just the materials," Millie said. "Just imagine what it would cost if we had to pay somebody to put it up? Even with the loan, it'll take years for us to break even on the barn." So while she had a steady income, she knew it likely wouldn't make that big a difference if the family got in trouble with the bank.

"Even if it takes ten years to pay off, we'll still be in the milk business," Mary Lou said. "It's our way of makin' a living."

"That and the garden," Anne said. "And with the camp closing soon, that money might be goin' away, too."

"It's a troublin' time," Mary Lou said, glancing over at Snaps. The girl twisted the edge of a quilt covering her legs. She had a pained expression as if the weight of the world bore down on her shoulders. "How are you feelin'?"

Snaps looked over at her mother. She thought, "*Not tonight, after all.*"

"Snaps," Anne said.

The girl looked first at Anne and then at Mary Lou and said, "It's a lot of money, and we won't break even anytime soon, maybe even add ten more head, but in the long run, it's probably for the best to build the barn."

"Maybe it's time to give up on milkin' and move on to beef cattle and the garden. I'll get my Social Security next year," Mary Lou said.

"We can still have milk cows for us, can't we?" Anne asked. While she wasn't a fan of churning the milk for butter, she liked how it would melt in a biscuit and sometimes run down her forearm.

The clock bonged, telling everyone it was half past the hour. The women looked at one another. Brother had forgotten to move the switch that kept the clock's bell from ringing.

"When was the last time he forgot to turn that off?" Mary Lou asked. She stood and put her Bible on the seat of her chair. She opened the door in front of the clock and flipped the switch. While she was standing there, she poked the fire in the hearth.

"It's cold tonight," Anne said, "for this early in the Fall."

"I can't remember the last time he forgot to turn off the top-of-the-hour bong," Millie said.

"Maybe he's got somethin' on his mind?" Mary Lou added.

Snaps thought, "*'tis fair to think on many things, but only one is clear. With one hand and one thought, all will fade.*"

Mary Lou looked at Snaps' face as her mouth twisted into a cruel grin. She would ask Anne to help take the girl to the doctor tomorrow and see if anything could be done.

She switched off the radio and shooed the girls out of the room and off to bed.

# Chapter 30

Snaps lay in bed that night, looking at the ceiling of her room. She considered the family's changes, the costs of the new barn and cows, and the possible positive and negative outcomes. She would soon be a single mother raising a child born of violence and sadness. She vowed she'd make sure he or she would never know of their father's background. The child would grow up believing his father died in the war and that his mother, grandmother, aunts, and uncles were all the family he'd ever need.

She knew how much her life would change with motherhood and what would happen to her reputation. She'd likely never marry. *"What man would have me?"* she thought.

She turned and looked out the window. Slants of moonlight cast shadows on the round, twill carpet in the center of the room. She remembered playing with wooden toys Brother had made for his nieces as they grew up, and now those same playthings would be handed down.

She imagined sitting in the middle of the floor and watching the baby stand for the first time. She envisioned how she would hold the toddler as they took their first steps. She closed her eyes.

Soon, she dreamed of the bright blue eyes and shock of blond hair and how much the child would look like their father. Then, her mind moved back to the trauma of the attack. "Maybe," she said as she looked down at the two of them as if she were a ghost hovering near the ceiling of the feed room. "Just maybe he loved me. Maybe that's why he chose that moment to express his love for me."

She watched as Ollie put his hand over her mouth, spread her legs with his knee, and used his other hand to pull down her pants and underwear. She had closed her eyes, but now, the ghost moved close to them. It watched as Ollie smiled, the corners of his eyes crinkling in that adorable way she had fallen in love with as he helped her at Camp Forrest.

The spirit moved around them, seeing how Ollie had his hand over her mouth and nose, cutting off her air. She had forgotten how her neck tensed and shoved her head back against the rough wooden floor. She must have been nearly unconscious as she struggled and eventually lost her will to live.

Did she fight back? She remembered pushing him away and how momentarily he stopped. Snaps punched the spot where the bayonet had entered his thigh and nearly killed him. She'd somehow found his weakest place and inflicted just enough pain to make him pause.

As she watched, she saw how he'd pinned her arms over her head. She pulled her left arm free and slapped him. She punched him in the side, and it didn't stop him. Why didn't she remember that? Did that really happen?

In her dream, she fought back. She tried to stop him, and when she pulled one arm free, she poked him in the eye. He yelped in pain, and she punched him again, this time hard in the side. He gasped and let go of her mouth and nose. She gulped air and hit him in the leg. She felt him moving up and away from her.

The fantasy continued as she scooted away from him and huddled in the corner near the door. She felt the rough wood on her naked buttocks and saw a thin trail of blood on the floor. She wasn't a virgin anymore, and that prize she'd hoped to save for her husband was lost.

She watched Ollie raise himself to his knees and move toward her. His pants hung around his knees, and she saw his erect penis waving from side to side. He smiled at her and said, "Mae West, who knew you were such a fighter?"

This is from a man who prides himself as a ruthless killer on the battlefield. A man who pledged his life to enacting and advancing the ambitions of Adolph Hitler to rule the world.

At that moment, Brother entered the feed room, shovel in hand, and smashed Ollie in the face. The boy's face became a mask of blood and exposed bone, and he dropped to the floor.

"He, he, he…" she stammered.

"There, there," Brother said. He crouched down next to Snaps and cradled her around her shoulders. "It's all over now."

But it didn't really happen that way. Snaps somehow knew that, and when she woke up, the actual events of the attack came flooding back to her.

She stared at the ceiling.

"I cannot bring this monster into the world," she whispered. She touched the slight swell in her abdomen as a single tear slid down her face.

# Chapter 31

Wildflowers hung from the bare rafters of the well house. Anne's eyes searched far and wide for the purple, blue, red, brown, black, and white plants. Her talent for arranging those same colors into bouquets or simple vases suddenly became another cash stream for the family.

Her hand-painted wicker basket swung from her left hand as she snipped flower stems and branches from bushes. She seldom left the farm, but there were occasions when she would find herself on other people's property or county-owned land. She'd been chastised and threatened when this happened but wasn't physically put upon. A pretty girl with a basket of flowers was so benign that even the cruelest neighbors or sheriff's deputy had difficulty getting mad at Anne for her collections.

The business found popularity when Anne took a chance and rented a small space at the farmer's market that operated every Saturday during the spring, summer, and fall. The family's space included their renowned vegetables and hand-churned butter. And while there was room for Anne's display, she wanted to branch out on her own with this new venture.

Anne's flowers somehow retained much of the aroma of the fresh blooms, adding another attractive feature to her wares. She would sometimes, if she had the time, offer some of her baked goods on those Saturday outings, but mostly it was freshly picked and dried flowers.

While there was little heavy lifting and toting to be done for Anne's booth, Jody welcomed the chance to spend time with her. Their relationship grew from being 'church friends' to a caring closeness, eventually evolving into a real, loving relationship.

He'd told her about how Brother accidentally dropped a hammer on his face months ago. While the bruising was long gone, the shadow of the small bump would sometimes take Anne's breath away.

Their affection toward each other grew, and while they enjoyed physical contact, they knew some limits had to be respected. Moving over that line could only happen after a walk down a church aisle.

"Look at her," Anne said as she stared at the family booth across the grassy expanse at the center of the Farmer's Market.

"Look at who? Oh, yeah, she looks happy today," Jody remarked. He'd worn clean jeans and a starched white shirt to the market. His black boots shone in the bright afternoon sun, and he'd even washed the mud from the laces.

Anne's attire reflected her modesty in a simple summer dress, as it was a warm day for fall, and she wore flat shoes. Her height drew attention after her middle school growth spurt, and she'd heard taunting through much of high school about being a 'bean pole.' She knew some boys didn't like girls taller than them, and she and Jody measured almost the same five feet ten inches in stocking feet.

"That's what bothers me," Anne said. She'd shared unpublicized details of the attack on Snaps with Jody, including her resulting pregnancy after swearing him to secrecy.

He'd assured her that he wouldn't say anything to anybody about the baby on the way. It was a big secret, but he knew the pain the information would cause if it somehow slipped out. Moreover, his lineage had embarrassing family stories, unlike what Anne's family was enduring.

"It's a pretty day," Jody assured her. "Maybe Snap is trying to get past what happened."

"That's hard to do when you can look down and see what's growing inside you," Anne said. A tone of anger and disgust crept into her voice. She knew Jody wouldn't take the comment as a personal attack on him. They had grown so comfortable with each other that offense wouldn't be taken.

A breeze brought the scent of the dried flowers back across the table, and Jody remembered how he'd accompanied her once on her traipsing around the woods. They'd stopped by a small pond and started kissing. His hand slipped from her waist 'accidentally,' and she moaned instead of slapping his hand away.

Inspired by the fragrance, Jody looked around and then put his hand on her butt. He smiled at her and expected the same excited kiss he'd received that afternoon.

Anne slapped his hand away. The sound wasn't loud enough to get the attention of anyone around them, much less her family across the way. "Watch it," she snapped. "We're in a public place. You don't want people talkin', do you?"

He shook his head as his hand drifted back to his side. "I don't know. I was just thinkin' about that time at the pond on the Jones' place."

"Now I'm thinkin' about that, too," Anne said. She looked down and then back at him through impishly arched eyebrows.

"Maybe we can get together tonight and think about that some more?" Jody asked.

"Maybe," Anne said.

They hadn't noticed Snaps standing at the edge of the table as they bantered. "Momma says we gotta pack up."

Anne took a step away from Jody. She tried to intuit what Snaps would feel, seeing her having fun with her boyfriend. She would do anything in the world if she could take away Snaps' pain.

"Will do," Anne said.

Snaps turned and walked back to the family booth.

"Whattaya' think she's gonna do?" Jody asked. He'd grown fond of the youngest of the sisters and cared about her future.

"I have no idea," Anne said. She began putting her vases and bouquets of dried flowers into a wooden box.

A single raisin muffin sat on a plate at the table's edge. Jody snatched it up and took a bite. "This one won't travel that well," he said with a smile. The muffin peeked from between his lips.

"I'll still have to charge you for it," Anne said playfully.

"Put it on my tab," he said and kept chewing.

"We'll settle up tonight," she said, picking up the box.

"Same time as usual?" he asked.

She walked toward the family booth and the truck. She liked to tease him, knowing she didn't have to answer.

# Chapter 32

Snaps held the ax with both hands as she approached the tree. She'd vowed dozens of times to take out what she considered a blockage of her view as she stood on the rock outcropping of her makeshift stage.

Her lips clenched, and her forehead furrowed as she approached. She spun the ax in her hands as she walked. It was the third time she'd ever tried chopping wood. Brother usually took care of that chore. He'd work most of the fall and into early winter, ensuring they'd have enough for the cold spells that would follow Christmas and the New Year.

Her eyes squinted almost shut as she moved the ax to her shoulder. She squeezed the handle, stopped before the dead tree, and set her feet apart.

"No harm in cutting down a dead tree," she thought. She eyed the trunk below her waist and let the ax fall from her shoulder. She reared back and swung the shaft through the humid air.

The ax blade bounced off the tree. Snaps felt the vibrations up the handle, almost making her drop the tool.

She frowned, put the ax back on her shoulder, and aimed at the same spot again. This time the ax moved, and a small chip of rotten wood fell to the ground.

"Ahhhhhh," she muttered in frustration. Her tone copied what she'd heard from her mother when the cows didn't go where they were supposed to go.

"Let's try again," Snaps said. She eyed the tree trunk and swung.

This time she missed the tree and spun herself twice before she regained her balance. "Ahhhhhhh, shit," she said much louder than she intended. "Ahhhhhh, shit, ah, shit, ah, shit!" she yelled.

She picked up the ax and planted her feet in front of the tree. This time she swung the ax and took a considerable chunk of bark out of the trunk.

"That's the way to do it," Brother said. He stood behind her, arms crossed, smiling at her.

"Oh," Snaps exclaimed, "no, ah, I'm just..."

"You're just cutting down this dead tree, ain't ya?"

He stepped forward and offered his open hand to her. He took the ax and moved her out of his way.

"Make sure you've got plenty of room. You don't wanna take somebody's head off with it."

In a way, he was wrong. Snaps did want to take someone's head off with the ax, but he'd already done that for her.

He was wearing his usual overalls, blue shirt, and boots. He hadn't shaved that day, so he looked a bit scruffy. His cap kept his hair away from his face; if he took it off, it would cover his forehead and maybe even his eyes. Mary Lou routinely gave him a haircut every two weeks, and he was due for a trim this Saturday.

"Now, you got the right idea about keeping your feet apart, but you gotta move your weight forward and follow through." He swung and chopped a good-sized piece from where Snaps had been aiming.

"You wanna cut up on one swing and tilt the head of the ax down on the next. That way, you'll get a nice cut all the way through. Now, you try it."

She took the ax from Brother and started swinging it around her. He stepped back, holding his hands in front of his body. "Careful, careful."

She nodded and focused on the notch he'd made.

"Slow and steady, and then," he moved his clasped hands in front of his legs. "Wham!"

Snaps stepped forward and took another swing. She angled the ax head down this time, and a chunk of the wood flew off and hit her in the face. She flinched but wouldn't rub her face or acknowledge that it hurt.

"That's all right," Brother said, "you keep goin'."

She swung again, letting out a little grunt as the ax head hit the trunk.

"That's it," he said. "You let it all out."

She smiled as she took the ax back behind her shoulder again. The weight felt good in her hands, and she felt the muscles tighten in her back and arm. She swung again. "Yahhhh!"

"Again," he said, nodding his head as she chopped large chunks of rotten wood from the tree.

"Yahhhhh!" Chop. "Yahhhhh!" Chop. "Yahhhhh!" Chop.

The ax fell to the ground, and her shoulders slumped. She was almost halfway through.

"Can I give it a try?"

He didn't wait for her to give him permission. He took the ax behind his back and put all his weight into the swing. "Yeeeehawww!" he yelled.

She smiled. It was the first time in weeks, the first time since she'd visited the doctor, and he told her the rabbit had died.

"Hit it again," she said, urging him on now.

He pushed his cap back. His sweaty hair fell below his eyebrows, and he brushed it back with his hand. She smiled at him and noticed a small scar on his hairline for the first time. "*Why haven't I noticed that before?*" she thought.

"You got it," she said in an encouraging tone.

Brother swung, taking a deep bite out of the trunk this time. The top of the bare, dead branches swayed. He took another swing, and then another, and another. He turned and offered her the ax. "You finish it."

She took the ax, spun it in her hands, and lifted it to her shoulder. She imagined Olaf's face there in the gray wood. She imagined what the ax would do to that sickening grin and those blue eyes. "Yaaaaaah!"

She swung the ax. Her weight shifted from her right foot to her left, and she extended her arms. The ax head slammed into the rotten wood and bit out a huge chunk.

The tree creaked. The top branches moved, and the tree slowly toppled over.

She stood there, looking at the fallen tree, and hefted the ax to her shoulder. She rubbed under her arm. She likely wouldn't be able to lift her hands over her head tomorrow, but it was worth it.

"Feels good, don't it?" Brother said. He stood next to her as she admired her work. "It feels good to let that out."

She nodded. She'd always liked Brother, but he was constantly too busy with his projects to spend time with her. She lived in her books and in her head; he was a creature of the earth and the forest.

"See that area right over there?" he asked, pointing to a stand of stumps, all about waist high. "That's what I done when I came back from Germany."

There were hundreds of tree stumps to the north of where they stood. And it finally dawned on her what he had done and now was doing with her. "You never talk about that."

"Well, ain't that much to talk about," he lied, "I just followed orders. That's it."

She nodded again, agreeing with him, even though she knew it wasn't likely that was all he did.

"That tree was always in my way," she said. She remembered how the branches blocked the setting sun and her imaginary spotlight. Even after it died, she found that the branches kept her in the dark.

"I'm glad it's gone," he said. "Let's go see what's for supper."

He turned, and she followed him through the fruit trees to the flower beds and into the back door of the well house.

"The flowers look pretty, don't they?" Snaps asked.

Brother's grouchy side returned, and he said, "Yeah, that's some mighty pretty flowers there."

# Chapter 33

Snaps sat in the rocking chair at the edge of the living room. The afternoon light from the window made it a prime reading spot. She had a new movie magazine; truthfully, she'd gotten it from Brenda, and it was months old, but it was new to her. She was reading an article about Greer Garson.

Snaps had mentioned how much she liked the actress, and Brenda was happy to provide distractions for her prized student.

"I thought I saw an article about her there," the teacher said.

Snaps smiled and dipped her chin. "Thanks," she said. She had cradled the magazine in her hands as if she were carrying a newborn infant.

"Think nothin' of it. Happy to," Brenda said and turned from her classroom door.

Snaps turned the magazine pages, eyes wide at the color pictures of the beautiful actress. She said without irony, "I'm glad I'll get to work with you one day." What were the odds of a young unknown from a small town in Tennessee making her way to Hollywood and co-starring with Greer Garson? A million to one, a billion to one? The mind reels.

Snaps read the next paragraph and found herself unable to breathe.

Her anxiety and stress of pending motherhood had caused insomnia and a slight tic on her cheek, but this was new. Sure, she'd had difficulty swallowing her food at times. Still, saliva went down her windpipe this time, and the oropharyngeal dysphagia slammed shut the tiny flap of cartilage that rested at the top of her esophagus.

She opened her mouth and tried sucking air as hard as she could. This made the problem worse, and she soon felt her eyes bulging. She sucked even harder with the veins in her throat distending. She flashed back to when Ollie held her down and put his hand over her mouth and nose. The memory made her panic, and she dropped the magazine and bent over the edge of the rocking chair.

"Would death be so bad now?" she asked herself. Her life as she dreamed it might be was over. She would be marked with a scarlet 'W' for whore for the rest of her life. She would have to raise a child conceived in hatred and violence and pretend she wouldn't see the father's face every time she looked at it. What service would she be to the world now? What usefulness would this child with a Nazi father have? She remembered Ollie's tattoo and how she'd asked him about it. He'd said it meant he was going to Heaven someday. She decided it would be better to die and take the baby and herself to Heaven.

As Snaps raised herself from the rocking chair, a headache pounded the back of her head, and she closed her eyes. "*Let it come*," she thought when Millie entered the room.

"Lord a' mighty, what's wrong?"

Snaps looked at her, felt the blood drain from her face, and pointed to her throat. Millie rushed across the room and slapped her sister on the back. It didn't help; in fact, it made the problem worse. Snaps winced in pain and glared at her sister.

"Slow down, honey, just relax and maybe try to breathe through your nose," Millie said.

Snaps glared at her older sibling and frowned. Her mouth worked like a fish hooked and slung on the riverbank. Her straining to get air into her lungs grew more desperate, and she could feel Ollie's touch again on her face and once again felt the pain he'd caused her.

"*So much pain*," she thought, "*just let it be over*."

Millie took both Snaps' hands in hers and looked her in the eye. Then, she started taking deep, steady breaths, hoping the Snaps would mirror her. "Slow down," she said, her voice as calm and soothing as possible. "Look at me."

Millie had heard Snaps talking to their mother about the attack and realized this might be connected. "You can do this," she said.

Snaps' gaze softened, and Millie worried she would lose her sister right here and now. "Ginger!" she yelled in the girl's face and yanked her hands down.

Snaps shut her mouth and felt the air move through her nose and into her lungs. She opened her mouth again, but Millie cautioned her. "Just through the nose, slowly, slowly, slowly."

Snaps looked at her sister and relaxed. She coughed and tried to speak. All she could manage was a croak.

"Get your breath, and then you can talk," Millie assured her.

Snaps nodded, and Anne walked into the room. "What's all the racket? What's going on here?" she asked. "What's wrong with you?"

Millie said, "Spit just went down the wrong way, didn't it, sweetie?"

Snaps coughed, followed by several deep, racking breaths. She coughed again, nodded, and sat back down in the chair. The memory of Ollie's hand over her mouth still played at the edges of her mind, but the air in her lungs caused most of it to drift away for now.

"My spit went down the wrong way," Snaps moaned. She didn't feel like talking about how ending her life might solve all her problems. She didn't want to burden her sisters.

"Don't do that again," Anne said.

"Yeah," Millie chimed in, "don't do that."

Snaps nodded, smiling now. "I didn't mean to do it this time."

"Stuff happens. Sometimes there ain't nothin' you can do about it," Anne said. The words left her mouth before she realized that this bit of philosophical wisdom might cause Snaps even more pain if she thought about Ollie's attack.

"You're right," Millie said, "sometimes there ain't nothin' you can do."

Snaps wheezed as she rocked and picked up her magazine. "I'm thinkin' about going to the picture show. Y'all wanna go?"

The Princess theater in the downtown business district was built over a cave, and shafts carried the air from underground through the building without fans. As a result, the temperature stayed a constant sixty-five degrees, winter or summer, causing some men and most women to wear a sweater or jackets. A concession stand provided fresh-popped popcorn, Cokes, and an assortment of theater-sized candy. Seating included a lower mezzanine and a balcony accommodating over 600 movie fans. Snaps and the girls had gone to the movies there semi-regularly for years, but it had been a while since they'd all attended.

Anne looked at Millie and nodded. She thought it was probably a good escape for Snaps.

"Yeah, let's go," they said in unison.

"*The Valley of Decision* with Greer Garson," Snaps announced without looking up from her magazine.

Both girls nodded, and Millie asked, "How about the seven o'clock show?"

"I'll be ready," Snaps said, rocking and reading. Her breathing had returned to normal, and the blood rushed back to her cheeks. Acting as if nothing had happened, she realized during her death-defying moment; she hadn't thought for one second about the baby. The fetus would have died along with her if she'd never caught her breath. She nodded to no one as she rocked, and her sisters left the room. "*Not for one second,*" she thought.

# Chapter 34

"We can't afford it, and we can't justify it," Mary Lou said. The plans for the new milk barn had come in the mail and covered much of the dining room table. Brother stood next to her and traced his finger over the rooflines and down to the foundation.

"I could cut some corners, maybe put off these interior walls here and here until next winter," Brother said as he pointed to the blueprint. "The milkin' machines would need electricity, and I'm sure they'll have an instruction book. I'm just not that familiar with wiring a building."

The Sunday afternoon sun slanted light across the dining room, the eight chairs, the china cabinet, and the sideboard. All the furniture had been built by Brother and featured extraordinary precision and professionalism. The barns, sheds, and houses he'd built throughout the neighborhood were viewed by passers-by with pride and sometimes envy that Brother hadn't constructed their projects. It took a lot for him to admit that he lacked electrical engineering knowledge in this crucial area of construction expertise.

"I know you can learn it," Mary Lou said. "If you can't, I'm sure we can trade it out with someone." She held a glass of iced tea and took a sip. She liked it with two sugars and a squeeze of lemon. She drank coffee in the morning and tea during the day. The caffeine helped her think.

"We'll need to add some more cows to increase the yield," Brother said.

"More cows means more feed in the winter," Millie said. She'd just entered the room and wanted her input on the project since some of her widow's pension would likely be needed to qualify for the loan.

"The machines will make the milking go faster," Brother said. He knew neither he nor Mary Lou was getting any younger, and freezing temperatures made it harder to sit comfortably on a milking stool.

Mary Lou rubbed her hands together. Her fingers ached late at night, and she had difficulty standing straight.

"Change isn't always a bad thing," Millie said. Now, she saw her future there on the farm and knew that long-term modernization would mean stability and growth.

Brother saw Mary Lou shift her weight from one foot to the other. He could tell she was trying to keep the family from seeing she was getting older and not as strong as she used to be. Mechanization of the milking would mean working smarter, not harder.

"Too bad Jess Comer done what he done," Brother said. He wished he could have snatched the words out of the air and shoved them back into his mouth. He didn't want to hurt Millie with this reminder. "Sorry, Millie, I didn't mean nothin'..."

She cut him off. "It's alright, Brother. You're right. Things would be a lot easier around here if'n it wasn't for his ornery ways."

"Now, now," Mary Lou tutted, "we ain't got no control over that man. Wouldn't want none."

They all laughed and returned to staring at the milk barn's floor plan. Millie broke the silence. "Milkin' machines will make life a whole lot easier."

"When do we have to give them an answer?" Brother asked. He'd already been told the deadline for their decision. Was his mind slipping, or did he just forget?

"End of November," Mary Lou said. She took a sip of her tea and pursed her lips. It was a sign she was deep in thought. Millie and Brother had seen that before and knew no final decision would be made today.

"And the loan papers are in the hands of the Co-op?" Millie asked. She remembered reading through the sheaf of forms and had signed, committing a portion of her pension to pay it back if the business faltered.

"I mailed it all in yesterday," Mary Lou said. She ran her finger down the list of dimensions and features of the new barn.

"We'll just have to wait and see," Brother said.

"And pray on it," Millie added. She turned and walked to the well-house. She found her mouth was dry and wanted to draw up some water from the well. She opened the back door and took the long aluminum tube from the hook. She checked the trigger at the top of the tube and checked the coiled rope next to the ceramic top of the well. She let the tube slip into the hole and down the forty feet to the underground stream. It had been a wet fall with plenty of rain to keep the well at the usual water level. Still, additional rope would be needed during dry spells to reach the county's most refreshing, clearest water.

Millie pulled the bucket from the well and aimed the tube at the pail. She pulled the trigger, and two gallons of water rushed into the pail. A small fish circled the bucket, and Millie watched it for a moment before she caught it in her hand and moved toward the open wellhead.

"I hope you make it," she said as she released it back into the well.

A truck with a tall tower had dug the well several years ago. It replaced the one Brother and Millie's father dug years before. It was an improvement, and while it cost to have the big rig come in, the investment paid off. She remembered how the well digger had divined that this was the best place to put the new well. He was Cherokee, and his reputation for successful water divination was known far and wide.

Millie and her sisters were small at that time and stared in wonder as the pile driver winched up the tower and released near the top. The weight thundered into the earth over and over and over. Snaps, the youngest, got bored first, followed by Anne, but Millie stayed around for the entire process. The mechanism and engineering intrigued her, and she grew used to the noise. In a few hours, the weight struck water.

"Forty-two feet," the well-digger said. His brown, wrinkled face broke into a smile. "I said it was around forty."

Frank, Millie's father, knew he'd made the right call bringing in this professional. His foresight in the importance of clean water for his family gave him the courage to commit financially.

"I didn't have a doubt in the world," Frank told the well-digger.

Millie took the pail filled with the still-cold water and placed it on the kitchen counter next to the stove. She took a dipper from a nail on the wall. She skimmed the top of the water, took a sip from the metal cup, and smiled.

She walked back into the dining room as Brother and Mary Lou stared at the blueprint. Brother moved to roll the paper into a tube and put a rubber band around it.

"We need to do this," Millie said, a bit louder than she meant to.

Both grown-ups turned and looked at her.

"I'll think on it," Mary Lou said.

"No," Millie said. She crossed her arms and looked first at Brother and then at Mary Lou. "We can make this work." She smiled and said, "I don't have a doubt in the world."

# Chapter 35

Snaps attended the little Baptist church, was baptized in the river, symbolizing her death and resurrection in Christ, and even remembered the Bible stories she'd heard in Sunday School. Her favorite was Abraham and Sarah. God promised the old man a son, but he and Sarah failed to conceive until the couple was visited by three men. One of the men told Abraham the couple would have a son when they returned the following year. Sarah overheard this and laughed to herself about having a child at their age. The visitor asked why she was laughing. He assured her that she would soon be pregnant even though she was past her childbearing years. And so she was. The child was named Isaac, which is Hebrew for 'laughter.' The birth of the child was a miracle, and the dramatic side of Snaps liked stories where miracles happened.

She continued to attend church and even sing in the choir, but her confidence grew more in herself than in Jesus. Now, after what had happened to her, she wanted that to change.

She walked along the creekbank and picked up a rock. "Oh, Lord, if this rock sinks, you'll make it so I don't have to have this baby."

She threw the stone in, and it sank. *"So much for a miracle,"* she thought.

It was a childish thing to think and say. She found her mind a jumble of emotions and illogic. Maybe there was a reason for what had happened to her that she couldn't see?

She kept walking. A light breeze brushed the hem of her dress, and she pulled the edges of her sweater closer to her shoulders. It was early Fall and the time of the year in Tennessee when temperatures on most days began in the forties or fifties and ended in the seventies or eighties. It was hard to dress for these days, and Snaps had chosen well that afternoon.

She loved the path she and her sisters had worn near the creek. The sound was soothing and allowed for deep contemplation. They'd talked about God and religion and decided they weren't one and the same. They knew churches did good deeds and society was better for their existence. Still, there were times when the organization failed to meet Snaps' needs. This seemed to be one of those times.

She tipped her face to the sun and basked in the warm glow. "*This will be my church*," she thought.

From that day forward, whenever she wished to talk with the Spirit, she would walk in nature and observe what the creative hand of God had wrought. She would remember her mother's symbiotic relationship with the plants and creatures of the Earth. She would remember Brother's comfort in his destruction of creation, knowing that whatever he could destroy in his feeble hands, nature would return to normal. She would place her sisters enjoying the freedom of gamboling in the fields for hours on end. And on this day, she would make a pact—if this role of motherhood passed from her, she would dedicate her life to bringing joy and comfort to others.

She did not want to be a mother. She wanted this part in the play that was her life to be unfulfilled.

She touched her abdomen. She didn't feel anything there, so maybe the doctor was wrong. Perhaps Ollie's attack on her didn't produce a fetus after all. Maybe it was all in her mind, compensation for allowing herself to aid in Ollie's escape.

She had to admit to flirting with him and enjoying the attention. He was different, clearly ambitious, with a magnetic personality. And his appearance was so perfect. She marveled at the symmetry of his face and body. One day when the temperature was in the nineties, Ollie was working outside the mess tent, cleaning chairs and tables with a hose.

He'd removed his shirt, and his skin glowed with perspiration and mist from the spray. Then, finally, he turned, looking like a Greek statue come to life.

Snaps walked up to the back of the kitchen door carrying a basket of eggs. She saw him, couldn't stop herself from staring in wonderment, and watched the water plume over the edge of the building, creating a rainbow.

Ollie turned and stared at her. She'd seen that hunger in a boy's eyes before, but never this feral, and she felt a similar wildness. They were young creatures with moral codes to live by, but deep down, they'd scratch the surface and find lions on the prowl.

God's hand had created this. She acknowledged his plan and the system he'd originated, if not with Adam and Eve, with the ape-like beings from which modern people descended.

She continued walking, enjoying the fresh air and the warm sunlight. "Creation," she said, "so beautiful and perfect."

God was all-powerful, as evidenced by her surroundings and travel through nature. In the doctrine, when Snaps emerged from that baptismal water, she was a different human being, and when she opened her eyes, her world was new. She claimed a pledge and believed you could count on it when God made a promise.

# Chapter 36

Saturday night baths meant taking buckets of water from the well house, pouring the water into big pans on the woodstove, and waiting for the water to heat. In the meantime, buckets of cold water filled the tub. Anne had a date with Jody, and while she hated a cold bath, she didn't have time to wait for hot water.

Anne gritted her teeth as she lowered herself below the waterline. She liked to be clean and fresh for Jody. She noticed he made a similar effort for her. It was appreciated.

Millie handed her the soap and went to get another bucket of cold water.

"The hot water should be ready in a minute," she said as she closed the door.

The tub was in the back corner of the pantry. Tin cans and clear jars of vegetables lined the walls. Home-made pickles covered one shelf. Brother liked pickles. Anne liked the canned tomatoes and green beans. Millie's favorites included pickled okra and beets.

Anne shivered as Millie brought in the next bucket.

"Hot-t-t-t-t water," she said through chattering teeth.

"Coming right up," Millie said. She dropped the bucket at the end of the tub, where the drain ran into the yard.

She returned in seconds, but it felt like an eternity for Anne. "Dump it, just dump it," she implored.

Millie did as asked, but she knew that even this boiling water wouldn't be enough to make the bath comfortable.

"I'll get some more water on the stove."

"Okay, but it won't matter for me," Anne said.

"I'll get the next bath," Millie said.

Adding a little hot water and letting out some cold water worked for the girls. By the time the last person made it, it was time for Brother to take his turn. They would leave the previous pan of hot water on the stove and let him have his privacy.

He cursed how late they were this afternoon. He would have to rush to be planted in front of the radio when the wrestling matches or 'rastlin' came on. Anne would be out while Millie and Mary Lou sat there listening but not reacting to the action as Brother did. In fact, the girls usually were knitting, darning socks, or writing when the headlocks turned into forearm bars. Snaps would be in her room with her nose in a book—just another Saturday night.

Except for tonight, it wasn't 'just' another Saturday night.

The routine over the last few months involved Jody picking up Anne in his family's pickup truck at the front gate and driving downtown. First, they would get ice cream or a soda at the drugstore. Then, they would go around the square a few times, park, talk, and drive around the square a couple more times to see if any friends showed up, then drive to their favorite spot.

The truck weaved from one side of the road to the other, dodging rocks and an occasional furrow deepened by rain. It was a dead-end road leading to a gate used by a farmer to get to a property separated by the new county road.

Anne sometimes thought Jody drove too fast and hit potholes, so she would bounce from the passenger side and end up closer to him. When he finally stopped, there was talk about the moon's brightness, how much the trees overhung the road, and how creepy it was. Anne sometimes grabbed Jody's arm when he tried to scare her, but she knew it was all just a ruse to get them together.

"I got somethin' special for us tonight," Jody said. His face split into a shy grin as he reached under the truck seat. "It's a small one. I only had two dollars."

It was a pint Ball jar of clear liquid with a brass cap and enamel cover.

"What is it?" Anne asked.

"'shine," Jody said. He had unintentionally deepened his voice when he spoke the 'forbidden' word. He knew it was illegal to buy and possess. He knew its purpose tonight was more for him than Anne.

"Where'd you get it?"

"Jess Comer. I mean, I know'd a boy, who know'd a boy who bought it."

"Sounds complicated."

He twisted off the cap and offered her the first slug. She shook her head and tipped her face forward. "I better not," she whispered.

He took a sip and then another. "Dang."

"That's probably enough," Anne said. She knew she had influence over him, but she wasn't sure how much.

"I'll take one more if you take one."

Anne didn't want to drink, but she knew that playing this game would likely benefit her more than not.

She took the small jar from Jody, placed the lip of the glass near her mouth, and sucked in air and a bit of the liquid. It was horrible. She felt like she'd drunk paint thinner. She coughed, tried to catch her breath, and handed the jar back to Jody.

Jody took another sip, choked back the burning sensation in his throat, and croaked, "Smooth, ain't it?"

She shook her head. Tears welled in her eyes, and she tried to catch her breath.

"I need some fresh air," Anne said. She scooted across the truck seat and grabbed the door handle. She was out, gulping air in seconds. Jody got out and rushed to her side.

"Are you gonna be all right?" he asked.

She nodded but was still too overcome to answer. Finally, she gagged and took a deep breath. "That was not smooth."

Jody laughed, "Yep, not smooth at all."

"I believe that's my first and last time tryin' that," she said. She fanned herself and leaned against the truck fender.

"Mine too," Jody agreed. He'd been talked into trying 'shine by the other boys and believed it would grow some hair on his chest. He'd have to check on that later.

"So, here we are," Anne said. Her eyes watered, and she wiped a stray tear with the back of her hand.

"Yes," Jody began. He thought the 'shine might help him. He believed he'd need an extra shot of courage on this night.

"Anne," he began. He kissed her. He took her hand and pressed it to his chest.

"Jody, what's.... "

"We've been goin' together for a while now. We get along good, and I think we should make it permanent," he said as he pulled a small gold ring from his pocket. He slipped it on her finger, asking her, "Will you marry me?"

Anne felt the smooth, cold metal on her hand. She glanced at the ring and then into Jody's eyes. Marriage was something she'd thought about. She'd even talked with Millie about how good she and Jody were together. Millie had looked sad at first, remembering her husband, but eventually enthusiastically agreed that Jody would be a good match.

"Let me think," she began. She closed her eyes. She remembered a day long ago when the family had traveled to a picnic area with a swimming hole below a cliff twenty feet or so above the water. The girls had worn their swimsuits under their clothes and wriggled out of them on the ridge. They'd held hands and jumped.

Anne remembered that long drop and the exhilaration of bobbing up to the surface. That same feeling grew in her chest at this moment.

"Yes, Jody, I will marry you," Anne said. She glanced again at the ring and then at Jody. He smiled and kissed her.

"I'm so happy," Jody said.

"Me, too," Anne agreed. "Me, too."

# Chapter 37

The paperwork for the loan involved two visits to the downtown office of an attorney the family had worked with for many years. Thad Williams, known for wearing a three-piece suit, striped shirt, and a bow tie, had written the letter to the Department of Defense, pleading Millie's case, claiming she was the rightful beneficiary of Stanley's life insurance policy. He had counseled Brother on any possible repercussions involving the death of the Nazi soldier Olaf Weber. He had written bills of sale for several of the current milk cow herd and the truck they bought last year. An attorney in a small town had to be a master of several legal arts.

The banker, Eb Short, also a man who had developed multiple talents, sat across the table from Brother, Mary Lou, Millie, and Anne in front of a stack of papers. Some of them were legal size. Bookcases filled with law books and framed pictures of Thad's family and friends looked down on them. A single window let a bar of bright, white sunlight illuminate a brocade sofa.

Eb picked up the papers and straightened them again. It was his third attempt to get them exactly right, and he placed them back on the table before him. Most forms had the US government department's names and seals affixed. Eb knew bureaucrats could sometimes reject paperwork that didn't have a signature in the proper place or a word or phrase that didn't meet their requirements. He wouldn't give them a chance to reject this proposal if he could help it.

He pulled a ball-point pen from his pocket and placed it caddy-cornered on the papers. His career as a loan officer began three decades before the Great Depression; he'd seen successful years and lean years for the local farmers and recently felt there might be an economic boom that would make his bank even more successful.

"I think you made the right decision to go with the new barn," Eb said. He believed this and wanted the Wright family to make a go of it.

Brother said, "The government didn't give us too much choice."

Eb cleared his throat. He didn't want to spook this deal for the bank by expressing any political statement that could turn off the borrowers.

"I sure do like that butter y'all make," Eb said. He turned the pen sideways on top of the papers.

Thad burst into the room with a secretary trailing behind him. She was short and round with black hair, glasses, and pale skin.

"Y'all ready to make this happen?" Thad asked.

There were slow, somber nods around the table. The weight of the process began to raise the temperature of the room. Mary Lou nodded and scooted her chair closer to the table.

Thad began, "A successful title search and loan application brings us to today's closing. Let's begin with the initial loan application."

Eb pushed the pen toward Mary Lou. He handed her the top sheaf of papers clipped together at the right corner. "You'll need to sign your name and initial where indicated."

The paper shuffling began. Mary Lou would sign or initial and then hand the pen to Brother, who would do same in the appropriate slot. This continued for several minutes until they reached the end of the process.

"Let's be careful," Brother said. He looked at Eb and narrowed his eyes. "Messed-up paperwork can cause a world of problems."

The town's gossip had thoroughly explored Millie's situation with Stanley's life insurance policy payout and how she'd been cheated because Stanley had failed to update his file. She was viewed as a victim and wasn't comfortable with that. Deep in her mind, maybe she didn't even realize it at the time. This act was a chance for her to reclaim some control.

Thad knew this was a delicate part of the process and that one wrong word could blow the whole deal. "I hear what you're sayin', but we all agree it's the right move."

Both Mary Lou and Millie nodded their heads. Brother looked at the women and reluctantly wagged his big noggin.

"That's it," Eb said, shuffling the papers into two stacks. He slid one to Mary Lou and kept the other.

Thad used almost all his teeth to smile and pronounce the proceedings a success. He shook hands with Millie, Mary Lou, and Brother. He turned to Eb and shook hands with him. They knew they had done something to better the community and help some good people, but they also knew their bank accounts would receive a nice infusion.

Standing outside the office building, Mary Lou clutched the papers to her chest and watched the loan officer make his way to the bank just two blocks away. "We're gonna have to work hard to make this pay off."

Millie touched her arm and said, "Don't worry about a thing. We'll be fine."

Brother watched the banker turn and spit in the gutter next to the sidewalk. "Bankers, they be the worst."

"Now, now," Mary Lou said, "We got the law and all this paper on our side. E'erthin's gonna be all right."

They turned and climbed into the cab of the truck. Brother turned the ignition key and backed into the nearly deserted street that circled the courthouse.

Millie took a deep breath, maybe feeling the weight of the family's well-being subconsciously shift to her shoulders.

# Chapter 38

Snaps stood next to the window and watched the moon rise over the stand of trees in the five-acre field. That area had become her favorite place in the whole world. She had practiced singing and all her stage work there. She'd even chopped down trees and shared a special moment with Brother. She longed to go there one last time, but she was afraid.

Her life was over.

She wore a long nightshirt and socks. Her hair was pulled back, and her skin was rosy from her bath just hours earlier. She took inventory of her situation. Unwed, pregnant, rape victim with another year of high school before graduation. Prospects are uncertain, and hope is on the wane.

Should she pack a bag, leave a note, and leave?

Maybe it would be better for everyone if she just ended it all before it was too late?

She rubbed her hands together. A wisp of cool air seeped around the windowsill. She wondered what it might feel like to take that cold, long sleep.

"To be or not to be," she whispered to her reflection in the window.

Those words took on new meaning for her now. Then, when she practiced the soliloquy for her class, she focused on performing and expressing the words; now, she understood Hamlet's feelings.

"To sleep, perchance to dream," she said, looking up at the moonrise. "For in that sleep of death, what dreams may come?"

In her mind, *"Ending my problem ends our family's problems."*

She felt like she was standing in a deep, dark well. She could look up and see moonlight, but it was too far away. She could stretch her arms over her head and cry for help, but deliverance seemed impossible. There were only two things she could do.

A knock on the door. Snaps jerked, roused from her existential musings, and touched her stomach—a reflex—a mother checking on the status of her baby.

"Yes," she said, turning from the window.

Brother opened the door a crack. He peeped his head around the jamb. "'rasslin' starts in about five minutes." He almost added, "according to the mantle clock," but that seemed unnecessary right now.

"Oh, yes, thanks," she said. She took a deep breath, realizing she was still touching her abdomen.

"Young Jackie Fargo's gonna take on Gorgeous Steven," he said. He stepped into the room as if the floor were eggshells. He wasn't a frequent visitor to any of the girls' rooms. Their smells and decorations always made the skin on his arms crinkle.

"You feelin' okay?" he asked. He was still in his overalls and a long-sleeved shirt. He'd taken off his shoes, and there was a hole in the toe of his sock.

"Yes," she said, just a bit too quickly.

If he'd been more perceptive, he might have picked up on Snaps' anxiety and been more empathetic. His mind didn't work that way.

"You still throwin' up in the morning?" he asked. He was genuinely interested in all the girls. They were his brother's children, and he felt responsible for ensuring they were doing as well as possible.

"No, that seems to have passed," she said. She had asked herself several times why the two of them had never talked about the attack and how he'd killed her assailant. "How are you feeling?" she asked.

"I'm awright," he drawled. "We finished all that paperwork today on the milk barn, so that's a load off."

"And another load on you since you're gonna have to put it all together," she said, smiling now. She knew from where she stood in the backlight that Brother would only see the outline of her face and body. She knew if Brother could see her, he'd feel some of the muddled thoughts she was having. He couldn't.

"I don't mind. It's the right move," Brother said. "Sometimes we gotta stick our necks out and hope for the best."

She thought, "*Could he have said anything better than that at this very moment?*"

She shuffled across the room and picked up a shawl Millie had knitted her for her birthday years ago. She'd worn a hole in one corner that needed mending but lacked the courage to ask Millie to fix it. Requesting anything of her older sister in the last few months seemed to add too much to her already overburdened shoulders.

"I felt some air comin' in around the windowsill," she noted, hooking her thumb over her shoulder.

Brother smiled, a problem he was best equipped to deal with. "I'll put it on my list."

He stood by the door and watched her walk by him. He'd held her as a baby, watched her learn to walk, helped her chop down a tree when she was angry, and looked forward to welcoming the baby she would bear in a few months.

She stopped, touched his hand, and said, "We better not keep Jackie waitin'."

Brother felt the touch of another so rarely. He'd get hugs on birthdays and occasionally on Christmas. He felt comfortable shaking hands with a few people, but that was just about all. He remembered his comrades on the battlefield and in the trenches. He cherished the back and shoulder pats because they made him feel he was part of the troop. Now, a simple touch from almost anyone made him feel unworthy because so many of his friends had died, and he somehow lived.

"Thanks, Snaps," he whispered.

"Do you think Jackie'll use his atomic drop tonight?" she asked. It was the wrestler's signature move and almost always ensured victory.

She looked up at Brother and knew she and the family would endure. Of course, there would be changes and new challenges, but if they worked together, they would persevere.

"I think I can pretty much guarantee it," he said, smiling.

She had no idea what that moment meant to him, but for her, that connection would play out in her mind for decades.

# Chapter 39

There was a time Millie dreamed of Stanley every night. Some were replays of their short time together. Some were nightmares of her imaginings of his suffering and his death. Some were dreams of the future that were now impossible.

Anne, still her roommate and tonight out way past her curfew, would sometimes have to shake her awake and console Millie when she cried. She went to bed after the wrestling matches and finished a shawl she was knitting for Snaps' Christmas present. She'd drunk a glass of warm milk, hoping it would help her sleep without dreams.

But that wasn't the case.

Millie was walking through an open field, but in the distance, she could see a small village with plumes of smoke rising from ancient stone buildings. She saw a church with three tall steeples. One of the spires looked like the top had been sheared off.

Millie heard gunfire and explosions as she walked. She jerked and pulled her sheet closer as if the covering would protect her. Her eyes moved under her closed lids, and her mouth worked, but no words came out.

In her dream, as she approached the village, she noticed a jeep with a litter strapped across the back. She saw a young man in the rear administering to the wounded soldier, and even from that distance, she knew it was her husband.

Running now, she leaped across a small ditch on the side of the road and, for some reason, believed she could catch up to the vehicle. Arms pumping and sucking air, she watched the jeep turn a corner and leave her sight. She kept running but slowed to a walk as she witnessed the city's destruction.

She saw a pile of bodies to her left and burned-out homes and vehicles to her right. She caught up to the now-empty jeep and heard screams of pain inside the church. She made her way up the steps and through the big, wooden doors.

"Stanley!" she yelled. There was certainty in her voice as she screamed his name again, "Stanley!"

She found cots with wounded men and women and doctors and nurses scampering to and fro, administering to as many as possible. Then, finally, she turned and saw Stanley. He was hunched over a young man in a brown uniform. The ᛋᛋ with Armanen runes symbol flashed on his shoulder.

She watched Stanley work, and a sense of pride rose in her heart. She saw the care he gave to each of the wounded and marveled at his expertise. She said, "I bet he'll be a doctor someday."

She moved closer.

In her bed, her fingers clutched the edge of the quilt her mother had made for her. Millie's breath quickened.

"Stanley," she said. He didn't look up. Instead, he was focused on this Nazi soldier, just a boy, and a wound he'd suffered to his leg.

Millie jerked as an explosion rocked the north side of the church. Stanley looked up and right at her.

She saw the soft, brown eyes and the crinkly lines formed there as he smiled at her. She loved his dimples and reached out to touch the side of his face.

"Stanley, I'm so proud of you," she said as he returned to his work.

She could see he was tired. The slump in his usually solid and broad shoulders told her he'd been carrying a weight and, because she knew him, would soon say what he always said, "I gotta lay this burden down."

She'd heard him say that so many times. She took a deep breath and turned back to the church's front doors.

Millie was smiling there in her sleep as Anne crept into their room. She was glad everyone in the house was asleep when she came in, but Anne still felt guilty as she looked at the clock on the mantle that read, "One o'clock."

"*Why should I feel guilty?*" she thought, "*I'm almost a married woman.*"

She glanced at Millie, lying on her back. The slant of moonlight illuminated her smiling face. Anne had been there to comfort her sister after horrible nightmares so many nights; it was good to see her having a happy dream.

She took off her clothes and hung them on a chair. Her nightgown was tucked under her pillow, and she slid it out as quietly as possible.

As she positioned herself under her covers, she looked at Millie again. She noticed her lips moving as if she were talking with someone. She knew past nightmares focused on Stanley, and Anne hoped that this meant Millie was having a nice talk with him.

She rolled over, and a knitting needle resting on a table between the beds fell, clattering on the hardwood floor. Anne winced, deciding whether to get out of bed and pick it up or let it lie until morning.

"Looks pretty late," Millie said.

Anne didn't look at her. "Yep, pretty late."

"What did y'all do?"

"We just done what we do most Friday nights, that's all," Anne said. She didn't feel it was right to tell Millie about her engagement tonight. It could wait until the morning when she could show everyone Jody's token of love.

"That's nice," Millie said.

"And I had some moonshine." Anne knew it was the wrong thing to admit at that moment, but it just popped out, and now she wished she could cram the words back into her mouth.

"Anne Wright!" Millie said. She threw back the covers on her bed and sat on the edge of the mattress. "What were you thinkin'?"

Anne turned down the covers on her bed. "I guess I was thinkin' I'd like to try it."

Millie scooted closer to the edge of the bed. "Well, how'd you like it?"

"Millie, it was awful. So bitter, and even with a little bit of flavor, maybe it was hickory or somethin', it tasted terrible."

Anne moved her legs over the edge of the mattress and faced Millie. She tried to hide her smile, but it was just too hard.

"You're not gonna do that again, are you?" Millie asked.

"No, 'course not."

At that moment, the moonlight flashed on Anne's left hand, and the highly polished surface of the gold ring sparkled. Anne noticed it first, and Millie saw it when she tried to shove it under the covers.

"What's that? What's goin' on?"

She slowly slid the ring out from under her covers and held it up to show Millie.

"Oh, my goodness!" Millie said, then realized how loud her voice was. She smiled and covered her lips.

"I know. Jody was so cute when he asked me," Anne said.

"Oh, Anne, I'm so happy for you," Millie whispered.

"He said he'd get a better one for my wedding band. Maybe with a diamond." And at that moment, Anne realized what Millie might be feeling and started to cry.

Millie got out of bed and sat next to Anne. Millie put Anne's head on her shoulder, just as her sister had done for her so many times. She was glad she was the first to know and had time to prepare for the news as Anne broke it to the rest of the family.

"I know now," Anne said between sobs. "I know."

And since they were sisters and had been through so much together in the last few months, Millie knew precisely what Anne was talking about.

"It's fine," Millie said, but she couldn't help but think about the night the same thing had happened to her. She recalled how Stanley had asked her and slid the tiny ring he'd bought her on her finger. She'd proudly put it on that night and still hadn't taken it off.

Millie felt the weight of the metal and cherished the memory it represented. She knew Anne was likely crying more for her than joy for herself, which was wrong. She understood.

"Don't you worry about me. You be happy. That's all you need to be right now," Millie said as she patted Anne's head.

Anne soon stopped crying, and Millie tucked her back into bed. "You try and get some rest now."

"You too," Anne said. She rolled over and pulled the covers to her face.

"I will," Millie said with confidence. Of course, she couldn't guarantee it, but she believed she might revisit Stanley tonight, and this time, she'd have news for him.

# Chapter 40

The following day at breakfast, Anne showed her ring to everyone and announced she was engaged. Smiles and hoots of joy accompanied the gathering around her as she sat next to Mary Lou at the head of the table.

"Lord'a mercy," Brother said.

"Oh, I'm so happy for you," Mary Lou said.

Millie smiled but said nothing. She knew that if she lied about already knowing about the impending nuptials, she would be found out, and she didn't want to spoil the news for everyone else.

Snaps smiled and said nothing, but that didn't keep her from thinking. She was happy for her sister, but the engagement caused her to think about her future. She would be an unwed mother with a tiny baby in a small town where everyone knew everything about everyone else. How could she keep up a ruse that would spare her and her family shame and ridicule? She wasn't that good an actress. No one was.

"Let me see," Snaps said, adding as much enthusiasm as possible to her voice. She rushed around the table and picked up Anne's hand. As Snaps grabbed Anne's finger, the palm of Anne's hand touched Snaps' abdomen. It was four months since the attack, and a swell had formed just south of Snaps' belly button.

Anne thought, "*Hot stove, hot stove, hot stove.*" She jerked and moved her hand down toward the table. She splayed her fingers and let the ring glow in the dim electric lights. Indirect sunlight burst through a window near the table and helped everyone focus on the ring.

"He bought this?" Mary Lou asked.

"Yep, with his own money," Anne said. She pushed her palm down into the oilcloth table covering. The ring made a slight impression on the material.

"Good for him," Brother said. He opened the cloth covering a basket and picked up a biscuit. He slathered butter on the now-open biscuit and dripped grape jam on the opposite side.

It was as if Snaps could feel the heat coming from Anne's reddening face. She took a step away from the table and stared at the ring. Would Anne want to have a child someday? Jody was attractive and would likely provide a good life for them if he continued working on his family's farm. Snaps considered they would have some bumps along the way, but the blending of these families would be suitable for both.

"Jody said he'd maybe buy me a ring with a diamond for a wedding band," Anne said. She moved her finger so the light would pick up the sheen from the gold.

"He's a good boy," Brother said, talking around the biscuit he was chewing. He swallowed and took a sip of his coffee.

"Have y'all talked about a date?" Millie asked. She finally felt she could add to the conversation. Millie hadn't talked to Anne about a wedding date and was curious. Her own wedding flashed in the back of her mind, but she quickly pushed it aside.

"No, not yet. There ain't no rush," Anne said. She slid her hand off the table and onto her lap.

Snaps turned and walked back to her chair. She picked up her coffee cup. "Good to the last drop," she said as she tipped the cup to her lips.

It was a strange non-sequitur, and most people wouldn't have noticed it, but Mary Lou had an ear for such strange utterances at odd times. These instances sometimes added to her poems, which popped up like daylilies.

She wanted to let Snaps know that what she said wasn't incorrect. Of course, she'd heard the commercial on the radio and the tagline "good to the last drop." The company used the phrase in their advertising because President Theodore Roosevelt, while visiting Andrew Jackson's homeplace, the Hermitage, in 1917, deemed the coffee he'd been served as "good to the last drop." But why did Snaps use the phrase now?

"Yep," Brother said, "sometimes they sing it on the radio."

Snaps swallowed hard, knowing it would be inappropriate for her to sing the commercial now. She didn't want to take anything away from Anne's moment. She swallowed again, but out it came.

Snaps sang, "Maxwell House, It's Good to the Last Drop." She smiled, picked up her cup, and took a sip.

Anne put her left hand under her thigh and picked up her fork. She poked at scrambled eggs and declared, "Needs salt and pepper. Snaps, could you pass me 'em?"

It was a simple request that, at any other breakfast, would have elicited a simple response. But today, Snaps couldn't stop herself from singing.

"Here's the salt and pepper," she sang. There was no recognizable tune to the response but a sing-song scale accompanying the words.

Brother stopped chewing, and so did Mary Lou. Millie sat next to Snaps and reached across the table to attempt to pat the troubled girl's arm. Snaps jerked back and stood.

It was as if she had taken all the air in the room. The rest of the family looked at each other.

"I've had enough," she declared. She scooted her chair back and stomped from the room.

When she was out of earshot, Brother asked, "What was that all about?"

"If'n I remember correctly, it was about at four months that I started to feel comfortable with the baby," Mary Lou said. Then, she shook her head and said, "Poor child."

Millie said, "Maybe she should see the doctor again."

Anne said, "Maybe she just needs some rest. Has she been sleepin'?"

Mary Lou shook her head and said, "No idea. I can't imagine her dreams are givin' her too much solace these days."

The word 'dreams' made Millie think about her recent visit with Stanley. She marveled at the vivid scene and how proud she was of Stanley working diligently with the wounded.

And at that moment, an idea formed in Millie's mind. It was madness, of course, but she couldn't help but allow the notion to take hold.

"Good to the last drop," Millie sang and attacked her breakfast with a new verve she hadn't displayed in months. Was she going mad, too?

# Chapter 41

With Fall approaching, Brother knew he needed to focus on getting the milk barn's concrete floor and foundation poured. Unfortunately, dropping temperatures and rainy weather could keep him from meeting the deadline set by the health department. He'd already bought a tarpaulin from the Army surplus store to cover the wood when it was scheduled to be delivered next week. He put his tools in the barn's feed room and sharpened all his cutting tools. But concrete was something where his experience was lacking.

The same went for wiring the barn for the milking machines. Just running a wire from the house system wouldn't be sufficient. There would be a need for a certified electrician to get involved. Brother didn't like bringing in other workers like an electrician or concrete finishers.

In the past, he'd mixed concrete for smaller projects in a wheelbarrow. Still, the new barn would need a concrete truck and professional finishers to ensure that the foundation and the floor didn't crack after a few years of use. The bank loan included these costs, but Brother liked to be in charge. He knew the adage 'Measure twice, cut once" also applied to projects like this where cutting corners now could cause problems later.

Brother rose early the day the truck was scheduled to arrive. He'd already measured and dug out all the trenches and laid off the lines for the finishers. He was standing by the gate when the truck rambled down the road.

The driver pulled the truck through the gate and stopped. He jumped out of the cab and held out a clipboard to Brother.

"You'll need to look over this and sign," the driver said.

"I ain't signin' anythin' until you're done to my satisfaction." Brother stood with his arms crossed over the front of his overalls.

"This is just the P.O. sayin' this is your concrete, and we're at the right place."

"Oh, well," Brother took the clipboard. He read the first few sentences and asked, "Got a pen?"

The driver took a pen from his coat pocket and handed it to Brother. "The money is in escrow, and the bill's paid outta that."

"Right," Brother said, handing the board back.

"Don't go too far. I'll need you to sign the approval when we finish."

"I ain't goin' nowhere."

The truck pulled up next to the foundation trench. The driver began tugging on levers, and the finisher pulled the chute back and forth. The concrete oozed from the big, spinning drum.

Brother wasn't accustomed to the engine noise and winced as the driver adjusted the throttle to even higher revs. That's why Brother was surprised when he found all three girls standing next to him.

They were together less now than they were just a few years ago. Then, with jobs, dating, and school, the time the young women spent together was relegated to Sundays and holidays. Today, they had all found time in their schedules to witness the foundation pouring. They watched the thick concrete fill the ditches and glisten in the sun.

"Y'all stay back now," Brother said. He waved a hand at them as they watched the machinery whirl, bounce, and shake. The engine and drum sound developed a loud squeal as the truck moved from one end of the plot to the other.

With Brother's back turned, the girls looked at each other.

Should they dare?

Snaps, almost always the leader in these instances, took a step toward the ditch and looked over the mound of earth that would eventually be pushed to the side of the building.

"Sure is deep. You wouldn't think that, would ya?" Snaps asked.

The girls watched as Snaps jumped over the black and brown dirt. She turned and offered her hand to Millie, who looked first at Anne and then Snaps. Should she dare?

Millie bounded over the dirt, her left foot catching a few clods that sat on top. The mud didn't fall into the ditch, and she let out a satisfying "Oh."

"Next," Millie said and offered Anne her hand.

Anne saw Brother talking with the truck driver. The noise kept her from hearing what they were saying, but she could tell they had found a common subject. Anne guessed it was likely the weather.

Anne jumped over the ditch and smiled at her sisters. "Now what?"

"That is always the question, isn't it?" Snaps said. Her ever-expanding waist didn't stop her from bending down and getting on her knees. She motioned for the other girls to join her.

"I saw something like this in a movie magazine," Snaps said. "They got this place in Hollywood where the stars put their hands in cement. It's in front of a movie theater."

"And then what happens?" Millie asked. She rarely paid attention to movie magazines and hadn't been to the movies in months. The thought of possibly seeing Stanley in a newsreel during the war made her cry. Now that the war was long over, she'd lost all interest in the silver screen.

"They usually just take some pictures," Anne said. She read the same movie magazines as Snaps, and she and Jody were avid picture show attendees.

"Let's do it," Snaps said. She put her left hand in the wet cement and then her right.

Anne followed just to the left and Millie to the left of her.

They didn't push hard on the concrete. The girls somehow knew they could ruin the finish or cause cracks in the foundation. They just wanted to make an impression.

"Feels kinda…" Anne said as Millie finished, "Squishy. I hope this comes off."

"It'll come off," Brother said. He stood looking down at them. His arms were folded in front of his overalls as before, but this time instead of a furrowed brow, he was smiling.

"We can smooth it out," Snaps said. Her bottom lip quivered as she struggled to pull herself back from the edge of the ditch.

"It's okay," Brother said. "Don't bother. It's fine."

A visible sign of relief passed through the girl's faces. Anne helped Snaps to her feet, and Millie crouched and then stood.

The young women stood and looked down at their handiwork. Brother offered them a rag, and they cleaned their hands as best they could. He sniffed and remembered all the other times they had shared an experience like this. They had picked blackberries when Snaps was little more than a toddler. She would snag a berry and yelp in pain as the thorns poked her tender fingers and arms, but she wouldn't stop eating.

"You know this is the foundation of the building. No one's gonna see this," Brother explained.

"*We'll* know," Snaps said.

"And a hundred years from now, somebody will tear down this building and put up somethin' else," Millie said. She had always had a sense of history and place. She remembered so much about growing up on the farm and the adventures the girls had experienced. She'd hoped one day to share those memories with her children.

"Yeah," Anne said. "We'll know it's there."

Snaps fantasized that one day she'd be a big movie star and put her hands in cement in front of the movie theater in Hollywood just as she had done here. She smiled, thinking about how people would travel for miles just for a chance to put their hands where hers once were.

# Chapter 42

The first delivery of wood and steel slid off the truck near the poured foundation and the still-curing floor. Brother was ready with the gray tarpaulin hanging over a fence post.

He met the driver at the gate and showed him where he wanted the load. "Right there," he said, pointing to a plot where he'd cut the grass short. The driver followed orders because Brother had a reputation for telling people what he wanted and expecting them to deliver on that promise.

Mary Lou heard the truck's arrival and walked through the corral that fed into the barn and through the gate. Many changes would be needed to get the new venture off the ground. A pump for the well would feed water into underground pipes leading to the milk barn. Running water in the house would come later. There might even be indoor plumbing in the future.

Brother could dig and help with the plumbing, haul pipe, and such. Still, again, an outsider with experience and knowledge would be hired to upgrade the facilities. He had accepted his limitations in this area, knowing that the help would cost money, but he wanted it done right, which meant hiring someone.

Mary Lou crossed her arms over her chest and said, "Looks good. Is that everything you asked for?"

"Not by a long shot," Brother said. "The next delivery has plumbing and roofing materials." He had to shout over the noise of the big engine backing the truck next to the building plot.

"Oh," Mary Lou said. "I'm glad you know what you're doin' 'cause I sure wouldn't." She also found herself shouting, with the engine shifting from a low, rough rumble to a high-pitched whine.

She watched the driver operate levers and handles that slid the packs of lumber from the back of the truck.

"What'a ya' say?" Brother asked.

"I said," Mary Lou shouting even louder, "I'm glad you know…!"

The last lumber touched down, and the engine returned to a low growl.

"what you're doin'!" still shouting even though the lot had quieted. "Oh, sorry," she said in her usual tone and volume.

"Yeah, me too," Brother said.

He signed the papers the driver handed him and looked at Mary Lou. "Wanna sign some of these?"

"No," she shook her head, "that's awright."

The driver climbed back into the cab and gunned the motor. He waved at Brother and drove toward the open gate. A plume of rock dust rose from the dry road as the truck turned a corner and disappeared.

A cow bellowed from behind the barn, and Brother looked at the small door in front. The memory came rushing back, and his bottom lip quivered.

"I better close that before a cow gets loose on the road," Brother said. His voice sounded like he had cotton in his throat.

Mary Lou looked at him as he struggled to find the words. "That sounds like Fibber. She won't get out," she said as if the possibility of a lost cow was the most important thing in the world.

Brother looked down at his shoes and then up at Mary Lou. "I didn't know what was goin' on." There was tension in his voice, and she saw a sting of pain at the corners of his eyes.

"I mean, when I first opened the barn door, I heard 'em. I thought somebody, you, had maybe left a cow locked up in a stall and forgot to let 'em out," he said, taking a deep breath. "

Mary Lou considered saying something that might help him unburden himself, but she let him speak uninterrupted.

"I opened the door, and I could tell the noise was comin' from the front part of the barn, not the back. It was strange, a stranglin', gurglin' sound, like somebody who couldn't catch their breath or was fightin' for air," he said, nodding his head almost imperceptibly.

"So, I come around the side of the doorway and down the hall to the feed room. I wish I'd put that closer to the stalls every time I walk down that way," he said.

"It's all right," she said. She couldn't help herself and prayed her interrupting him wouldn't stop his story.

"I come down the hallway, and the noise got louder. I picked up a shovel, and for some reason, I thought there might be a snake after a chicken or something like that. I spied through the slats in the doorway, and I could see Snaps just fightin' a boy that was holdin' her down. The boy had his hand over her face, and she looked kinda' blue on her skin. She punched him in the leg, and I saw him stop for a second. His face just turned pale. I seen plenty of looks like that in the war. They have an arrogance like they have a right to own everythin' in the world."

Brother looked down and then back up at Mary Lou. He had failed her. He had been unable to keep one of her girls safe and felt awful.

"He still had his hand over Snaps' face; like I said, she was pale as a sheet. I should'a said somethin'. I should'a pushed him off. I wasn't thinkin', and I hit him with the shovel." He winced in pain.

"I hit him with the wooden end. I thought it woulda' just knocked him out or at least make him stop. I guess I hit him too hard."

Mary Lou moved closer to Brother, but he stepped back.

"I hit him too hard. And he just rolled off Snaps." Brother choked on the girl's name. "I should'a got there sooner, done somethin' different." He was sobbing between words now, and tears streamed from both eyes.

"I killed lots of Germans in the war. Up close and far away, but not a one of them was easy. I still see them sometimes. Even in the daylight," Brother wheezed and took a deep breath.

"It's alright," she said, reaching for his arm again, but he pulled back. "You did awright."

"I just wish," he turned and walked toward the barn.

She thought of something Pete the milkman had said, "Snaps is a strong girl. Just give her time."

Brother was moving away from her and toward the front of the barn. He refused to look back at her.

She remembered how Pete had said, "Snaps done good, but Brother did better," but she couldn't think of a way to phrase it so that Brother would understand.

She pulled up a corner of the tarpaulin and sat on the wood. The aroma of the damp canvas and the freshly cut wood filled her nose. She pulled a small journal and a short, stubby pencil from her pocket. She looked at the sky and then down at her paper. She wrote a few phrases Brother had said and then her impressions of his actions. This was how she chronicled the emotions of her family, and she didn't know how, but she believed one day, these notes would help her understand.

# Chapter 43

Mary Lou's Journal, September 9, 1945

List of things to be grateful for:

Sunshine, moonlight, wind, rain, snow, plants, animals, family, friends, books, radio, pictures, knowledge, love, and faith.

Memory. Promises. Love.

Good days and bad days.

Poetry that helps me make sense of it all.

*The Faithful Few*
*Those who say nothing can be done,*
*Don't have their faith in the holy one.*
*Clouds that cover a rainbow due,*
*Will see the sun soon breaking through.*

Mary Lou stopped. Her pencil hovered over the paper, and she sighed. She looked at the evenly spaced block letters that made up the words that spoke to her heart. Unfortunately, even this most tried and true method wasn't working for her today.

She stared at the barn and saw Brother leaning face-first against the door. She couldn't see what he was doing from this distance, but she saw his shoulders bounce up and down. Finally, she heard him sniff and open the door. He walked through with his head bent low.

Failure.

She had failed the one promise she'd made Frank. They had talked about how they would raise the girls. She'd looked into his dark brown eyes and seen her reflection. She was one with him on so many levels. They even finished each other sentences at times. The days before the births of the girls were filled with long walks and conversations about everything under the sun.

They'd even discussed what the other would do if something happened. They'd made a promise so many years before to love and care for each other until 'death do us part,' not realizing that Frank's days were shorter than Mary Lou's.

She'd never dealt with failure well. There were new agricultural methods and crops she'd tried that didn't take root. She'd tried different ways of cooking the family favorites, and the recipes that didn't work were quickly dropped. The children would squirm and say they enjoyed the flank steak or chitlins when she knew they didn't. She'd tried different methods of darning socks and making quilts; when she failed, she always felt she'd failed her family. Now, she *knew* she'd failed. There was clear and growing evidence in Snaps' womb.

She returned to her poem. There were times she'd find the ending before she wrote the beginning. She put her pencil to her bottom lip.

*Where there are gathered one or two,*
*You will find the faithful few.*

It was a bit 'sing-song' and not up to her usual standards. She liked the turn of a phrase she might have heard on the radio or in conversation at church. The girls were an endless inspiration for new ideas and expressions. There were days she'd rush to her journal to write down something one of them had said before she forgot.

She remembered how she'd promised Frank she would take care and protect the girls, and in that pledge, she'd failed miserably. How could she make it right? She'd hold on to Snaps and never let her feel pain or danger again. She believed she could do that until death parted them.

She turned the page and wrote, "She will never leave my sight again," without thinking about what that might entail.

# Chapter 44

Brother would mumble to himself as he nailed the two-by-fours together. His inner dialogue seemed too rough for words that others might hear, so he masked them with sounds that, if people were close enough, might mistake for the rantings of a madman.

He couldn't do the entire project alone, so he asked Millie, Anne, and Snaps to be his extra set of hands and feet. The girls alternated days, finding Millie the most helpful, Anne the most distracted by her thoughts on her flower and baking businesses and her fiancé, and Snaps being the least helpful and most preoccupied.

"Just hold that up there, Snaps," Brother said.

She tried, but the plank was heavier and had potential splinters. She hated splinters.

"I said, hold it, girl."

"I am," she retorted. She knew she wasn't doing a good job, but she'd found out long ago there were jobs where if you weren't helping, you wouldn't be asked back. Anne and Millie would be crushed by not being helpful, but Snaps had no such qualms. As her stomach grew, it became even more difficult for her to focus.

"Hand me the screwdriver, the flat-head, Snaps," Brother said, holding out his hand. He was on a ladder, and while most of the corner connections required ten-penny nails, the corner where the electrical connection would come into the building needed more support and insulation.

"Flathead. Got it," she said. She rummaged through the toolbox beside the ladder. Did she pick up the Phillip's head on purpose?

Jody strolled up to the construction site as Brother frowned and handed the screwdriver back to Snaps. "Jody, can you hand me the flathead screwdriver?"

"Sure," he said as he pulled the tool from the top of the box. "Here ya' go."

He handed it up to Brother. The moment the hammer struck him in the face flashed in his mind. "*When will that finally go away?*" he asked himself.

Jody said to Snaps, "You should'a been there when he dropped that hammer on my nose."

Brother winced. Making such a big mistake still tarnished his confidence in his abilities. There were many things in which Brother felt inadequate, but carpentry wasn't one of them.

"Right there," Snaps said with a lilt in her voice. She smiled and poked Jody's nose.

"Yep, he set it too. I went to the doctor, but he said it'd probably be alright," Jody said.

"If I don't get a roof on this thing before the rains come, ain't nothin' gonna be alright." It was Brother's attempt at a joke. It wasn't funny, and the children didn't understand why it was such a bad thing for the wood to get wet. Not only wasn't rain good for the wood, but it also made Brother's joints ache. Damp weather was affecting him more often than it did in the past, and he didn't like it. He'd seen his father crippled by arthritis, and he didn't want that as he neared the end of his life.

"Snaps, why don't you go get us some water," Brother said. "You're thirsty, ain't ya?"

"Yeah, sure," Jody said.

Snaps turned and walked to the fence separating the yard from the pasture. The gate squeaked as she opened it. She would bring out the oil can and the bucket of water.

"She's puttin' on a few pounds," Jody said as he watched Snaps turn and slip through the gate.

Brother debated telling Jody about Snaps' pregnancy. Even if they hadn't set a date, he was engaged to Anne. Brother believed trusting him with this secret might help him understand some of the strange looks and hushed whispers in the family circle. It was still a small town, though, and while he liked Jody, he didn't want to put him in the awkward position of holding his tongue.

"She's just fillin' out a bit," Brother lied. It really wasn't Jody's business.

"She probably needs to cut back on the bread and butter," Jody said with a smile. Brother looked down at him, frowning.

"I got another hammer up here," Brother said. He was joking, but his delivery never matched the words he had in his head. He knew most people saw him as just an old grump, but he thought he was funny sometimes.

Jody grimaced and touched his nose. He looked up at Brother and saw he was smiling. Jody smiled too.

"Here's the water," Snaps said as she put the bucket down near the pile of lumber. She picked up the ladle and scooped up a cup of liquid. She held the handle out to Jody.

The fiancé took a sip and said, "Always the best in the county."

"That's true," Brother said as he finished screwing the metal plate to the top of the wooden frame. He climbed down and took the ladle from Jody. He scooped up the water and took a long draft. "Ah, that's good."

"What's next?" Jody asked. He'd come to visit Anne but considered scoring some points with Brother might help him fit in with the rest of the family.

"Crossbeams to hold up the side walls. I'd like you to help if you've got the time," Brother said. He wasn't used to asking for help and hoped he'd soon be at a place where it wouldn't be necessary.

Snaps turned to leave again. Jody said, "Hey, girl, you might want to cut back on those biscuits and gravy."

It was a playground tease, and he meant nothing of it. Jody knew he could be funny and believed it was one reason Anne fell in love with him.

"I'll do that," Snaps said, but her voice broke on the word 'that,' and she rushed away.

Jody could see her shoulders shaking as she ran and heard three great sobs as she pulled open the gate. She looked down as she spun through the opening, refusing to look up or back at Jody.

"What'd I say? I was just jokin'." Jody said.

Brother knew what Snaps was upset about, and here was yet another opportunity to let this boy into his confidence. "I don't know, Jody. I can't figure out women," Brother lied.

# Chapter 45

The Army investigator came up the steps and softly rapped the screen door. The sheriff stood behind the lieutenant with his hat in his hand. Both wore uniforms, indicating their rank and place in society. The lieutenant was pale and clean-shaven. The sheriff was red-faced, with greasy hair, and his shirt was wrinkled. The lieutenant took off his hat and put it under his arm.

Mary Lou pulled aside the curtain covering the window in the top half of the door. She twisted the knob and stepped across the threshold.

"Hello, ma'am, my name is Lieutenant Gregory P. Morrison." He said, putting out his hand, "I'm with the Judge Advocate General's office of the U.S. Army."

Mary Lou took the young man's hand and shook it. "What can I do for you?"

"If we might come in," the lieutenant asked.

Mary Lou looked over her shoulder at the family gathered around the radio. Millie had a pan filled with green peas. Two bowls sat at her feet, one with shells and the other half filled with peas. Anne sat enthralled by the soap opera playing on the radio. Snaps sat in her favorite rocking chair. She sipped at a cup of tea she hoped might settle her stomach. Brother also sat listening to the radio and turned to see the Army man at the door. He stood. "What do you need?"

"I'm finishing up an investigation of the escape of a prisoner from Camp Forrest. This happened on…," he said, reading from a clipboard in his left hand.

The sheriff said, "Maybe we should talk out on the porch." Months had passed since his visit following Olaf's death. He'd won reelection and continued display-ing his well-known prowess in fighting with drunks and his sensitivity when deal-ing with victims of violent crimes. He hadn't had time to check in on Ginger and felt guilty about it.

Mary Lou and Brother started for the door. The lieutenant said, "And Miss Ginger, too, please."

Snaps looked up and saw the people gathered at the doorway. She'd heard her name and noticed Mary Lou beckoning her, indicating she was to come along.

Mary Lou and Snaps sat on the porch swing. The sheriff and the lieutenant stood next to a white pillar holding up the porch roof. Brother sat on a step that led to the yard. A breeze rustled the leaves of the trees, and across the road, a neighbor's stand of wheat undulated in the wind.

"Let me assure you the guards who let this incident happen have been reprimanded and suffered a loss in rank and privileges," the lieutenant began. The clipboard was still in his right hand, and he referred to it when needed.

"Miss Ginger Wright," he addressed Snaps.

She wouldn't look at him.

"The incident occurred on May second while you were delivering foodstuffs from the farm."

"Yes," Snaps whispered.

"A prisoner, Olaf Weber, escaped in your truck and hid in your barn."

"Yes," Brother said. He looked up at the lieutenant and squared his shoulders as if he might need to get up and fight.

"You had met the prisoner, correct? He was one of the aides in the kitchen?" the lieutenant asked.

Brother thought, "*Was he going to accuse Snaps of helping the prisoner escape?*"

"He'd help me unload the truck sometimes," Snaps said. Her voice was louder now, and she looked the lieutenant in the eye.

"You didn't notice him in the back of the truck?" The lieutenant asked.

"No," Snaps said.

"Good, Olaf had help from the other prisoners when they created a distraction, but I have to ask if he had help. I hope you understand."

"I did not help him," Snaps said. There was an edge to her voice, and Snaps felt her cheeks grow red.

"I see. Sorry again that I'm required to ask. The prisoner hid in the barn for two days and attacked you?"

"Yes," Mary Lou said, "I saw the bruises."

"No broken bones, no need for a doctor?"

"She saw the doctor," Brother said. There was now a noticeable edge in his voice, too. His shoulders hunched forward, and he moved his right foot to the top of the step.

"There was a sexual part of the attack," the sheriff said.

The lieutenant flipped through pages on his clipboard. "That's not mentioned in your report here."

"I left it out," the sheriff said.

The lieutenant knew this was a severe violation of the law and protocol. Still, he also understood the sheriff didn't want to cause any additional harm to the girl.

"I see. Well, that does change certain aspects of the case." The lieutenant was a graduate of Yale law and had practiced two years before the war. He'd dealt with clients and knew areas where sexual assault was sometimes handled differently by the police. Shame and gossip were always hard to deal with, and the lieutenant didn't want to inflict any more harm on this victim.

"Good, I will file a report, but I need you to sign on this form attesting to your recollections of the attack. I will say, this is a sealed report, and while I'll have to add the sexual aspect of the attack, my superiors will be the only people to ever read the details."

The sheriff nodded, and Snaps saw in his eyes that she should trust the lieutenant. Maybe they had dealings in the past, so she nodded and looked at the soldier.

"Whatever I need to do," she said.

"There's nothing I can say or do that would express how sorry the U.S. Army is that this incident took place. The nature of the crime is horrific, and I'm sorry you had to experience that."

Snaps nodded.

"I see. The nature of the attack presents the possibility of more complications," he said. He turned to Snaps and looked directly at her.

"I'm a good girl, Lieutenant."

"I see. I see," the lieutenant cleared his throat. "I've been approved to offer you this check for one-thousand-seven-hundred-and-fifty dollars as, uh, compensation for your troubles. Thanks to the sheriff, the details of the attack are not known by the public. Still, the Army has regulations involving incidents like this. A service is provided if the attack results in a pregnancy that approved Army doctors would perform. It's a safe medical procedure that would end your situation should this happen."

Snaps hands shook, and she stared at the floor. Her mouth twisted, but she couldn't find any words. She felt a bubble of anger in her stomach. "*How dare they offer me money,*" she thought.

"I see," Mary Lou said. She touched Snaps' hand and nodded. "We'll know about that in about another week or so. She's usually as regular as the phases of the moon."

The lieutenant handed Mary Lou a business card and said, "There is a time limit on the performance of this procedure, obviously."

"Is that legal?" The sheriff asked.

"This would occur on an Army base with Army doctors involved. It's not considered an illegal procedure under those circumstances," the lieutenant said. Turning to Snaps, he told her, "Four months is the latest the procedure can occur under this regulation."

"I guess the Army thinks of everything," Brother said. He'd relaxed a bit and looked at the wheat field.

The lieutenant held the pen to Snaps and showed her where to sign. "Here, here, and here," he said as Snaps scrawled her autograph on the form. The lieutenant drug a piece of paper from the clipboard and handed it to Snaps. "Again, the Army is so sorry that you're going through this."

She looked at the check. She noticed her name and the name of the man who'd signed it. She saw how the numbers were spelled out at the bottom of the paper.

A bubble of anger moved up Snaps' abdomen, but she quickly swallowed it. This man wasn't there, and it wasn't his fault. She was angry at the guards who'd failed in their duty but was glad she'd stopped driving the truck to the camp. Anne made the last trip a week ago. At that time, she was told the facility was closing soon, and the produce, milk, and eggs wouldn't be needed. "*Too many bad memories,*" Snaps thought.

The lieutenant turned and stepped off the porch. The sheriff followed him to a black two-door Ford parked on the other side of the yard gate.

The military man stopped and turned. He said, "I checked the autopsy report and Weber's medical records. He had a serious wound in his leg that had mostly healed, but there was new bruising around the injury."

"What's that supposed to mean?" Brother asked.

"When Snaps fought him, she probably saved her life when she struck the criminal in the leg," the lieutenant said.

"I didn't know that," Snaps muttered.

"There was no way you could have," the lieutenant assured her.

Snaps thought of this last statement as she stood in front of her mirror and looked at her silhouette. She touched her abdomen. Who or what might have told her that hitting Olaf in the leg might cause him enough pain that he would let her breathe? Was it a miracle or just luck?

Two months and twenty-nine days had passed since the day of the lieutenant's visit. While she wasn't showing yet, the time to decide was almost up.

"Half of this young'un's gonna be a Wright," she said to her reflection.

# Chapter 46

Construction of the milk barn advanced quickly as Brother's innate talent blended with the detailed instructions that came with the building materials package. Soon, he was working alone. But sometimes, his carpenter's apron carried nails, screws, a hammer, four screwdrivers, and other assorted tools. Even then, he didn't feel the need to ask for aid.

The girls would visit the site from time to time and talk with Brother as he worked. They would help if asked, but that offer was rarely needed as the walls and roof took shape. The shingles covered half the top when the first cold rain came, but no significant damage was found after a short inspection. Brother covered the rest of the sheeting the next day, grumbling to himself most of the time. More of the inner passages and equipment began to fill the space, and it was clear that the deadline to get the milk barn operational was within reach.

The county building inspector, an agent with the milk cooperative, and a health department inspector visited the day before operations began. Each had a clipboard with several pieces of paper attached. Two of the men had pens in their pockets, one carried a pen behind his ear, and the health department inspector wore glasses. One walked with a limp. Mary Lou, dressed in a gingham dress and black shoes, greeted the men at the front gate and ushered them to the construction site.

"Come in, gentlemen," she said as she swung open the gate from the road to the front pasture. "Right this way."

"Thank you, Mrs. Wright. Lovely weather today, huh?" the inspector said.

"Yes, fine as frog hair, yes indeed."

They walked through the knee-high alfalfa, high-stepping around an occasional cow pile. "Watch your step," Mary Lou implored. She didn't know how much country living this group was exposed to every day.

"Yes, thank you," said the one with the pen behind his ear.

They approached the construction site. Brother moved down the roof eave and climbed down the ladder. He offered his hand for each man to shake and returned their smiles.

"I'm pretty close to finished," Brother said. "Y'all timed it just right."

The inspectors didn't respond but began their walk around the building. One stared for a moment at the wiring attached to the corner of the frame. Another went to the spigot that sat at the end of the building. He turned it on, and water gushed out, splashing his shoes.

"You'd have thought I'd knowed better than to do somethin' like that by now," he poked fun at himself.

The third looked at the opposite corner of the roof. There was a small discolored area running under the edge of the plywood sheeting.

"There might be some mold growing here," he said, pointing to the portion of the roof that had been rained on and covered the next day. "We can't have mold around the milk."

"I'll be happy to pull that up for you to take a gander at," Brother said. He moved the ladder to the corner and held it.

The inspector took the pen from his pocket and lifted a few shingles. "Yes, it looks like there could be some damage that needs to be replaced here."

Brother huffed, trying to cover his response as much as possible. He didn't believe the discoloration was mold, and he wanted to challenge this pipsqueak of a man. He didn't want to test the man's expertise, but something boiled up inside him.

"Looks fine to me," Brother said. His grip on the ladder tightened with his knuckles whitening.

"I'll be the judge of that," the inspector said.

Brother knew from other projects on this farm and others he had completed over the years that a persnickety inspector could cost time and money, so he swallowed hard.

"I see," Brother mumbled.

The inspector climbed down the ladder and checked several boxes on his form. "We have to take every precaution. Our milk will soon be traveling dozens of miles across the country. Stores need to know they can trust our products won't make them sick."

Brother bristled at the references to 'our' milk but again held his tongue. He remembered tussling with this same inspector on a job for the Warren farm. He judged a fitting on the roof eave was wrong, and Brother had to pull the entire section. He didn't want to do that here. That delay would put them on the other side of their deadline and keep them from bringing in any money.

"There was a bit of rain before I could get the roof all the way on," Brother explained. "I ensured it was all dry before I put down the roofing paper."

The inspector didn't respond but entered the large sliding door at the north end of the building.

"It was dry," Brother said, this time a bit louder than he intended.

The inspector ignored Brother and turned to the interior corner where the patch of mold would have leaked through. He didn't see anything and, again, made a note.

Brother entered the building and was about to buttonhole the inspector when Mary Lou moved in front of him. "Let him be," she said. "If'n he finds anything, we'll fix it."

"He ain't gonna find anything," Brother said.

Mary Lou could see his fists drifting up to his beltline. She took a deep breath and tried to distract him. "The water and electric look good. At least we picked the right folks to do that," she said with a smile.

Brother could have taken this slander of his lack of plumbing and electrical construction skills as an affront. He finally realized confrontation right now wouldn't be helpful.

"Awright," he said.

Mary Lou could see he was calming, and she turned back to the building inspector. "I hope everythin' is to your likin'.'

"I'm still working," the inspector said.

"Hey," the plumbing inspector said from across the open mall that would eventually usher the cows to their stalls. "Is that barn over there where you gave that goddamn German hell?"

"Did I what?" Brother asked. Now, his fists returned to his waist, and his eyes reddened. In his mind, he'd grabbed the inspector by the collar and swung him to the ground. He fantasized about taking the man by the throat and choking the life out of him.

"Gave that boy that beat up Snaps hell," the inspector said, smiling. He pulled up his pant leg and tapped on the prosthetic. "I'd a done the same thing."

Brother turned away from the group and looked up at the corner of the building. He feared it was not going to pass inspection. Without turning back, he said, "I was just doin' what was right."

The building inspector watched from a distance and pulled his clipboard up to his waist. He tutted to himself and said, "I don't see any problems here." He turned to Brother, "You did a good job."

"I did the best I could," Brother said. His breathing returned to normal, and he kicked the earth with the toe of his shoe. "Concrete boys did a good job, didn't they?"

The plumbing inspector nodded and said, "Ain't gonna be any cracks in that for years."

The electrical inspector nodded, too, intuiting the pain Brother still felt for his response to the attack on Snaps.

"I was in the South Pacific," the building inspector said. "We done some horrible things out there. So far away from home. I'm glad it's all over."

"Yeah," the plumbing inspector said, "A number one all the way around. Y'all gonna get a lot of service out of this barn."

"That's the plan," Mary Lou said. "Can I get y'all a cup of water or maybe some tea?"

"Water's right there on the corner," the plumbing inspector said, hooking a thumb over his shoulder.

"Right you are," Mary Lou said.

"We've got to get moving on," the building inspector said. He offered his hand to Brother. The men eyed each other for a moment, and Brother shook his hand. "You did a great job."

"Thank ye," Brother said, "I gotta get back to it."

Mary Lou ushered the men back to their car at the pasture gate. They smiled, signed forms, and handed receipts to her.

"I hope you remember the good thing Brother done for you here," the building inspector said as he shook Mary Lou's hand.

"I think about that every day," she said. She swung the door closed behind the men and watched as the car kicked up a plume of dust as it moved past the corner.

# Chapter 47

Mary Lou watched Millie use an electric mixer to make butter. On one level, it was sacrilege, but on another, it was progress. Next time, she would do away with the churn and try the new method.

"It shore does make a racket," Mary Lou said. The beaters clanged against the sides of the thick, porcelain bowl. It was not her favorite noise. She always tried to think of pleasant sounds. She loved the sound of walking through the grass early in the morning. She loved the sound of her cows mooing to be let into the barn. She loved the sound of the creek as it babbled behind the barn and split the 140 acres of their property in two.

Mary Lou remembered the sound of the scythes as the long grass fell before the cutters. She had wielded a blade since she was eleven. She'd usually use the blade to cut underbrush and weeds that grew in the pastures. Then, the grass dried in the fall, and it was time for harvest.

The traveling men Father hired to cut the hay all dressed the same, and they emitted a sound as they cut. They inhaled on their backswing, and all said a "huff" as they stepped forward and exhaled. Mary Lou asked one of the men, and he said the sound helped them find the rhythm of their simultaneous swings.

She joined them in the harvest the following year. Soon, she, too, was inhaling on her backswing and exhaling as the blade cut the long, green grass. "Huff."

Mary Lou helped cut the hay this way for ten years. The faces of the men aged, but the group stayed intact. One year, Father found a farmer with a horse-drawn cutter and hay baler, and the men were told when they arrived that their services would no longer be needed.

She found the sound of the tractor and hay baler too loud and disturbing. She told her father the sound the men made was more pleasing. Her father said, "That sound the horse-drawn cutter makes is the sound of progress."

She still didn't like that sound, even though it was faster, cleaner, and more productive for the farmer. Sometimes the old way was best.

She had not yet gotten accustomed to the sound of churning butter like this, and she didn't think she ever would.

"It sure does save time," Millie said.

Not only did the hand mixer make so much noise that it made it hard to hear someone talk, but it also drowned out the radio. The gentle sloshing of the churn let the normal rhythm of the conversation continue. The tradeoff between the churn and the mixer was the amount of time saved. The new refrigerator and stove helped save time too, but for what reason?

Mary Lou decided the taste was the same, and the butter had a smoother consistency. "*The only constant in life is change,*" Mary Lou thought. She wanted to write that phrase down in her journal, but that would have to wait a few minutes. The butter was almost done, and Millie brought the butter plate and sat it on the dining room table in front of Mary Lou. She heard a strange new rhythm in the tiny motor as it spun the curved blades. It wasn't like anything in nature she could recall, but it seemed natural.

"That's gonna cut the time by half," Mary Lou said as she slid the lump of butter onto the plate.

"You see, I told you," Millie replied.

Mary Lou considered Millie's response. She asked herself, "*Would I have spoken to my mother that way?*" When she was growing up, rural electrification was still decades off, and it wasn't unusual for a family to live in a house with a dirt floor.

"*What will the future bring?*" she asked herself.

"Here," Millie said, "let me."

Mary Lou stopped the motor and looked down into the bowl. The girl had a pitcher of milk and slowly poured the liquid into the container.

They traded places, with Millie sitting in the rocking chair and letting the low hum of the motor drive the beaters against the side of the bowl. Her apron would catch any milk that sloshed over the side of the bowl. This second round of churning would produce butter for sale. Since the POW camp was closing soon, the produce and milk products needed to find a new outlet.

"Shake a little salt in there," Mary Lou said, rocking in the chair near the radio. The afternoon soap opera featured the scandalous adventures of Lisa and her family of thieving scoundrels.

"I'm gonna name one of the cows Lisa," Mary Lou said. She'd picked up her sewing and listened as Lisa announced her intention to marry her sister's estranged husband.

"That's just bein' mean out of spite," Millie said. She watched the beaters circle the bowl. Her mind drifted, and she remembered how arm-weary she and the other girls would become with churning butter.

"That new cow, she's got a meanness in her too," Mary Lou said. "She tried to butt me the other day. Did I tell you that?"

"I don't remember you mentionin' that," Millie said. She picked up the salt-shaker from the table and shook a couple more dashes into the mix.

Mary Lou thought, "*That's gonna make that butter too salty.*" But she didn't say anything. She'd learned that there were times when it was best to let her children find their own way without her giving orders or making plans.

"That looks pretty good," Mary Lou said.

Millie looked up; drops of cream splattered her dress, hands, and face. She smiled.

Mary Lou realized it had been months since she'd seen Millie smile.

"Looks good enough to eat," the mother said.

# Chapter 48

The cows twisted their heads in wonder and confusion as they were herded into the milk barn for the first time. They knew their places in the old barn but had to be taken by the ear and led into the new milking stalls.

Mary Lou started the machine. The whirring sound of the pump reminded her of the hand mixer beaters. "Come on, Lisa," she said as she patted the cow's hindquarters. "It's not the day to be trifflin'."

Lisa dipped her head into the trough and took a mouthful of the mixed-grain feed there. She kicked her leg back as Mary Lou attached the teat cups and watched the milk surge through the clear tubes. There was no question this was easier on her back and her hands, but something about the process was off-putting.

"It'll never be the same," Brother said as he pulled the ladder down from the corner of the room. He was checking on the cleaning job he'd done on the mold the building inspector had uncovered. He should have seen and dealt with it before the walk-through, but old age was creeping toward him, and he couldn't do what he used to do now.

"That's the truth," Mary Lou said.

He looked down at his hands. The swollen knuckles ached when it was going to rain and sometimes even when it wasn't. He looked at Mary Lou's hands and saw the same inflammation.

"It's probably gonna keep us workin' for a while longer." He held up his hand to show her his arthritic joints. "I remember my father's hands got so bad the fingers turned down into his palm. He could barely lift a spoon near the end."

She looked at her hands and said, "I know. Arthur's a terrible travelin' companion. I think about that sometimes when I'm sewin' quilts or knittin'."

"We just gotta keep goin' as long as we can," Brother said, "these children need our help."

She turned to check on the pump and collection tanks. The walls in the tank room were unpainted. Brother hadn't found the time before the equipment was delivered. Because the pump and tanks rested against the wall, it would be difficult to slide a paintbrush behind it now.

Mary Lou opened the door and walked in. She felt the vibration of the motor with the palm of her hand. It was warming and soon would likely be too hot to touch.

"I'm gonna get to paintin' in here next week," Brother said. He stood by the door and wiped his hands with a handkerchief he'd pulled from his overall pocket.

"Ain't no rush as far as I can tell," she said. She smiled at the tubes filling with milk roaring into the silver tanks.

"Inspectors come around always lookin' for somethin'," he said as he tucked the cloth back into his pocket. "That's their job. I seen that when I was overseas."

"Sometimes, you're doin' the best you can with all you've got, and it still isn't enough."

She considered the possible future Millie might have now that she was adjusting to the idea of being a widow. She might have looked at her mother and saw that even when confronting death, it was possible to keep going. Unfortunately, Mary Lou was not a person who embraced change and wanted to know where she was going and who she might be traveling with as she moved forward.

She looked at Brother. She saw the almost white hair now and how his shoulders stooped. He was only fifteen when he served in the Army, and while still strong as he approached his fifties, she knew how hard life had been for him. She wished he would stop smoking. She knew it made his skin leathery, and she heard him coughing as he struggled to get out of bed. She was the one who washed his pillowcases yellowed by the nicotine he'd sweat out through the night.

He'd developed the habit in France with his fellow soldiers, finding comfort in the taste and the smell. He gagged and coughed on his first cigarette but struggled through. By his third one, he had mastered the act. It took him a few more unsuccessful attempts at rolling his own, but he soon learned that.

Brother took his pouch of Bull Durham from his pocket and folded a paper in his hands. He tapped the tobacco into the furrow and rolled it into a tight tube. He stuck the cigarette into the corner of his mouth and struck a match with his fingernail.

She never liked the smell and had a rule about smoking in the house. She sometimes worried about the open flame around the hay, but Brother was always careful. He talked about when he was a boy and how his homeplace had burned when a candle tipped over. He left his wallet on a bedstand with a hundred dollars and forty-two cents in the pockets. He retrieved the coins from the ashes, but the paper money was lost.

"That smokin'," she said.

"You don't have to go any farther," he said. "I know what you're gonna say."

He had heard the complaint in the past and promised to be careful. But he refused to stop, sometimes saying it was his only pleasure in life.

"And you don't have to say what you're gonna say," Mary Lou said.

"I guess we're just gonna have to agree to disagree," Brother said as he turned and walked to the side of the barn that was his designated smoking spot.

She considered a poem about the push and pull of change in people's lives. She reached into her pocket for her notebook, but somehow, she'd forgotten it this morning, with all the excitement and anxiety of opening the new barn.

"I guess I'll just have to remember it," she muttered, patting the large, silver tank. Then, finally, she turned and walked to the stalls to change the cows. Two more rounds, and she'd be finished until this afternoon.

# Chapter 49

Snaps' belly continued to grow, and while her dreams of violence refused to subside, she soon fell into a routine around the farm that filled her hours. She walked near the creek and through the woods. She chopped at trees from time to time. She recited poetry. She sang songs, acted out scenes from plays, and performed all the parts herself.

She, of course, couldn't work in town or be seen at church or any of the stores. Her staffing the booth at the Farmer's Market ended too. She'd gained weight in her hips and thighs. When her clothes stretched too far, she'd ask Millie to alter them. Some became too small for even that temporary fix.

"I can't button my pants," Snaps complained to her mother.

Mary Lou, Millie, and Snaps stood in the storage room next to the bathtub. As Millie pinned the edge of her skirt, Snaps stood on a wooden box.

"Maybe some elastic in the back," Mary Lou said. Her own time in a 'family way' had taught her just how uncomfortable pregnancy could be. She had familiar experiences with all her pregnancies, but each girl produced different symptoms, and all ended with Mary Lou giving birth in the upstairs bedroom. Sometimes the doctor made it there in time, but most times, he did not.

"You look fine," Millie assured Snaps, then asked, "How does it feel?"

There was a time Snaps knew her feelings well. She could find a matching feeling and express herself on stage with a similar emotion the character was experiencing. Now, all those feelings and her access to them were unreachable.

"It's not too tight, for now," Snaps tried to make a joke. She could feel the tension in the house and tried not to react when conversations stopped when she entered the room.

"You still got a ways to go, honey," Mary Lou said. Given the time of the attack, the birthdate could be calculated within days. But given the nature of gestation,

Mary Lou knew from her pregnancies and dealing with cows that the exact time would be hard to pinpoint.

"I don't feel right," Snaps said. She stepped from the box and turned. She was a few inches taller than Mary Lou and a few inches shorter than Millie. She looked first at her sister and then her mother.

"It's natural. You have good days and bad days. That's the way it goes," Mary Lou said.

"I've never, you know," Millie said. The conversation was drawing close to the nub of pain that dwelt in the pit of her stomach. She couldn't eat for days after the chaplain's visit; there were others when she felt queasy whenever she swallowed, and several times she vomited. Time passed, and her stomach returned to normal, except for those days when something happened that reminded her that she was a widow and unlikely to ever be a mother. "We'll f-f-fix it," Millie finally stammered.

"I don't see how," Snaps said. Her gaze dropped to the floor. It was as if she could see her dreams fade away there in the slats of the hardwood flooring.

"Now, you'll be fine," Mary Lou said. She put her arms around Snaps' shoulders and squeezed. She wanted to help the girl accept her fate that while childbirth was complicated, she would survive and make a life for her baby and herself here on the farm.

"I know, I know," Snaps said.

Millie put her arms around Snaps as Mary Lou's embrace ended. She whispered, "It's gonna be all right." And she meant it. She believed in God and that while everyone had personal problems, he would guide them through them. "God's gonna help us find a way," she said.

"I guess," Snaps said and shook her shoulders, loosening Millie's now painful grip. Unfortunately, Millie sometimes didn't know her own strength and could cause discomfort when she wasn't careful.

Snap's first thought was that Millie might be hurting the baby. Deep down, she knew that wasn't possible, but her maternal instinct kicked in before she could think it through.

"Oh, sorry," Millie said. She felt blood rush to her cheeks and looked down at the floor. She loved her sister and wanted to let her know it, but she would need to find a better way.

Brother appeared in the doorway. He wore his favorite overalls, and his wide-brimmed straw hat covered his forehead. He held out his right hand. Between the thumb and forefinger, he held a letter.

Mary Lou asked, "What is it?"

Millie looked Brother in the eye. She could see the pain and winced as he said, "It's for Millie."

She had received several life-changing letters in the past few months. Many involved her appeal for Stanley's life insurance policy and various letters of condolences and support from the Army.

"Who's it from?"

He choked a bit as he said, "Stanley."

# Chapter 50

Millie's knees turned to jelly. She stared at the address. Yes, it was Stanley's hand-writing.

"How?" she muttered as she tried to steady herself by putting her hand on the doorframe.

Brother grabbed Millie's arm and steadied her. He moved her through the door and sat her at the head of the dining room table. Mary Lou, Snaps, and Brother sat near her.

"Maybe we should let her…," Mary Lou said, trying to think of her daughter's feelings with everyone gathered around.

"No, it's fine," Millie said. She stared at the envelope for a moment. "It just showed up?"

Brother answered, "The mailman said it happens sometimes. The mail service was slow, and some letters from Europe got lost for a while."

Millie nodded slowly. Her mind was a jumble of feelings, memories, and sup-positions. She thought, "*How could this be?*" She checked the postmark. It was several days after Stanley had reportedly been captured. She turned the envelope over and paused.

"Open it," Snaps said. She didn't mean to be so abrupt; none of this was her business, but she couldn't hold back. "I'm sorry."

"It's okay," Millie told her. She picked up a knife left over from breakfast and slit open the end of the envelope. Millie's habit of opening the opposite side of the envelope was her way of preserving the postmark. Stanley had traveled to so many different places. This was her way of living vicariously through him.

Millie changed her mind. She looked at everyone around the table, stood up, and walked through the living room and out into the yard. She stopped at the big elm tree near the front gate and unfolded the paper.

*Dearest Millie,*

*We're in Belgium and facing a major push by the Germans. I miss you and think about you all the time. It's freezing now, and while we wear coats most of the time, it's still not enough.*

*There are many casualties, and it's part of our job to help both American and German troops. I felt the need to write to you because of the strangest thing, actually two things that happened.*

*I was shadowing a patrol, and we saw this young German boy lying in a ditch. I jumped out of the jeep. He still had a pulse, but he was bleeding from a wound on his leg. It looked like the soldier had been stabbed with a bayonet. I put a tourniquet on his thigh, and the soldier I was with helped me put him on a stretcher and transport him to a makeshift hospital we'd set up in a church.*

Millie stopped reading for a moment and recalled her dream. How could it be? She remembered she had watched Stanley working with wounded men in a church. She shook her head and returned her focus to the letter.

*The boy was very handsome and robust but didn't speak much English. I did the movement from the Tarzan movie, 'Me Stanley and you....' He said his name was Olaf Weber. He let me know that some of his friends called him Ollie.*

*I was pretty proud of myself for getting his name and all. We didn't work on many German soldiers, so it was good to see that some of them were good people.*

*I only had learned one phrase in German, Millie.* **Beginnen sie mit zehn neun acht sieben**, *which means; start with ten, nine, eight, seven. It's a countdown we ask the soldiers to say before we give them the ether before their operation. I've never seen one soldier get past eight, Millie, I swear.*

*But Olaf was so strong he got almost all the way to three. As he was going under, he made this gesture with his hand. I'd never seen anything like it, and I wanted to tell you. He looked at me and moved his hand horizontally to the ground. I took it to mean he wanted us to let him go. He didn't want to live. The Germans knew they were losing, and this last big push would likely fail. The war wouldn't...couldn't go on much longer.*

*The surgeon didn't see the boy make the movement, but I wasn't gonna let him die. The doctor got in there and did this thing where he patched the artery instead of amputating the leg. I'd never seen anything like it before.*

*We fixed the boy's leg, and the surgeon gave me the best compliment. He said when we get back to the States, he will pull some strings and see if he can get me into medical school. Ain't that something? You could be married to a doctor someday.*

*Anyway, I just wanted to tell you the good news and how I'll be home soon.*

*Love you always, Stanley.*

Millie leaned against the tree trunk. She felt the rough bark against her arm and the back of her shoulder. Her mind was a whirlwind.

She knew from the newspaper account of the attack on Snaps that the boy's name was Olaf Weber. But it was such a big world. There's no way it was the same one. Stanley said he was a good boy, and Stanley was always a good judge of character. But Snaps had told her about how she was fighting the boy and hit him in the leg. That's what made him let her go, and Brother killed him. But there's no way it was the same soldier.

She reread the letter's last paragraph and loved Stanley more than ever. She noticed her family gathered on the porch looking at her.

It was impossible to describe their faces and how they each looked like they wanted to rush to her side. She looked at them and shook her head. *No.*

Millie turned and touched a tree branch and smiled. A light breeze wafted the smell of lilac toward her and helped her relive the moment once again....

It was late in the day, but the sun still shone over the house's eaves. They had been talking for a long time, and he kissed her.

"Hey," Stanley said. "I bet you can't get up on that limb, there."

Millie liked a challenge, and while it had been a long time since she'd tried to climb any tree and over five years since she last climbed this tree. The skill came back to her instantly. When she was younger, Brother told her she was more like a monkey than a girl.

She grabbed the limb like she had a hundred times before and hefted herself up. She sat there and arranged her skirt. She wiggled her ankles as her feet dangled near his face. She looked down at him and smiled. He was smiling too, and she patted the top of the limb next to her.

"Come on up," Millie said.

"No, I'll stay right down here," Stanley said. He pinched the toe of her shoe, and as she closed her eyes and yelped in pain, he pulled a gold ring from his pocket.

"Millie Wright, I've loved you for so long," he said. Tears were in his eyes because he knew their engagement wouldn't be long since he'd recently signed up for the Army. Still, he knew they'd have years together when he got back. And a great story for anyone who asked about how they got engaged.

He asked the question, "Will you be my wife?"

She took a deep breath. The aroma of lilac from the bushes near the pasture fence filled her with joy and peace. She'd stood by the tree many times since Stanley's passing and always remembered how she felt that day.

Of course, her family already knew what Stanley was planning and was standing there watching and smiling as witnesses to the happiest moment in Millie's life.

She looked up now. They stood there, just as they had before, but this time they hesitated, not knowing what to do.

Millie raised her hand and motioned for them to come to her.

Anne led the way, followed by Mary Lou, Snaps, and Brother. Millie opened her arms, and they grabbed and held on, knowing that this was probably one of Millie's biggest jolts in a year full of shocks.

Brother laid his big hand on the back of her head. He knew so much of the pain and sorrow she was feeling. It was like a phantom limb, the feeling many amputees experienced when an arm or leg was taken. He'd heard some of the ship boys talking about it when he was returning from the war.

"It's all right," Mary Lou said. "We're right here."

"I know," Millie said, "I know."

# Chapter 51

Snaps tried to slide the letter out of Millie's hand, but she gripped the paper hard and said, "No." Millie insisted, "Please."

The rest of the family had turned away from Snaps, so they didn't see the exchange of glances between her and Millie. Snaps immediately stopped and smiled at her sister. "Sorry, I was just curious."

"I know," Millie said. "Maybe someday." But Snaps had already turned and was moving away from the tree.

The family finished hugging Millie, patted her on the back, turned, and walked back to the porch. Brother headed for the swing. While it was his usual nap time, he didn't believe he'd be able to sleep today. Anne and Snaps raced to the front steps. Even though she was slowed by her expanding belly, Snaps won. Mary Lou said as she brought up the rear, "'Bout time for lunch."

Brother turned and decided, yes, lunch before nap. Now, that made sense. But so much of the past few months refused to make sense. Late at night, Brother would lie in his bed and wonder what he might have done for the family to have suffered so much. Was it something he'd done in the war? But, he never came to a definitive conclusion.

Millie couldn't be less interested in eating right then, but she said, "Yes, that sounds good."

Plates from breakfast were stacked in the sink, and clean ones reset the table. Mary Lou brought warmed bowls of vegetables and a plate of biscuits. Millie's 'mixer churned' butter had been a big hit for several weeks, even though Mary Lou still thought the girl used too much salt.

They sat in their usual places, with Brother at one end and Mary Lou at the other end of the table. Millie slipped Stanley's letter into her pocket and scooted up. Snaps and Anne sat in the middle chairs and acted as facilitators on opposite sides of the table.

The new water pump clicked on, filling a tank that sat next to the machinery in the well house. It was tight in there, but the plumber made it all fit. If the door to the pantry was opened, the pump's motor interrupted most conversations. The noise was jarring initially, but the family quickly became accustomed to the rattle. And the water continued to be the coldest and the best in the area even after the well bucket was retired.

Running water in the house was next, first in the kitchen, then a toilet, a hot water heater, and soon after that, a shower. Finally, a septic tank would be sunk in the pasture east of the house. Brother hadn't dug one of these, and he'd likely need help from someone with a tractor and a backhoe.

All this was a significant expense, and contemplating these improvements seemed financially at least a few months away. Of course, Snaps offered the money the Army had given her in compensation for the attack. Still, the family rejected it, knowing the strings attached. They convinced her to hang on to the money and use it for a big purchase, vocational course, or college, which might help her get a job. She was still considering her options.

The local economy had dipped in reaction to the national transition from war material production to peacetime products. Still, the farmer's market continued to flourish, and Anne's dried flowers and arrangements continued to grow in popularity. With the closure of Camp Forrest, the family found a new place for their truck garden produce and eggs at an expanded Junior's Market. The proprietor's son returned from the South Pacific and convinced his father it was time to use the money he'd earned in the Navy to increase their square footage. After that, Junior's could accommodate whatever the Wright family had to offer.

Millie looked around the table and realized everyone there had visions of their futures except her. Anne's marriage was just weeks away. She'd soon be living in a house Jody was building on his father's property. Snaps would soon be a mother, and her time would be consumed with raising her baby. Momma and Brother were aging but still spry and hard-working with no plans for retiring anytime soon. But what would she do?

Millie took a bite of butter beans and chewed while she thought. She couldn't tell Snaps that it might have been Stanley that saved the life of her attacker. "*Who would believe it?*" she asked herself as she pinched off a bit of biscuit and popped it in her mouth.

"Weight of the world," Anne said and immediately regretted it. She had no interest in adding to her sister's grief, but sometimes her mouth blurted something out before her brain fully engaged.

"What?" Millie asked, pretending she didn't hear what Anne had said.

"Oh, nothing," Anne said, cramming a slice of tomato into her mouth before she could say anything else that would embarrass her.

"She sai…," Brother began, but a stern look from Mary Lou stopped him before he could finish the sentence. He returned his gaze to his plate.

"Well," Anne said. She felt she was off the hook from her previous gaffe. Maybe it was time to ask Millie about the letter. "*Or, maybe not,*" she thought.

"I think it's time to open up the back forty," Brother said. Grass in the east pasture was getting short, and the cow's food supply needed to be rotated. The hay from the west field would sustain the cows through the worst weeks of winter.

"Good idea," Mary Lou said. She took a bite of potato salad and cleaned her plate with half a biscuit.

"I'm going to go to Belgium," Millie announced. It was something she'd thought about in the past, but now Stanley's letter made her need to go there even more necessary. Everyone at the table turned and looked at her. This statement was from a woman who'd never crossed the Tennessee state line. Now, she wanted to cross the Atlantic Ocean.

"I have my own money now, and we're doin' p-p-pretty good," she stammered, picked up her glass of tea, and took a big swig. "*What in the world?*" she thought.

"It's…," Brother started to say something. He'd crossed the ocean and knew just how perilous and uncomfortable it would be for Millie. She'd never ridden in a boat bigger than a canoe.

"It's, ah…," Mary Lou started, but she had a hard time mounting an offense at this moment. She had heard Brother talking about the high waves and long distances and knew Millie wouldn't like it.

"I think she should go," Snaps said. She smiled and finished her biscuit. "She needs to go," she added.

"Yes," Millie said, "I need to go."

Anne asked, "What are you gonna do when you get there?"

In Millie's mind, there were many questions to ask, and the only answers were in Europe. "I need to go."

# Chapter 52

Anne's wedding didn't have the same sense of urgency as Millie's. No looming deployment date pushed them to make the arrangements and plan the perfect honeymoon getaway. Jody tried to be helpful and supportive but was confused about his role at the beginning of the process. He'd need to find a best man. He'd choose his father. And he'd need three groomsmen. That would mean two boys he'd attended high school with and Cousin Bruce, who'd visited from Baltimore almost every summer in the last ten years.

Bruce was a city kid but loved his summer visits with Cousin Jody, mostly because he liked caring for the animals. His visits had prompted him to study biology, with an eventual veterinary school graduation a few years away.

Bruce's visit in the Fall of 1945 included hanging out with Jody and the rest of the boys at the dam. The rushing water made everyone talk loudly, so no secrets could be safely shared.

"I think I gotta girl back home," Bruce said. He pushed his glasses back on his face after they almost slid off his nose. He wore a plain white T-shirt, jeans, and Army surplus black boots. He thought they looked cool, but they were shiny and not comfortable.

"You *think* you got a girl?" Jody asked. He wore a similar outfit, and his cowboy boots were comfortable but not shiny. It was one of those Fall nights that started out warm and would end up cold after midnight. The boys had jackets in Jody's car.

"Yeah," Bruce said, picking up a rock and chucking it into the rushing water.

"When do you think you'll know?" Jody asked.

"When she tells me," Bruce said, chuckling to himself.

"You got that right," Jody replied, also chuckling. "Hey, I got somethin' in the car."

"What is it?"

"Shine. Have you ever had any?" Jody asked.

"I've heard of it. We studied alcohol in chemistry class. The teacher set a dish of it on fire," Bruce said, showing off his schooling.

"That's what we do here, too," Jody agreed. "You can't trust moonshiners. Sometimes you gotta test it."

"Okay, how do ya' do that?"

Jody opened the passenger side door of his car and pulled out a Mason jar of the clear liquid. He shook it and held it up to the full moon.

"Looks good," he said.

"Looks like water," Bruce told him.

"It ain't water," Jody replied, pulling a spoon from the glove box. "You gotta put a match to it. If'n it burns blue, it's good to go. If it burns yellow or red, it's got lead in it. The old saying is, 'Lead burns red and makes you dead.'"

"I'm not interested in drinkin' poison," Bruce said with a tone of knowledge and maturity.

"It ain't poison, well, really, in a way, I guess it is, but what'a ya' got to lose?" Jody asked. The water rushing over the dam continued to force the boys to raise their voices to be heard.

He opened the lid and dipped the spoon into the moonshine. He set the jar on the passenger seat and struck a match with his thumbnail.

The 'shine burned yellow. Bruce looked at Jody and said, "I guess that's it."

Jody tossed the match to the ground and took a swig of the moonshine.

"You just said it would kill you," Bruce said.

"I said it *could* kill ya," Jody said, smacking his lips as the burning sensation in his chest seemed to reach down to his toes. "It'll likely just make ya' go blind."

Again, Bruce's eyes widened, and he frowned. "I'll pass."

Jody said, "Suit yourself." He took another draw and screwed the lid back on. He opened his eyes wide and pantomimed, trying to find the car. "Where is it?"

Jody yelled, "I can't see!" He couldn't keep the ruse up for long. He had to see Bruce's face as he stumbled around play-acting.

"All right, smart ass," Bruce said and got into the passenger side, slamming the door behind him.

Jody rounded the car and jumped into the driver's seat. "How can I drive when I can't see?" He asked, joking with his cousin.

"It ain't funny," Bruce said.

Jody pulled the car back from the dam and parked near a tree leading to a slab that crossed the river. He reached for the moonshine, but Bruce jerked it away and put it on the floor.

"I need to know how you and Anne got together," Bruce said. He rolled down his window.

"She was goin' door-to-door sellin' muffins. I asked her to go to church with me, and we started goin' out. Simple as that," Jody said, rolling down his window. A breeze caught the smell of adjacent cedar bushes.

"And that was six months ago?"

"Yeah, thereabouts. You thinkin' of askin' out your 'almost girlfriend'?"

"No, not yet," Bruce said. "And how did you ask her?"

Jody pointed north. "There's a lane where they run cattle and sometimes have to put in tractors and hay trucks. We were at the end of the road, and I just asked her."

"Easy as that?" Bruce asked.

"We had some 'shine. She didn't need it, but I did. I was nervous. We're talkin' about the rest of our lives together."

"I know, forever," Bruce said, elongating the word 'forever.'

Jody punched his cousin in the arm. "I know."

"Why do ya' think you needed the 'shine?"

"I don't know," Jody said. "I'd heard it called 'liquid courage' 'afore. When they're right, they're right. I do feel a little bit bad, though. I bought it off this man who done Millie—that's Anne's sister—wrong."

"What'd he do?"

"Millie's husband forgot to change the beneficiary on his life insurance policy, and when he got killed in Belgium, his father, the moonshiner, got the money."

"That don't seem right," Bruce said.

"It ain't right at all," Jody agreed.

"What are you gonna do about it?"

"I've been studyin' on that."

"As you buy moonshine from him?" Bruce asked.

"Yeah, smartass," Jody looked at the water rushing over the dam. "I'm gonna come up with somethin' and soon."

# Chapter 53

Snaps tried to talk as she pinned the hem of Anne's wedding dress. It was impossible and dangerous. She had a dozen straight pins between her lips.

"Just put'em in the pincushion," Anne said.

As Snaps continued placing the pins, Millie circled the girl on the wooden box.

"Gotta get this right," Snap mumbled around the pins in her mouth. It was unintelligible.

"This place here in front needs tacking," Millie said, pointing out an area that, up close, would look uneven. She had perspective and was able to coach Snaps' handiwork.

"We've got a week to finish it," Anne said. She was tired of the preparations and decorations. She had sketched the arrangements and bouquets and would gather the flowers the day before the wedding so they'd look good. She'd keep them in the giant refrigerator at the church. She'd done it for other weddings, and the system worked well.

"That still doesn't look right," Snaps said. She had put most of the pins in the overstuffed, red pincushion, making it easier to understand her.

"I know," Millie said. She took another step back, and her leg brushed against the lip of the bathtub.

"I can't figure it out," Snaps said.

"You will," Anne said, encouraging her. She knew of Snaps' recent difficulties with her pregnancy, and she wanted to be supportive.

Millie helped Snaps to her feet, and they both circled Anne. They looked from her feet to her shoulders, trying to find the seam or pleat that was drawing the front of the dress from its proper place.

"Maybe it's on backward," Snaps joked. It was her attempt to ease the tensions they'd all been feeling lately.

Anne's eyebrows shot up, and she was about to take offense when she realized the joke was about her still-developing bosom. Of course, Snaps hadn't had that problem for years.

Anne grabbed her chest and said, "Maybe you could lend me some of yours?"

They all laughed. "Girl, if I could," Snaps said, "I would."

Millie grabbed the seam on Anne's right shoulder and yanked. The front of the dress slid into place, and Snaps dropped to one knee and pinned the hem.

"Easy peasy," she said and picked up the pincushion. Again, Millie helped Snaps to her feet.

"Get that thing off, and we'll get to work on it," Millie said.

"Maybe we could get Ma to help. She's really good," Anne suggested.

"Of course, we will," Snaps said. She stretched and rubbed her lower back. Millie squeezed Snaps' shoulders.

A shard of sadness moved like a spike through Millie's chest. She feared she might have to sit down and let it pass, but she knew if she showed weakness or any kind of emotion, it would reflect poorly on both of her sisters. She swallowed and resolved to deal with these feelings later and not spoil their moments. She knew she would need to do the same at Anne's wedding and on the day Snaps gave birth.

"You look good," Millie said, but there was a strained tone in her voice that she couldn't cover.

Snaps and Anne looked at each other and decided not to dig into the feelings they knew Millie was likely having. They were sensitive to everyone as much as they could. However, they knew Millie was still grieving Stanley. Therefore, her recent declaration that she would visit his grave in Belgium could not be challenged.

"I'm just lucky," Anne said.

Millie and Snaps knew this was also true, but neither had the words to express their pain and sorrow. So instead, they would soon break it into smaller pieces and deal with it later, like a jigsaw puzzle.

Millie remembered her wedding day and that her wedding dress was put away in a cardboard box under her bed. She'd pull it out and look at it alone in the house. It still smelled of her perfume that day, and she would hold the bodice to her face. Soon after the visit from the Army chaplain, Millie couldn't even look at the dress without bursting into tears. Now, the sight and smell soothed her. It was strange how a reminder of memory and loss could transform in her hands.

"Momma says she'll start on the cake on Friday," Anne said. She'd already talked with Mary Lou about flavoring and appearance. She asked Millie for permission to use the bride and groom from her cake as a topper.

"It sounds like everything is going along," Snaps said. There was a hitch in her voice on the word 'everything.' She sometimes found herself knowing no man would have her after the baby was born. She was tainted and would never marry.

Millie picked up the pincushion and placed it near a table Mary Lou used for her sewing supplies. Unfortunately, one of the pins stuck sideways and pricked Millie's finger.

"Ouch," she reacted. She pulled her hand away and stuck her finger in her mouth.

"Are you okay?" Anne asked.

"Yes, take that thing off before I get blood on it," Millie said around the index finger stuck in her mouth.

Anne pulled the dress over her head, hung it on a hanger, and headed toward her room.

Millie whispered to Snaps, "Do you think they've done it yet?"

Snaps shook her head, "No, that hasn't happened. Wouldn't she have told us?"

"I'm not sure," Millie replied. She looked at the dress hanging near a shelf of pickled peaches. "She's gonna be a beautiful bride."

Snaps said wistfully, "Yes, she's going to be perfect."

The women knew their circumstances had ruined their status in local society. Snaps would never marry, likely never have another caller, and Millie was fast approaching the age when women resigned themselves to spinsterhood.

Millie put her hand on Snaps' shoulder and said, "She's going to be perfect."

# Chapter 54

Snaps felt the baby kick. She was lying on her back in bed, reading, and the baby let her know it was there.

The movement startled her. She shouldn't have been surprised. She knew it was just part of the baby's development and natural. She touched her belly and marveled at the new life growing inside her.

How could she find joy in this baby? How could she ever look at it and not remember?

She put her book down, rolled over, and struggled to reach her feet. She walked down the stairs and out the front door. Morning sickness had ended months ago as her body adjusted to the changes inside her. Still, tonight she felt sick to her stomach.

Sitting on the porch swing, Brother held a cigarette, the red tip glowing and illuminating his face. He was staring at the front yard, the large elm tree, and the front gate.

"Are you gonna make a run for it?" Snaps asked. Her nausea passed, and she slithered down the column that held up the porch.

"Just thinkin'."

"I know, me too," Snaps said. She looked down at her bare feet and straightened the edge of her nightgown. "Do you think anyone would care if I just ran off?" Snaps asked.

"I'd care. You're the funnest one of the three," Brother said as he drew smoke from the cigarette.

"That's true," Snaps agreed, chuckling.

"Everything's gonna work out, Snaps," Brother said. "We'll work it out."

"My life...I had plans," Snaps said, looking down at the gray planks beneath her feet. A lightning bug fluttered near her foot, and she reached down and picked it up. It flashed, illuminating her red-rimmed eyes.

"You ain't been cryin', have ya?"

"No," she lied, "I'm doin' all right." She let the lightning bug go. She watched as it circled a rose bush and then flew away.

"Good," he said. He blew a smoke ring and poked it with his finger.

"I'm never gonna fall in love. I'm never gonna have a husband. I'm never gonna have a job," Snaps blurted out. Tears burned her cheeks, but she wouldn't look at him.

"That's a whole lot of never," Brother said. He kicked the porch and started the swing. The hooks that held the chains squeaked as he moved. He needed to replace the little squares of leather he'd used before to absorb the friction.

"I know I shouldn't complain. I could be dead if that boy had his way," Snaps said, sniffing and wiping her nose with the hem of her nightgown.

"As long as you're pushin' air, anything can happen," Brother told her. He blew another smoke ring, but the trick ended with him coughing. He looked like he might not catch his breath, and Snaps turned to look at him struggling. "You okay?" she asked. He nodded and continued swinging.

"If'n you could do what you wanted, what would it be?" Brother asked.

Snaps turned and looked at the elm tree and then the front gate. She couldn't look at him because she'd never said what she was about to say to another living soul. "I think I'd like to be in the movies."

"Really, well, how would you go about doin' that?" he asked. He had been to two movies in the past. One starred John Wayne, and the other had Errol Flynn in the lead. He liked the stories, but he had a hard time getting his eyes to adjust to the light. And the sound, the music always seemed too loud. He liked the radio, where you could change the volume.

"I'm not sure. Can't do it around here, though," she said. A tone of resignation crept into her voice.

"Maybe you need to talk to someone," Brother said. He kicked the porch again, and the squeak cranked up in volume. "That's about to drive me crazy."

"What?"

"That squeak," he said. "Don't you hear that?"

"Yeah," she said, "I guess I wasn't noticin'."

"What did that teacher tell you?"

"Mrs. Northcutt, the English teacher. She doubled as the director of our school play," Snaps said. New energy marched into her voice, and she smiled.

"I remember," Brother said.

"She said I was a good singer and dancer. We did that musical, remember?"

"Yes," Brother said, "I remember."

"She had a baby, you know. Her husband died at Pearl Harbor. He was a ship's mate and a gunner. She said the men who survived said he was a hero."

"I bet he was," Brother said.

"She's raisin' their baby all by herself," Snaps said. "Maybe I could do that."

"Snaps," he stopped swinging, "you can do anything you set your mind to."

"I can, can't I?" she said. She turned and looked at him, but he was already getting up from the swing and moving toward the elm tree.

"I gotta make the water," he said, unbuttoning the fly on his overalls.

Snaps always thought that expression was strange. "*Was he really making water?*" She thought. "*Wasn't he just returning the water to the Earth where it came from in the first place?*"

"I'm goin' back in," Snaps announced to Brother, but he was out of earshot. She pushed herself up by holding on to the column. "Whew, I'll be glad to get this baby out."

And then, she thought about the pain and near-death experience women endured during childbirth. She knew every human being in history had begun this way. While that thought was somewhat comforting, she also knew this baby's background.

The baby kicked as if answering. "I hear you," she said, rubbing her now protruding belly button, "You're half Wright, and you'll be out soon enough."

# Chapter 55

They were parked at their spot. The air was cooler that night, and the moon shone brightly now that most leaves had fallen from the trees.

Anne and Jody kissed. It was a week before their wedding, and while they had talked about their wedding night and waiting, for some reason tonight, there was an additional urgency on both sides.

"Hold on," Anne said, "just a minute."

Jody focused on Anne's neck, ensuring he didn't leave any marks, but he knew it was a vulnerable spot for her. So he kissed her, and she moaned.

The cab of the pick-up truck was spotless, as usual, but there was a new smell. He'd painted something, and it hadn't thoroughly dried. She sniffed and pushed him away.

He sulked a bit and leaned against the driver's side door. "Sorry, I guess I'm just too excited."

"You can cool your jets for a few more days," she said, smiling as sweetly as possible, "I believe in you."

"I know you do." His excitement shifted, "that's why my cousin Bruce and me made a plan. He'll be in for the wedding, and we'll do it then."

"What are you talkin' about?" she asked. She straightened her skirt and crossed her legs underneath her.

"Jess Comer, we're gonna put him out of business," Jody said, smiling. He'd wanted to tell Anne about how he'd have revenge on the moonshiner for what he did to Millie.

"How? Wait a minute, who came up with this?"

"I did, well, Bruce did, he's in college studyin' to be a veterinarian, and he's had some chemistry courses. He said if we slip some lead powder into Jess's still, it'll make people sick, and they won't buy his 'shine."

"And they might die," Anne said. She was shocked at Jody's plan and reconsidered next week's wedding. She asked herself, "How can I marry someone that could think something like that?"

"We're just goin' to put some lead powder in the tubing. People will get a little sick, but they won't die," Jody said.

"I am very disappointed in you, Jody White."

Jody knew from the tone in Anne's voice he'd overstepped. He'd learned from dealing with his father that the quicker you can make a wrong a right, the sooner you can move past it.

"I'm sorry, it's just that, what he did to M-M-Millie," he stammered.

"And you came up with that idea?" Anne asked.

Jody had mentioned the situation in passing while hanging out with his cousin. "Bruce came up with the idea because he works part-time at a golf course, and they use lead sometimes to balance the heads of the clubs. But, look, we knew most people test their shine before they drink it, and then folks would have to pour it out. Nobody likes spending hard-earned money on somethin' and then havin' to throw it away."

She looked at him. Moonlight shone on the planes of his face, accentuating the sharp angles and bringing out the liquid brown of his eyes. Her heart skipped a beat, but she knew she'd have to lay down the law.

"Bruce is out of the party. I can't have someone around that thinks that way." She continued the scolding by employing the royal 'we.' "We do not even consider hurting someone else out of revenge like that. Millie's doin' fine, and while the money owed her would'a come in handy, she's got family, and that's all she needs."

"I know," Jody mumbled. He'd never seen Anne so mad, and he didn't want to see her like that ever again. "I'll do better."

Anne heard him and believed him. She didn't know she could love him even more today than she did yesterday, but she did. "I believe you," she said. She slid across the seat, took his hand, and placed it on her breast.

Jody's eyes flew open, and he looked at her. They'd played around in the past, but he knew this was serious. "What'a you think you're doing?"

She loved him because he listened to her and was willing to see her point of view. She knew then that there wasn't anything they couldn't tackle and would be together forever. She kissed him. "Do you have a blanket or something?"

"I've got one behind the seat, but… what?" he said.

Anne batted her eyes and said, "It's a beautiful night. Maybe we could go in back and look at the stars?"

He wanted her as he'd never wanted her before, but he also knew they'd be together forever. "It's clean and everythin', but I just scraped off some rust and painted over it. The bed's probably not dry yet."

She took it as a sign. "Well, probably for the best. We can wait," Anne said. She was satisfied with the decision and somehow knew that waiting until the next Saturday night was the best thing they could do.

He kissed her again and patted her on the shoulder. "I'm gonna take you home now."

She nodded, slid back across the bench seat, and looked out the window. She thought, "*It's our world now. Our world.*"

# Chapter 56

Snaps decided to wear her best Sunday dress to the wedding. It had been altered in the bosom, and Millie had used matching fabric to push the front panel out over her growing abdomen. She'd hold her bouquet in front of her stomach and not turn sideways so any wedding party pictures would indicate her current state.

She was eight months along now and becoming extraordinarily uncomfortable. All she could think of was her mother, who had told her how she struggled through her last months during the summer.

The day began with a light frost, and Mary Lou worried people sitting in the front yard would be uncomfortable. The temperature rose quickly as the sun crept over the roof eaves and warmed the area adjacent to the front porch.

"The chairs are all lined up," Brother said. He was wearing his Sunday best, but his tie was crooked. Mary Lou straightened it.

"Now you're perfect," she said, smiling at him.

"I doubt that," he joked back.

The dining room table featured an assortment of snacks circling a two-layer wedding cake. Anne had picked the flavors and the white icing, but Jody provided the tenderized beef and flour rolls combined to make the best biscuits and steaks they'd ever put in their mouths.

Preacher Kemper arrived forty-five minutes early with all the necessary paper-work. He shuffled between Anne and Jody for signatures and last-minute instructions or changes.

"You're the prettiest bride I've ever seen," Preacher said. He glanced at Snaps as she adjusted her dress. He was a good man and knew it was his job to encourage sinners to repent, but he also knew there was a time and place for that, and this was neither.

"See ya' out there," he said, clasping his Bible to his chest and walking toward the front porch.

Preacher Kemper remembered the horrible day he'd had to notify Millie of her husband's passing. He'd prayed hard that night to know the right thing to do or say that might help her deal with the sadness of her loss. He was still waiting for an answer.

Jody's father and mother sat in the front chairs. His mother wiped tears from the corners of her eyes. His father crossed his legs and tapped on the side of his boot. He was proud of all his son's accomplishments and believed he'd done an excellent job raising Jody. He thought Jody could handle just about anything life could throw his way.

Mary Lou sat next to Millie as they watched Brother stand beside Anne and offer his arm.

"I'm very proud of you," he told her.

Anne had promised herself she'd not cry during the proceedings, but she couldn't help it. "Thank you," she choked and took a deep breath. She swiped at her cheek and took his elbow.

The preacher stood on the porch as Anne met Jody near the bottom step. "Who gives this woman in marriage?" he asked.

Millie and Mary Lou sat in the front row of the chairs. "I do," Mary Lou said. She took Millie's hand and squeezed.

Snaps smiled as she glanced over at them. Millie daubed a handkerchief at the corner of her eye, and Momma took a deep breath and smiled. Snaps hadn't seen her mother smile that much lately. Most times, by looking at her slumped shoulders and stoic demeanor, Mary Lou seemed to carry the weight of the world. But not today.

Millie grabbed the borrowed camera and stood up. She moved to the side of the wedding party and quietly took pictures. The preacher repeated his usual speech about the sanctity of marriage and how what God has brought together let no man put asunder.

Snaps realized that this was likely the only marriage ceremony she'd ever be a part of, so she knew she had to enjoy each moment. She smiled at the camera and greeted Jody's parents, thanking them for contributing to the reception.

As the ceremony and celebration ended, Jody brought his truck around the corner of the house. He drove up to the porch, and Anne jumped into the bed. Anne threw the bouquet to Millie and smiled as she waved to her family. "Y'all take care!" she yelled over the sound of the truck's exhaust.

"You too!" Snaps yelled. She didn't know what Jody had planned for their trip, but she knew they'd have a good time if they were together.

Jody's mother approached Snaps at the end of the dining room table. She was a devout Baptist and believed everything the Bible said, so she felt it was up to her to bring up the fact that Snaps looked to be in a family way without a husband.

"I see, well," Snaps began her defense, but Preacher Kemper put his hand on Snaps' forearm.

He'd prepared himself for any possible criticism and judgment coming Snaps' way. So he had done the math when he visited Anne and Jody for their pre-ceremony interview, and Snaps passed through the living room. He believed he could protect her from shame and humiliation better than anyone else in the area.

"Young women can experience changes in metabolism as they mature, Mrs. White," he said. He allowed the authority that accompanied his standing in the community to color his voice. He turned to Snaps. "Maybe too much bread, butter, and cheese."

For some reason, Snaps hadn't prepared a come-back for a challenge to her condition and welcomed the preacher's rescue. "Yes," she said, "I plan on starting a new diet tomorrow. There was just too much goin' on for me to focus on myself."

"That's goin' to change now, isn't it, Snaps?" Preacher Kemper asked with a knowing twinkle in his eye. He liked the idea that he could provide more than just spiritual guidance and judgment.

"Why yes," Snaps agreed. She cast her gaze to the floor and then back up at Mrs. Jones. "You can be sure you'll see a whole new me in the next few weeks."

The preacher stifled a chuckle and turned his shoulders back toward the dining room table. "These steaks and biscuits are marvelous," he said. He picked up the next to the last one and took a bite. "Heaven on earth."

Mr. White said, "The breed's what makes it so tender, white-faced Herefords."

Still chewing, he glanced at Snaps and said, "Yes, so much of life is determined by nature."

# Chapter 57

Snaps parked the truck on the square's north side and rolled down the window. Her belly was too big now to go out in public. Still, she could enjoy watching people strolling around the two-story government building that housed all the county offices and courtrooms. It was designed in the Classical Revival style in 1859 after the original building burned to the ground. At the time of construction, the installation cost fifty-thousand dollars and served as headquarters for both sides during the Civil War. Nathan Bedford Forrest occupied the building first in 1862 through the following year. Union forces took over and stayed until the end of the war, and there were several minie ball holes left in the red brick walls. A tornado in 1913 almost took down the clock tower. Ten years later, a man calling himself the Human Fly said he would climb to the top of the tower for a small fee. A collection was taken by the people standing around the square, and the amount was sufficient for the Human Fly to attempt his ascent. He successfully made his way to the peak but slipped and fell to his death on the way down. The sheriff witnessed the accident and helped put the man in the back of his car. He delivered the Human Fly to the doctor's office, where he was pronounced dead. The daredevil carried no identification, and it took a week for the name of the man to be discovered. In the newspaper, the sheriff was quoted as saying, "I guess he didn't plan on falling."

Snaps had heard all the stories and even read three books on the town's history. At the time, she believed knowing her origins would help her acting. Maybe learning more about where she was from would help her decide what to do with the rest of her life.

The music from the car radio caught her attention first. It was the Grand Ole Opry, and tonight the featured artists were Roy Acuff and Hank Williams.

Snaps patted the window frame in time with the music. She took a deep breath and considered singing along but realized she didn't want to draw attention to herself. How would she explain that she couldn't get out?

She saw the passenger side door of the black Chevrolet open, and a boy hopped out. He was blond, and he had a dollar bill in his hand. With the door open, Snaps could see the driver was Mrs. Northcutt.

Snaps grabbed the key still in the ignition and cranked the truck motor. She drove around the square and parked next to the Chevy. Mrs. Northcutt saw who was in the truck and rolled down her window.

"I haven't seen you in a coon's age," Snaps said.

"That's not a very nice word," Mrs. Northcutt said. "My husband wrote to me about the Negro men he served with and how some of them found that word 'Coon' was hurtful."

Snaps had heard the expression dozens of times, and it never occurred to her that it might be offensive. She always thought it was about the life span of a raccoon and not about anything else.

"Oh, it never, well," Snaps stammered, "I'll not use it again."

"They fought as hard as the white men," Mrs. Northcutt said. She looked away from Snaps' gaze and turned up the radio.

"Hank Williams," Snaps said, trying to reengage her former teacher.

"He's a true poet," Mrs. Northcutt said. "*I'm So Lonesome I Could Cry* is just as moving and evocative as Shakespeare."

"That's true," Snaps agreed.

Mrs. Northcutt's son came out of the Woolworths with a cone of vanilla ice cream. He hadn't taken a lick yet and presented the treat to his mother as if it were an Olympic medal. "That's okay," she began, "that looks so good. But why don't you give that one to Snaps here and get us another."

The boy's face shifted through so many emotions. First, pride followed by joy, then sorrow followed by pleasure as he realized he'd get to go back into the store with the soda fountain.

"No, that's okay," Snaps said. She had rested her hand on her belly, and the thought of eating ice cream at this hour would only add to her weight gain.

"No, Miss Snaps, I insist. Besides," Mrs. Northcutt said, "I think Bobby here might even get some candy on the way out."

The boy's face lit up again, and he passed the cone to Snaps. He glanced through the passenger window, and his mouth dropped open. He looked back at Snaps' face, but it was too late. She took the cone from Bobby and nodded to him in thanks.

The boy rushed back through the double doors and could be seen hovering around the candy counter before he picked up a chocolate bar. Then, he sauntered to the soda fountain like a rooster surveying the hen house.

"He's a good boy," Snaps said between licks of the ice cream.

"I'm doin' the best I can. I've gotta admit, there are times when I could use a man around the house, but we'll get there." Mrs. Northcutt watched as Bobby placed the candy bar on the counter and raised two fingers to the soda jerk.

On the radio, Hank accepted the uproarious applause of the Opry fans and began another hit song, *Lovesick Blues*.

Mrs. Northcutt said, "A singing poet."

"From Alabama," Snaps said, overlaying a tone of incredulity because of the state's backwardness.

"It doesn't matter where you're from. If you believe in yourself and your talent, you must try." Mrs. Northcutt considered telling Snaps the story of the Human Fly again, but she realized she'd used that one in drama class. She thought, "*Would Snaps remember that?*" Local history was so easily forgotten.

"I hope you're still working on your singing and acting," Mrs. Northcutt said. Snaps was the most talented student she'd ever worked with, and she knew her gift had to be refined and honed for her to be successful.

"Sometimes," Snaps said. Her teenage girl's voice and attitude crept in at the most inopportune times.

"I'm telling you," Mrs. Northcutt began, realizing her emotions were over the top and might even turn off Snaps. She pulled a slip of paper from her purse and a pen from the ashtray.

"Here, hang on to this," she said as she handed the paper to Snaps.

"What is it?" Snaps asked.

The light from Woolworths was too dim for Snaps to read what was written on the note. Instead, she tucked it into her shirt pocket.

Bobby bounded from the front door with both hands full of ice cream cones and a chocolate bar in his shirt pocket.

He handed his mother her cone and zipped around the car. He slipped into the passenger seat and said, "Let's go home."

Mrs. Northcutt picked up on the opportunity and nodded at Snaps. "Good to see you, dear." She cranked the engine and put the car in reverse.

Snaps watched Bobby talking with his mother, but the engine's sound drowned out what he was saying. Her head nodded as she listened, the engine idling as Bobby spoke.

Mrs. Northcutt turned and looked at Snaps sitting there. Her eyes widened, and she painted a pained smile on her face as she pulled her car into the street.

Snaps scooted across the bench seat and put her hand on the steering wheel. "If she can do it, maybe I can, too," she whispered.

She turned up the radio as Hank finished his song. Again, the applause made the radio speaker crackle. She could imagine Hank on the stage, bowing to the fans and knowing he'd made the right choice to leave Alabama.

# Chapter 58

While Millie's wedding night was passionate and caring, Anne's was not. Poor boy, even growing up on a farm and experiencing first-hand the joy of sex; after a few minutes, Anne was convinced Jody didn't know anything.

They were in the Starlight Motel on the Tennessee/Kentucky border. Jody chose this location near the lake and thought he'd like to show Anne his prowess as a fisherman.

His expertise as a lover was lacking, and Anne let him know her disappointment.

"I don't think that's the way that's supposed to go," she said.

They lay naked side-by-side with just a sliver of light from the bathroom illuminating the small room. The furniture and décor played up the area's sportfishing. Anne knew Jody had gotten a deal since it was off-season.

"Maybe you're too cold," Jody said. He pulled back the covers on his side and pointed his foot toward the floor.

"Get back in here," she said, grabbing his arm and pulling him back. "I'm fine. Maybe you're the cold one?"

"I feel fine," Jody said. There was an edge to his voice. It reminded Anne of the moment he'd told her about his plan for revenge against Jess Comer.

She turned to him and said, "Show me how you love me."

Anne knew bulls were sometimes teased by cows in heat before farmers would bring in the thoroughbreds. She knew Jody needed to be distracted from his performance and relax. He was overthinking, and she believed she could achieve her goal if she changed her approach.

She put her hand on his face. "Show me how you love me," she repeated. Her tone, this time, was tender and encouraging. She kissed him, and he responded with the same passion and eagerness he'd shown the night he'd asked her to get married.

"Show me how you love me," he said. He rubbed her shoulder and let his hand drift down her back. He drew her close and took a deep breath.

"Do you think we should have had music?" she asked. "We could'a got Snaps to sing something."

"What, the service?" he exclaimed. "Oh, well, I guess, but I think everything went okay."

She reached down and touched him. He tensed and tried to pull away from her fingers. "Hey, too cold," he said.

"They'll get warmer," she cooed and kissed him again. She was right, of course, and she could feel him responding. "There we go," she whispered.

She moved her hand as she kissed him, first the back of her hand and then the front. Her fingers lingered over him, and even in the dim light, she could see him smiling.

"Yeehaw!" he shouted.

She put her finger to his lips and said, "Not so loud." She looked at the ceiling and whispered, "Neighbors."

"Right," he said as he rolled over and knelt between her legs. "I'm not too heavy, am I?"

Anne shook her head no and guided him toward her. Her breath quickened, and she winced as he entered her.

"Yeehaw," he said but didn't yell this time.

"You are so funny," she said as she felt him move inside her. "I love you."

He felt himself inside her now and focused on the moment's pleasure. "I love you, too," he said, but the expression felt rote and disconnected. He wasn't thinking about love right now.

Jody finished, and Anne patted him on the back as if to say, "Good boy." She wasn't condescending or demeaning, but she knew she couldn't use this technique too many times in the future—he'd eventually see through her tactics.

The following day they made love again, laughing and smiling, which lasted much longer than the night before. Anne didn't feel the same discomfort and enjoyed the closeness and seeing Jody's face as he finished.

"You can't call me a 'girl' anymore," Anne said.

"Nope," Jody said, "you will forever be a woman after today."

Anne considered what had happened to her sisters, and while they were 'women' in many ways, they both had been cheated of the full range of the experience. Millie had loved Stanley without children, and Snaps was about to have a child without love.

"Life isn't fair," Anne said as she pulled back the covers and swung her legs over the side of the bed.

"And it's short," Jody said. He was lying back and looking at the ceiling. His arms were crossed behind his head, and his tumescence had yet to subside. "Hey," he said, reaching for her hand and letting her know he would enjoy another session.

"Don't ya' think we should go get your tackle?" she asked. "The fish ain't gonna jump out of that lake all by themselves."

Jody grabbed her and pulled her back onto his chest. "I just lost all interest in fishing."

# Chapter 59

Snaps waddled across the field to the rock outcropping she had used as a prosce-nium since she was a child. Most of her plays and concerts included dancing, but now she couldn't even see her feet.

She took her stance, knees flexible but firm, her shoulders back, and her eyes wide. She scanned her audience. She liked to pick a single member and focus on them. Then, if they seemed uninterested or weren't reacting as planned, she'd work harder to draw them in. She rarely failed.

She hummed to herself, searching for the note to begin her song. The baby kicked, letting her know he disapproved of her choice. The baby wasn't interested in hearing her sing, and wanted to nap. Snaps wasn't having it.

"You stop that right now," she muttered to the fetus. She could see his feet and head movements as they shifted the cloth at the front of her clean white shirt. Her jeans were stretched, and the top button had long passed its usefulness. "Stop it," she said.

"Who are you talkin' to?" Millie asked. She wore a similar outfit, 'farmworker chic,' but had secured all her buttons and snaps.

"Nobody," Snaps said. Her cheeks colored a bit. "Just hangin' out."

"I see," Millie said. She sat on the edge of the rock outcropping and looked at her sister. She could see the weight she'd gained in her face and legs. And, of course, her distended belly was impossible to look around at that angle.

"I was just gonna," Snaps began and then lost her energy to lie, "I don't know."

"I heard you tuning up there."

"I was tryin' to find the note," Snaps said.

"You were gonna sing. Is the baby tryin' to keep you from it?"

"Maybe," Snaps continued. She looked down at her audience of one. "I think he wants to take a nap."

"Make him stay awake a little while longer," Millie said. She leaned back and looked up at the songstress.

The sun slowly dropped behind the treetops, and a single beam struck Snaps' face. It was as if the world wanted to hear her and had provided a spotlight.

"This land is your land," Snaps began singing. She'd found the key where she could sing comfortably and hit the high notes.

She continued, but something was wrong. The ease with which she could add vibrato to her voice had left her. She hadn't sung in months, and now with her breathing restricted, it was gone.

"I can't," Snaps said. The light showed the hollows of her eyes and the shadow of her furrowed brow.

She tried singing again; her voice cracked on 'New York,' and she stopped.

Losing her voice, losing the one ability she thought she could always count on, overwhelmed her. She looked up at the sky as if asking why she was the victim of this cruel loss.

Millie picked up from where Snaps had stopped. She felt the vocal limitations of her own talent, but she knew how important singing was to Snaps. She egged her sister on, knowing how essential her ability was to her. She struggled to stay on pitch.

"Don't, Millie," Snaps implored. "It's okay."

But Millie wouldn't stop. Woodie Guthrie was her favorite, and she'd heard this song many times on the radio. In many ways, it was her song.

Millie sang, putting as much of her heart and soul into the song as she possibly could, and finally, Snaps took a deep breath and joined her.

Snaps sang, and her raspy voice cleared. She helped Millie to her feet.

They stood arm-in-arm and sang. Millie took the second part, not a natural harmony but more like a call-and-response she'd heard some singers use when visiting the church.

Snaps sang "the golden valley," as Millie repeated "the golden valley" just a second after her sister.

They both sang, again, not in true harmony, but as two voices who shared parents and inherited a timbre from their mother and father.

They sang, ending the last line together this time, laughing as they finished.

"You keep going," Millie said and moved to the side of the stage. She watched Snaps' voice grow stronger and regain some of the power and emotion she'd developed over many hours of practice.

Snaps kept going, feeling the strength and confidence continue to grow in her soul. She would sing, and she would keep singing, no matter what.

She glanced over at her sister as Millie stood, arms crossed, beaming with pride and joy at the part of Snaps that at one time seemed lost but now was found.

As she finished the song, Snaps raised her arms to her sister, and they embraced. Millie felt the baby kick and smiled, knowing that maybe he was just as pleased as she was that his mother had found her voice again.

# Chapter 60

Snaps wasn't sure what was happening. She felt a sharp pain in her abdomen, and water ran down her leg. She looked at the puddle forming there on the porch. "*It's too early*," she thought. She looked at her mother standing there and asked, "Isn't it too early?"

Mary Lou took a deep breath and said, "It happens when it happens. Let's get you cleaned up and in bed."

Snaps nodded and put her arm around her mother's shoulder. She noted how thin her mother was and how protruding the bone in her shoulder felt.

"I'll send Brother for the doctor," Mary Lou said. She knew from experience labor could take minutes or hours. She'd had help with two of the three girls, but Snaps popped out so quickly that the doctor only arrived in time to snip the umbilical cord and missed the main event. Mary Lou hoped that wouldn't be the case today.

They decided going up the back steps would be too much for Snaps, so they went to Mary Lou's room. Millie and Brother had heard the commotion and were given their assignments. Brother was dispatched, and Millie fetched clean sheets, towels, a string, and scissors. "And boil some water," Mary Lou said as she guided Snaps to the edge of the bed. "We'll need to sterilize the scissors and a wet towel to clean up her legs."

"They're all sticky," Snaps said. Her voice sounded small and distant, and Mary Lou remembered when the girl was little, and she'd fallen while chasing a cow, skinning her knee.

"I know, child."

"Is it supposed to hurt like this?" Snaps said through gritted teeth just before another wave of contractions hit.

"*Too soon,*" Mary Lou thought. She couldn't say anything now that might upset Snaps. "It's fine," she said, comforting her child by patting her cheek. She looked her in the eye and said, "Everything's gonna be all right."

"Okay," Snaps said, but she sounded unconvinced. She'd felt pain before, falling and breaking her left wrist, cutting herself while chopping vegetables and such. But this pain was deep and made her body shiver.

Millie brought in the towels and sheets. She spread the cloth behind Snaps and propped up pillows that would help support her. Snaps shook her head and grasped one of the wooden posts at the foot of the bed.

"Put the sheet and the towels on the floor," Snaps said as her fingers turned white, gripping the post.

"Aren't we gonna wait for the doctor?" Millie asked, realizing just how dumb the statement sounded as it left her lips.

"We're gonna do the best we can," Mary Lou said.

Snaps looked up from her crouching position. Agony and fear registered in her eyes. "Am I gonna die?" she asked.

"No, no," Mary Lou said, "you're gonna be fine."

Snaps stood, still gripping the bedpost, and bellowed like a bull.

"Let it out," Mary Lou said. She remembered how she'd reacted to the labor with Millie. Frank wasn't all that helpful, but surprisingly, Brother was. Fortunately, he seemed to see the act more like a building project. "Go. Stop Brother before he leaves. You go get the doctor, Millie."

Millie stood, stunned, taking the new assignment as an affront. She froze.

"Go get him," Mary Lou said with even more emphasis.

Millie turned and rushed out of the room, down the hall, and through the front door. Brother had just put the key in the truck's ignition.

"Momma wants you," she said, breathless from her run.

"Me?" he asked, then remembering his witnessing Millie's birth, "Oh, all right."

He slid out of the truck cab and raced to the house, not looking back. Millie watched him run, and as he entered the front door, she turned and jumped into the truck.

Brother entered Mary Lou's room and saw a small pool of blood on a sheet that was spread near the bed. He saw Snaps' head shiver in pain. She raised her head, her eyes bulging and red-rimmed, and glared at him.

She blurted out, "Why didn't you kill him sooner?"

Was it a valid question? Would any of this have happened if he'd acted more quickly? Brother had asked himself those same questions for months and had failed to come up with a suitable answer.

"I don't know," Brother muttered.

"It don't matter right now!" Mary Lou shouted. In truth, she thought, "*It ain't never gonna matter,*" but she refrained from saying it.

"It just happened," Brother said.

Snaps growled in pain. Even though the temperature in the room was cold, a sheen of sweat popped out on her forehead. Another wave of contractions came, and Mary Lou reached under Snaps dress. "We got to get these off."

She yanked down Snaps' bloody panties and tossed them on the rocking chair. "Go check on the water."

Brother nodded and left, relieved he could escape Snaps' piercing glare.

"Okay, honey, this is happenin' pretty fast," Mary Lou said. She had her wrist on Snaps' forearm and could feel her pounding pulse. "You gotta breathe, honey. Focus on me," she said. She puffed out her cheeks and smiled at Snaps.

The girl closed her eyes, dipped her head, and gritted her teeth. She looked up at her mother and squatted.

"She's gonna have it right here," Brother said. It was a goofy and obvious thing to say, and he knew it. He didn't know what the reaction might be, though.

Mary Lou giggled first, followed by a smile from Snaps and then a loud "Ha!"

The women looked at each other, and it was as if they could read each other's minds. "Yes, men are useless."

He put the pan of hot water on the floor next to the rocking chair and took Snaps' hand. She gripped his fingers, and he thought she might break them. It was another stupid thing to do or say in a series of dumb things.

Mary Lou lifted Snaps' skirt and said, "I can see the head." She unbuttoned the skirt and pulled it from Snaps' bulging belly.

"Too fast," Brother said. "The doctor ain't here."

Mary Lou sighed. "He'll be here. Okay, sweetheart, you're gonna need to push now."

Mary Lou touched the wet and bloody head, and a face slid toward her fingers. "Lordy mercy," she said.

She touched the nose, and his left shoulder slipped out, quickly followed by his right.

"Here comes another one," Snaps gasped.

The contraction caused Snaps to sway, but her grip on the bedpost continued. Mary Lou cradled the child's head as the rest of his body slid into her hands.

"He's here," Mary Lou said.

"Holy Moley," Brother said. "Well, at least I ain't so outnumbered now."

Again, a stupid thing to say, but Brother's subconscious seemed in overdrive. The good news was it made both Snaps and Mary Lou laugh.

Snaps slid down the bedpost and rested with her knees up in the air. She looked at the baby and smiled. For a moment, the pain left her body. The placenta slid out of her uterus, and she took her first deep breath in over thirty minutes.

"Here," Mary Lou said as she wrapped him in the towel and wiped his face and body. "You need to hold him."

Snaps didn't fight her mother on this command. Her motherly instincts overcame her, and she reached for him. She looked at him and his piercing blue eyes and cried. "I can't," she muttered.

"Well, you can and you will, young lady," Mary Lou said. This was her first grandchild, and she knew how important the bond had to be between mother and child.

"I can't, don't you get it!" Snaps screeched. "I can't!"

# Chapter 61

Snaps' brief break with her responsibility to care for the baby faded quickly. She took the infant to her chest and began feeding him. She tried to look away but knew he depended on her and couldn't let him down.

"Okay, baby," Snaps said, touching his forehead. He had a sprig of blond hair and a blunt nose. The only thing now that reminded her of his father was the blue eyes.

She watched him innocently suckling. His eyes were closed, and he grinned with joy. He farted softly, and Mary Lou knew what that meant.

"We better get a diaper on that child," she said, knowing the foul nature of the first bowel movement.

"I'll go get one," Brother said. He left the room and rushed through the hallway to the linen closet. He rifled through the towels and found the stack of diapers in the back corner of the bottom shelf. Since the baby was early, there hadn't seemed to be any need to prepare for his arrival.

"And don't forget the pins!" Mary Lou shouted. The noise frightened the baby, and he separated from Snaps' nipple and let out a high-pitched cry.

Even though they were at different ends of the house, Brother heard the boy's complaint and said, "Oh crap."

Mary Lou had tied the string around the umbilical cord and deftly snipped the tissue. She'd seen the doctor perform the same procedure with her children and even had Frank help with one of them when the doctor was late.

Brother pushed a stray sprig of hair from his forehead, almost dropping the diapers and pins as he raced through the house.

"All right, all right," Brother said. He dropped the diapers on the rocking chair's seat and put the pins nearby on top of a chest of drawers.

His discomfort with Snaps' nakedness and even more possible embarrassment spooked him. "I gotta get out of here," he whined.

"We're gonna need a washcloth to clean him up," Mary Lou said. She unconsciously mimicked Brother's nervous response by pushing a sprig of hair from her forehead.

"All right," he complained, "I wish you'd said somethin' about that when I was in the linen closet."

"It's my job to make you crazy," Mary Lou said. She let a slight smile tickle the edges of her lips. After all the stress of Snaps giving birth, she couldn't help but tease the old fellow a bit.

She took the baby from Snaps and unswaddled him. The baby had a quizzical look, and Mary Lou surmised it was about to happen.

"Hold on there," she said as she unfolded the diaper and laid him down. She gathered the cloth into folds like the professional she was. She was just in time for the baby to produce the most foul-smelling, tar-like, dark green substance. She had seen and smelled it before, so she knew what was coming. Snaps did not.

"Oh crap," Snaps said. She was a country girl living on a farm in rural Tennessee, and she had never smelled anything as horrible or caustic. "Oh, my, gosh, that's horrible!"

"It's natural," Mary Lou said as she dipped the washcloth in the now-tepid water. She cleaned up the baby's bottom and picked up another cloth to wash the rest of his body.

"He's a beauty," Mary Lou said. She swaddled him again and put him on her shoulder. When she looked back at Snaps, she was lying on her side and sound asleep.

"Do you wanna hold him?" she whispered to Brother.

"Do you think it'll be all right?" he asked in return, but she was already placing the baby in Brother's large, callused hands.

"He's tiny," Brother whispered, looking at the baby's unfocused eyes.

"I bet Snaps thinks he was pretty big," Mary Lou said. She pointed toward the door and led Brother out to the front porch.

The old man sat in the swing and kicked the floor with his big, black boot. The baby quickly fell asleep and started making sucking noises.

"He's already dreamin' about dinner," Mary Lou said. She sat beside Brother and pulled back a corner of the blanket to better look at him.

"So, I guess the obvious question is," Brother asked, "don't you think she should give him away?"

Mary Lou had considered this many times since it was discovered that Snaps' rape had conceived a child. There were dozens of young couples in the area she knew would welcome a baby into their homes because they couldn't have one of their own. She even talked to the minister at church about what he thought might be best for the baby. She hadn't spoken with Snaps about it, though. She knew the pain was just below the surface for her, and she feared the girl might do something rash if confronted.

"God gave him to us, and I believe God wants him to stay here." She was emphatic, and she let a tone of determination leak into her voice. "I'll take him myself if she don't want him."

"Aren't we gettin' too old for that?" Brother asked. The baby nestled against his chest and listened to Brother's heart as the swing swayed back-and-forth and back-and-forth.

"Snaps will help. She'll get over that...." Mary Lou paused and looked out into the front yard. From the corner of her eye, she could see the plume of dust the truck kicked up as it approached the meadow near the road. "Looks like the doctor's here."

A part of Brother wanted to stay on the porch, kicking the floor and setting the swing in motion every so often. He knew the baby and Snaps needed to be checked out by the doctor, but a part of him was at peace. It was a feeling that had eluded him for years now, the years since the war.

The doctor, dressed in a black suit, white shirt, and string tie, jumped from the still-rolling truck and sprinted to the porch. He had just graduated from medical school since his stint in the Army and found the small community just what he wanted for his new wife and new baby girl. He stopped when he saw Brother holding the baby and Mary Lou's grinning face.

"I guess I'm better late than never," the doctor said.

"She only took about ten minutes," Mary Lou whispered. She feared a loud noise like before might disturb the sleeping infant.

"Let's take a look at him," the doctor put his bag on the floor. "Boy?"

"Yes, a boy," Brother said.

The doctor took out his stethoscope and put the ear tips into his ears. He unwrapped the top of the swaddling clothes, and after warming up the bell in the palm of his hand, he applied it to the baby's chest.

"No name yet?" the doctor asked, but he wasn't listening. Instead, the gently ta-thump, ta-thump, ta-thump of a clear and healthy heart echoed in his eardrums.

A name hadn't occurred to either Mary Lou, Millie, who was now standing at the bottom step leading to the porch, or Brother. "Can we just call him Baby Wright for now?" Mary Lou asked.

"Of course," The doctor said, grinning, "we can fill in the paperwork later." He hung the stethoscope around his neck and turned toward the front door.

"We'll do a full exam later. She's in here?" he asked, walking into the house.

"Keep a-goin'." Mary Lou said. She looked at Millie and asked, "Do you wanna hold him?"

Millie hesitated for a moment. She had toyed with being an aunt and all that entailed, but she wasn't fully prepared since he'd turned up earlier than planned.

"Yes, of course," she replied, moving toward the swing.

Brother, the childcare expert now, said, "Support his little head." And turned the baby over to Millie.

She nodded to Brother, sat on the swing, and kicked the apparatus into motion.

"Here we are," she said without looking down at the baby's face.

# Chapter 62

Anne returned from her honeymoon, rested, and ready to claim her duties as an aunt to Baby Wright. She "oohed" and "cooed" and held him, helped bathe and clothe him. She walked him around the house when he had gas and felt she could record a significant accomplishment when the baby burped.

"He's a little smaller than I was expectin'," Anne said as she looked down at him sleeping. And then it dawned on her how she knew the exact moment of his conception and worried that even mentioning something as innocent as what she expressed could cause harm.

Snaps sat across from Anne's rocking chair and watched as she paced, swaying from left to right and smiling at the baby. The coal-fired stove drove the brisk fall temperatures from the living room. A kettle, whistle open, sat on the stovetop, and increased humidity, adding more comfort to the atmosphere.

Snaps pulled the edges of her shawl tighter around her shoulders. She turned her gaze to the northside window and marveled at the frost melting before her eyes.

"We'll fatten him up," Snaps said. There was a distant, hollow tone in her voice, and when she looked back at Anne, she winced as if feeling a splinter enter her finger.

The baby awoke with a start and started crying. It wasn't a hungry cry or a sleepy cry. It wasn't even a soiled diaper cry. While the baby felt comfortable in Anne's arms, he wanted his mother. Anne intuited this and approached Snaps as she sat there rocking.

Anne offered the baby to Snaps, saying, "Here he is."

Snaps looked up at her. Anne could see her eyes squint in pain for just a second, and then Snaps painted on a smile.

"Come here, little one," Snaps said. She modulated her tone in hopes of quieting the baby. She kicked the floor and began rocking, thinking he might respond. Instead, he cried even louder.

"Hey now," Snaps said. She pulled back the swaddling clothes and took a sniff. "He's not dirty or wet," she said. She looked up at Anne, seemingly at a loss.

"I don't know," Anne said as she sat in a straight-backed chair next to Snaps.

Jody entered the room and looked at the two women and the crying baby. "Whatsamatter with him?"

"Sometimes they just have to cry," Snaps said. She was guessing and felt it was up to her to decode what might have been going on in the mind of an infant.

"He's sure got some good lungs. I could hear him outside even with the windows closed," Jody said. He stuck his thumb in a belt loop on his jeans and adjusted his cowboy hat. While he was still a boy in many aspects, Jody felt a new confidence and swagger. He tried asking Anne to do more things he and his father had been doing around the house, like cooking and cleaning. She let the 'orders' pass but noted that she'd have to set him down a peg if they continued. But, of course, things would be different when they moved into their own home, even if it was just a few hundred yards from Jody's parents' house.

"He's a complainer," Anne said.

She watched Snaps lose focus and let the baby slip from her grasp. It wasn't much, just a few inches, but it worried Anne. She reflexively moved to shore up Snaps' support for the baby but pulled back. She wanted Snaps to feel the weight of the baby in her arms. Snaps needed to support him on her own without Anne's prompting.

"Maybe if you walked him around," Jody said. He tugged at his white, long-sleeved shirt and grinned at his suggestion.

"I was doin' that a'fore you came in," Anne said. The baby slipped again, and Snaps seemed fascinated by something in the yard. The frost on the tree limbs glistened in the slanting, rising sunlight. The sparkles mesmerized her as if she had left her body.

There was that feeling of a splinter entering Snaps' finger. She winced again at the thought. She attempted to put it out of her mind, but no matter how hard she tried, there it was. Now, the feeling moved down to her arm, and the weight of the baby was replaced with her elbow digging into the floor of the feed room. Ollie was on top of her again, pushing himself into her. Finally, she stopped rocking, and the baby slid from her side.

Anne caught him before he left the confines of the rocking chair, but it was evident in her mind that Snaps had had some sort of spell. The baby cried louder, and Jody took a step back.

"Somethin's the matter with him," Jody said. It was an innocent statement, especially from someone with little experience with babies.

"No," Anne said as she looked down at the baby. "He's perfect." She stood, rushed past Jody, and into the hallway with the linen closet. She opened the door and pulled out a clean diaper. *"Maybe he just doesn't like the feel of the diaper he has on,"* she thought.

Anne laid him on top of a chest of drawers they'd used as a changing table and unwrapped him. He was dry. The stub of his umbilical cord was still attached, but it looked like it might fall off soon. "What's goin' on?" she asked the infant as he stared up at her, red-faced and crying. "You just ate, so you can't be hungry."

As a draft of chilly air moved through the room, the baby peed, and an arc of clear liquid almost struck Anne in the face. But instead, she quickly covered him and absorbed the stream. "That's pretty good, you little booger," she said, smiling. "You almost got me that time."

The baby stopped crying and smiled at Anne. It amazed her how easily the child's emotions could turn on and off like a spigot.

"Whatever you did, you done it right," Jody said. He was standing in the doorframe. The babyface Anne had loved for many months was now aging. His fat cheeks were smoothing, and he was shaving every day now.

"Babies are a mystery," Anne said. She wrapped him in a new blanket and placed him on her shoulder.

"I guess this is good practice, now that we're gonna have one," Jody said.

This was news to Anne. While they had had sex almost a dozen times since their wedding night, she wondered, does he really believe that women can get pregnant whenever they want to?

"I'm not pregnant," Anne said. She stood in the middle of the bedroom where Snaps had given birth and patted the now-sleeping baby.

"Well, I know, but it don't take more 'an once for cows."

Anne knew he wasn't ignorant, but his frame of reference working on the farm had skewed his perception. Nevertheless, she said, "We'll have a baby. There's no tellin' when, but it'll likely happen someday."

"But not now?" Jody asked.

"I'm on my period, so not this month," Anne said.

Jody knew when cows and horses were in heat. You could tell how they acted, especially around other fertile animals.

"Aw, right," Jody said. He moved to the side of the doorframe as Anne moved through. "*There are times I wished I didn't love her so much,*" he thought.

# Chapter 63

Mary Lou shook the feed into a bucket. It was a mixture of grains and molasses that she augmented with hay harvested earlier in the year. The cows nibbled at the dying grass and sometimes even leaves from bushes. But, they mainly depended on the feed at this time of the year.

It took her three trips to the feed room to fill the troughs. She winced as she moved the bucket from her left hand to her right. Then, an old injury caught her. A borrowed bull had butted her so hard that she rolled three times before stopping in the middle of the barn's hallway.

The cows now knew their place in line and rarely tried to move ahead of the leader Mary Lou had named 'Lisa' from the radio soap opera.

"Hey up there, Lisa," she said to the cow as she opened the rear barn door. The cows, with bags swollen and teats distended, sauntered to their designated slot and poked their heads through the slats. They ate leisurely and had become accustomed to the sound of the gate closing, trapping them in that stance until the milking machine was finished with them.

Mary Lou attached the teat cup shells and put away the feed bucket. She could spend the rest of the time inspecting the cows for injuries or disease and preparing for the afternoon milking. Farming was a 365-day-a-year job, rain or shine, snow or hail. It didn't matter to the animals and was the only way to stay in business.

"God's sure been good to us," she said, marveling at the line of twitching, shaking, and shitting animals as they ate.

"He sure has," Brother said. He walked with his fingers hooked into the loops of his overalls and around the steaming piles. He had an unlit cigarette in the corner of his mouth—he was trying to stop smoking, and this 'pacifier' helped him keep his hands busy.

"Where are the girls?"

"Millie's right behind me," Brother said. "She wanted to see how the milking machine was workin'."

"It's workin' just fine."

"I think she wants to take over the afternoon chores," Brother said. He reached inside the pouch on the front of his overalls and fished around for a match. Then, he remembered how he wasn't supposed to smoke and snapped the pouch shut.

"She knows what to do," Mary Lou said. She surmised there might be a hidden motive for the visit.

"She may have somethin' else in mind, too," he said. He tried to wipe the grin off his face and navigated to the back door. He pulled it shut and walked to the front door where Millie was arriving.

"The mornin' dishes are all washed," she announced. It was a duty that the girls had shared growing up, but now with Anne living with Jody and Snaps primarily lost in her own world, that task and many others had fallen to Millie.

"Hey, Momma," she said with as much enthusiasm as she could muster.

"Hey, daughter."

"I'm here to help. But I need to learn more about this stuff," Millie said.

"Yes, you do. What brought this on?"

"Oh, well, things gotta get done around here," she said. She stepped around a puddle of urine and picked up the feed bucket.

"Pretty simple, really," Mary Lou said. "Put out the feed, let the cows in, hook'em up, and turn on the machine."

"Got it. Did Brother mention anything else?"

"No," Mary Lou said. She turned and looked at her eldest. This poor child had been through so much and had been so sad for so long. Now, she seemed giddy about something, and Mary Lou was curious.

"We got a letter, and it's good news."

"What's it about?"

"A survey crew was working their way through the area and down by the creek. They found zinc," Millie said.

"Miners?"

Brother stood next to Millie. "It really is good news. If we sell them the rights, they'll dig just north of the creek and back into the woods before the eighty."

The eighty was the acreage where they harvested hay and let the cows roam when they could eat grass. "I see," Mary Lou said.

"The letter says they can fence off the area, and it won't disturb the cows or hurt the water supply," Millie said. "All we need is signatures."

"How much money are we talkin' about?" Mary Lou asked.

"It's enough that we can get a bathroom and a hot water heater," Millie said. She remembered luxuriating in the tub at the motel where she and Stanley celebrated their honeymoon. She liked the bubble bath salts, and she even liked dunking her head. It was heaven.

"What about the field? What's it gonna look like when they finish?" Mary Lou asked. A cow swung her tail at Mary Lou's shoulder. She wasn't fast enough to dodge it, and the appendage whacked her.

"Momma, are you all right?" Millie asked.

"That looked bad," Brother said.

"It's fine," Mary Lou said as she rubbed her shoulder. Was this God telling her not to investigate this deal?

"The man's coming by, a geologist, tomorrow to fill us in and answer any questions we might have," Millie said. "This is so exciting."

"Of course," Brother started, "we'll need to convert the storage room and put up a wall. Then, we'll have to dig a place for the septic tank. It's a big project."

"It sounds like it is," Mary Lou said. She patted the offending cow on the hindquarter and heard the machine's vacuum draw air instead of milk. Finally, it was time to turn the cows back into the field.

"You're not dead set against it?" Millie asked. She couldn't keep herself from smiling.

"No, of course not. If it's God's will for this to work out, I'm for it."

Mary Lou opened the headgates on both sides of the barn, and the cows backed away from the feed troughs. They made their way to the door that Brother now held open.

"A flush toilet. No more walkin' the path," Millie said. She wished she could stop smiling so broadly.

"Yep," Mary Lou said, "I wouldn't miss that in the least."

The meeting with the geologist went well, and the papers were signed. A down payment on the mineral rights changed hands that morning. In addition, there were promises of additional money depending on how well the prospecting progressed.

The installation of indoor plumbing took three weeks. Still, the results were met with glee from each family member, including Snaps' little boy. He received a rubber ducky to play with and soon "oohed" and "ahhed" as the bubbles rose around his chubby face.

"God's been good to us," Mary Lou said as she watched the baby play in the new bathtub.

Snaps convinced herself she couldn't hear what was said over the roar of the water rushing into the tub. She shook her head and piled bubbles on the baby's head.

# Chapter 64

The doctor didn't like blank spaces in his paperwork. He stared at the clipboard. He needed to file this form with the county public health officials, but he couldn't if these slots were empty.

He gripped the steering wheel as he drove to the farm with knuckles turned white. He had an excuse for the visit. It was time for the three month-checkup. The baby could be evaluated for possible birth defects or potential problems passed down by the parents. He'd enjoyed his rotation in pediatrics, and there was a time when he thought of specializing but decided he wanted to be an 'old country doctor' like his father.

He glanced down at his clipboard on the car's front seat next to him. He turned off the motor, grabbed his little black bag, and opened the door. He stepped out and looked at the front of the Wright's house. It was early, but he knew country folk usually awoke at dawn, and babies were also notoriously early risers. He had two other families to visit that morning, and his afternoon schedule was packed. If he had to, the doctor could put off filling out the forms until his next visit. He closed the door and stepped toward the front porch that circled three-quarters of the house.

And then he turned around and opened the car door. "Yank that bandage off quick and get it over with," he heard his father's voice in his memory. Of course, it wasn't advisable with every aspect of wound care, but sometimes it was the best way.

He stepped on the gray planks. One squeaked under his weight. He knocked on the door. He waited until Millie pushed the curtain away from the window and smiled at him.

"Doctor," she said. She smoothed her apron and took a step back. His demeanor impressed her, and she thought about his deep, green eyes. The doctor was nothing like Stanley, yet something about him reminded her of him.

"I'm not new anymore. Maybe you could just call me Robert," the doctor said. He put the clipboard on the rocking chair's seat in the living room.

"Okay, Robert," Millie said. She looked at his shoes. She felt she could tell a lot about a man by how he cared for his shoes. He was likely messy and disorganized if they were muddy, unkempt, and had holes in the soles or cracks in the uppers. But, on the other hand, if his shoes were clean, polished, and well-kept, he was likely that way in other aspects of his life. "The baby's in here."

The bassinet in the dining room sat in a dark corner to encourage the baby to sleep later. Still, he was an early riser, as the doctor suspected he might be. He looked down at the grinning, fat-cheeked face and "cooed" and "aahed" at him. The baby responded and giggled along with the doctor.

The doctor placed his stethoscope around his neck and put the ear tips in his ears. Then, he checked the baby's chest. "Heart and lungs are normal."

"He's a good crier," Millie said. "I mean, he's loud when he wants to be."

"I see, and Ginger is okay? She's not up yet?" The doctor asked as he lifted the baby and held him up to the light.

Millie glanced down at the doctor's shoes. She felt her cheeks redden and put her left hand in her apron pocket. "No, she's still sleeping."

"I see," the doctor said. He knew every mother was different, and some dealt with childcare stress in their own way.

"I'm sure she'll be right down if you need to ask her anythin'."

"I just wanna check on how she's doin'. Any trouble expressing milk?" he asked. He'd found that sometimes new mothers would be too tense to feed their baby and unable to lactate.

"No, she's fine. We supplement with milk from Junior's market."

"And he's regular. No loose stool or constipation?"

Millie felt her cheeks redden again. She took a step back from the bassinet. The slant of early morning sunlight struck her, and as the doctor turned, he saw her, really saw her, for the first time. She wasn't a patient or just another woman on the street. His heart almost leaped from his chest, and he smiled. Millie smiled back, but she didn't know at the time why.

"Regular as the sunrise," Millie said. She felt him staring at her and realized it was the same way Stanley had looked at her as he picked her up for their first date. She felt her heart race and put her other hand in her apron pocket.

"I s-s-see," the doctor said as he weighed the baby, who felt appropriate for his age, and as he unwrapped the swaddling, he found no defects or problems, the same as the first time he'd laid eyes on him.

"Let's go see if Snaps is awake," Millie said.

"Snaps? I always call her Ginger. Oh, now I get it," the doctor said, nodding.

"It was a nickname our father gave her with she was young. She's always been, I guess you could say, energetic."

Doctor Robert followed Millie to Snaps' room. She opened the door, and the hinge squeaked. Millie winced at the sound and slowly walked in. "Snaps," she said, "are you awake?"

Snaps rolled over and looked at the couple. Her eyes were red-rimmed from crying herself to sleep that night. "I'm awake," she mumbled.

She struggled, pushed herself to a sitting position, and let her feet dangle over the edge of the mattress. She had lost much of her baby weight, and her stomach and hips were as slim as before her pregnancy.

"Can you stand up for me?" The doctor asked.

"Yes," Snaps said. She scooted over the side of the bed and stood in her night-gown. Her toes clenched on the cold, hardwood floor.

"Stick out your tongue," the doctor said. He turned her toward the sunlight coming from her window.

"Say ah," Doctor Robert said.

Snaps complied, but she wouldn't look the doctor in the eye. She intuited there was more to this visit than just a routine checkup on her and the baby.

"I've got a form downstairs I need to fill out and file with the county records office." He placed the stethoscope around his neck and put the bell over her heart.

In medical school, he learned about the different heart sounds and what they could tell him about his patients. Physically, Snaps' heart sounded fine, but he felt something was off.

"Can you help me with that?" he asked as innocently as possible.

"I'll try."

"We don't have to put the father's name on the paper. He's just baby Wright, but we must give him a first name."

Snaps slowly shook her head. Then, she pulled away from him and walked out of the bedroom.

"I guess we'll have to wait a little longer on that," Millie said. She frowned and turned, following Snaps through the door.

The doctor put his stethoscope back around his neck and picked up his bag from the rumpled sheets on the bed. The quilt covering the end of the bed featured a wedding ring pattern. He'd seen this before in farmhouse bedrooms and marveled at the ability of the quilter to connect the curves into the matching design.

"Wedding ring quilt," the doctor said to himself.

# Chapter 65

Preparing for Christmas included the creation of new ornaments for the tree and the butchering of the largest hen in the coop.

Brother's expertise with his crosscut saw meant he and one of the girls, usually Millie, would stomp through the woods near the house on a frosty morning and decide which cedar tree would be best suited to set in the front hallway.

"This is the first year for the baby," Millie said.

"He's too little to know what's goin' on," Brother replied as he pushed a branch out of his way. The wooded area was adjacent to the family farm and drew dove hunters from the town in droves. This wasn't the season, so it was safe to roam the area, but when in season, the air was thick with the sounds of gunfire and yelping dogs.

"I'll take pictures," she said. She ducked under the branch Brother had pushed and grabbed her hat, which was just about to fall from her head.

"I guess he'll need some presents," the old man grumbled. He wanted a cigarette, but he knew it wasn't good for his lungs, so he chewed on a toothpick.

"Yes, he'll need some." Millie smirked, "Very funny."

"Some people think I'm not funny."

"You can be hilarious," Millie said as she scanned the tree line, "when you wanna be."

"How about that one?" he asked, pointing to the northern edge of the stand.

"We can't get the first one we run across."

"Well, if'n it's the right one," Brother argued.

"We got to see some more so we can get the best one," Millie said.

"And if'n this one is the best one?"

Millie nodded, "Then we'll come back for it."

"Great," Brother said. He didn't have any other plans for the day, so this was as good a way to kill the hours as any other. But, of course, there was always something that needed fixing or building on a farm. Still, even Brother needed an occasional day off.

They found four other trees that met Millie's height, limb thickness, and smell requirements but returned to the first tree. Brother sawed the trunk at ground level, and the tree fell on the soft, brown grass. A tangle of briars encircled the branches, but Millie used her knife to cut the limbs free. For Millie, it was a perfect tree.

They dragged the cedar across the meadow and up on the front porch. Then, finally, Brother hammered two boards to the bottom of the cut, and they dragged the tree into the house.

Millie, Mary Lou, and Snaps took ornaments from a cardboard box and trimmed the tree. There were glass ornaments and tinsel left over from last year and the previous year added to the string of freshly popped corn.

The chattering continued as the baby slept in a rocking chair, propped up on pillows. His mouth would move in a sucking motion as he slept. Finally, his hands were free, and his thumb found his mouth.

"Are Anne and Jody coming over tonight?" Millie asked. She draped tinsel on the top limbs because she was the tallest of the girls.

"Maybe, it depends on a delivery of some bull Jody's father ordered," Snaps said. She squatted in front of the tree and hung homemade ornaments the girls had made over the years.

Brother sat next to the baby. He folded his newspaper and watched the conclusion of the decorating.

"Lookin' pretty good there," he said. It was a perfect tree. But, there was a time he wondered if Millie would ever become enough of her old self to decide as simple a thing as which tree to bring home for Christmas.

"You done good, girl," Mary Lou said. The family tradition was almost complete. It was up to Snaps now. Could she, would she, was the question?

Millie and Mary Lou stepped back and looked at the tree. Snaps reached her tiptoes and placed the star on the tree's peak.

Snaps knew what they were expecting. It was something she'd done every year since she was small. It was one of those family traditions that had grown and flourished as Snaps' innate talent became honed and fully developed.

"O holy night, the stars are brightly shining," Snaps started the song without searching for the right key. She started low because she knew she'd end on a high note. "It is the night of our dear Savior's birth." She paused as if a piano was playing, and the connecting bridge filled the room with music. "Long lay the world in sin and error pining," she sang, closing her eyes now. "Till He appeared and the soul felt its worth."

Mary Lou watched in amazement as Snaps sang. It was as if she could see the child reaching deep into her soul and rejoicing in the birth of Jesus.

"A thrill of hope the weary world rejoices," Snaps' voice added a rhythm that reminded Brother's untrained ears of the long marches and drills he'd performed in the Army.

"For yonder breaks a new and glorious morn," Snaps' voice quivered on the word 'glorious,' and Millie wondered if she would make it through the chorus. Was there enough of the old Snaps left in there?

"Fall on your knees," Snaps opened her mouth, and the phrase became an acknowledgment of her sorrow of the last year. She felt it all now, and there was no going back to how she was.

"O hear the angels' voices," she sang, and Brother rocked. He watched Mary Lou as she listened, now with her eyes closed and silently mouthing the words.

"O night divine," Snaps held the word 'divine' for a full five seconds. Then, she took a deep breath, losing herself in her performance. "O night when Christ was born," she sang, now softer and lower, building to, for this performance, the ending. Strong and mighty now, "O night divine, o night," soft and slow now, holding the last note, "O night divine."

The baby's eyes fixed on Snaps. His rhythmic sucking matched the pace of the song. Finally, as Snaps finished, the baby removed his thumb from his mouth and laughed with joy.

Brother had stopped rocking and felt a tear fall from the corner of his eye. It was unusual for him to cry. He'd lost friends in the trenches and more when they were ordered to advance. He'd often wondered why he was alive, and they were all gone. Now, he didn't wonder but was merely grateful.

Mary Lou stepped back and looked at the tree. The lamplight shone on the tinsel, and the star at the top seemed to be winking at her. She knew in her heart that her youngest daughter was back. She had returned from the dark place and had decided to rejoin the world. All that had happened to her was a prologue. Now she would return to the townspeople who loved her, the church members who marveled at her, and the Lord who had given her the talent to lead others to Christ.

Millie crossed her arms and put one foot in front of the other. She felt grateful but less for the season and the birth of Christ. She had an idea.

# Chapter 66

Snaps sat on the edge of her bed. She had no idea how often she'd looked at the slip of paper. It might have been hundreds. But, on the other hand, it might have been thousands of times.

The name was unfamiliar to her, but she knew the city and what the address denoted. The office on Broadway was likely over the theater downstairs, meaning it was over nine hundred miles away. That was, supposed Snaps, if she wanted to go, it would be a long train ride.

She looked at the paper and mouthed the name. She held the form up to the moonlight and realized her chance of traveling there was as likely as her stepping on the moon.

Millie sat in the rocking chair and watched Snaps look at the paper. She held the baby and marveled at how his fingers clutched his bottle. "*So small and so perfect,*" she thought, "*how could something so wonderful come from hatred and violence?*"

"You have a gift," Millie said.

She couldn't read Snaps' thoughts, but she surmised the paper in Mrs. Northcutt's block-letter handwriting meant something to Snaps.

"So," Snaps said, "I'm a mother, too. What else am I?"

The day ended with the opening of presents and Mary Lou's ordering the family to bed early so that everyone would be rested when Anne and Jody showed up the following day. Jody's family traditionally opened presents on Christmas morning, while the Wrights were a Christmas Eve family. The Wright family historically saved Christmas morning for church. New family members meant changes in habits and routines.

Mary Lou stuck her head in the doorway and said, "Girls, get to bed. We've got a big day tomorrow."

"I want to go to New York," Snaps said. She was looking out the window when she said it and couldn't turn around and face her mother.

"You're needed here," Mary Lou said as she stepped into the room. "Your baby needs you."

"I want to go," Snaps said and turned around. She looked at her mother and Millie as she rocked the baby. She could tell in the dim light that he had finished his bottle and would be asleep soon.

"That's just not goin' to happen. You've got responsibilities. I've got a responsibility to keep this family together no matter what," Mary Lou said, her voice gaining in volume but low enough to not wake up the baby.

"I need to go," Snaps said. She placed her feet shoulder-width apart and squared her shoulders. It was as if she were standing on stage, and the iris of the spotlight slipped open. She prepared herself for conflict. "If I don't, I'll never know if I could have done it. That'd nag at me the rest of my life."

"No," Mary Lou said. She had squared her shoulders, too. Her face tipped down, and she looked at Snaps through shielded eyelids. "That baby is a Wright, and he needs a momma."

"I'll take him," Millie said.

Mary Lou turned and glared at Millie. "You stay out of this. God says we need to stay together, and that's how it's gonna be."

Brother appeared in the doorway. "What's all the ruckus?"

His long, striped nightshirt hung just past his knees. The girls had rarely seen him in this outfit, and if it weren't for the seriousness of the conversation, someone would have made a snide remark.

"Snaps here wants to go to New York," Mary Lou said. A tone of disappointment crept into her voice, and she turned her glare to Brother as if that might help bolster her argument.

"She's almost eighteen," Brother started, "after that, she can do pretty much anything she wants."

"She ain't goin' anywhere except to bed, so we can have Anne and Jody over tomorrow and then go to church," Mary Lou said emphatically.

"I ain't goin' to church tomorrow either," Snaps said. She was still standing in her fighting position, and her arms were crossed over her chest. She seldom used the word 'ain't' and never challenged her mother.

"You'll do as you're told or...."

Snaps cut her off, "I'll have to leave?"

"Now, hold on, the two of you," Brother started. They were all aware of the sleeping baby, so the volume of the voices didn't match the intensity of the words. "Y'all don't wanna start sayin' somethin' you can't take back. I've been down that road, and it's a lonely place."

The baby murmured in Millie's arms, and she stood, walked across the room, and placed him in the bassinet. She looked first at Brother, then Mary Lou, and finally at Snaps.

"I'll take him. I'll be his momma."

"No, that settles it. Now, everybody get to bed," Mary Lou said as if anyone could close their eyes tonight.

"Snaps, I can look at him and not see the face of a bastard who's trying to kill me," Millie said. "*You* can't."

Snaps' eyes softened, and her voice quivered. "But what about going to Europe?"

Millie smiled and said, "I'll go, just not today, this month, or this year. But I'll go someday."

"I can take him with me to New York. Mrs. Northcutt's raisin' her son all by herself. If'n she can do it, so can I," Snaps implored.

"She's not raisin' a child in New York," Millie said. "And she has family here to help. You won't."

"I can't saddle you with somethin' like this, Millie," Snaps said. But, of course, she'd stopped watching her mother and Brother by now.

"You have a gift. I see it every time you sing, dance, or do crazy speeches on your rock. The world needs to hear you," Millie said. She took Snaps' hand and squeezed. "Please, let me do this."

"But," Snaps said. Tears gathered in her eyes, and she wiped at one with her free hand.

"We'll call him Stanley Frank Wright," Millie said. She paused and emphasized each of the names. "He'll know me as his mother until the time you tell him and not before."

"But what about the people in town," Snaps said. She knew the damage to Millie's reputation if she showed up with a baby.

"Pish posh," Millie said, smiling. "I ain't worried about that. And you shouldn't either. It ain't nobody's business, and that's for sure."

They both laughed. Mary Lou considered jumping in again and pleading her case, but before she could, Brother said, "Then it's settled, and we can all go to bed now."

"But...," Mary Lou began, but a look from Brother stopped her.

"Let's all go now," Brother said, "we've got a big day tomorrow. It's baby Stanley's first Christmas."

Brother's time overseas, seeing so much death and hatred, had given him a way of imagining the big picture. He had lived and known everyone's time on Earth was short. He knew Snaps' talent could take her far, but the clock was ticking, and he knew the pain and sorrow of lost opportunities.

As he crossed the threshold, he felt a hand grab his elbow. He turned. Snaps put her arms around Brother's neck and hugged him. It had been years since someone had embraced Brother that way.

He remembered how he was just a boy standing in the lobby of Union Station. He started shaking, and his mother took him in her arms until he stopped.

"You'll be all right," she said. "I'll be right here when you get back."

She was gone when the war ended and he'd returned from Germany. But he would remember that hug for the rest of his life, just as he'd remember this one from Snaps.

"My daddy Frank would be proud," Snaps said. Her voice cracked, and she could feel Brother crying, too.

"Yes, he'd be proud of you, too," Brother said. He nodded and walked into the hallway. He threw his shoulders back as he'd been taught in France and marched to his room.

# Chapter 67

The outer double doors of the church were open even though the temperature was nippy. Families brought casseroles and baked goods. Anne's famous muffins were always a hit and sat at their usual place at the head of the table. Children in the Sunday school classes expected little gifts from the church and were not disappointed. Everyone got something. This tradition started during the Depression when many members knew poor families would have nothing under their trees.

Snaps sat in her usual spot, the first chair of the choir, and she sang her solo, "O Holy Night," with the same verve and emotion she brought to every delivery.

Millie sat next to Mary Lou and Brother and beamed at Snaps' stellar performance. The discussion about her possibly leaving her baby and her hometown was still going on, but Millie felt Mary Lou wavering. They knew this would always be Snaps' home, but her future was elsewhere.

The preacher's message this Christmas included the usual reading of the story of Jesus' birth, how his life came from humble beginnings, and how he changed the world. Snaps sat staring at the minister's back, occasionally glancing at the quiet baby sleeping in Millie's arms.

The preacher turned to the future and said he believed 1947 would be another excellent year for believers. Brother squirmed in his seat as the young man began rattling off all the great things God would do for everyone. Brother only attended church for the big holidays and was found wandering the woods on most Sunday mornings, but he knew how important it was to make a good impression on the townsfolk, and he didn't want to be one of the only sinners in town.

The meeting ended with the children clutching their presents and their mouths filled with candy they'd been ordered to hold in their pockets until they got outside. Then, finally, the preacher stood on the steps and shook hands with the parishioners. They all told him they loved his message and how much his service meant to them.

Across the parking lot, a lone figure moved through the clusters of families and children, darting from one side of the gravel square to the other. Brother saw him first and took off his hat. A part of him said he needed to be ready for a fight. Mary Lou saw him second, and she too knotted her hands into fists, though there was little she could do if it really did escalate into fisticuffs. Millie and the baby came next, nodding and chatting with the minister, followed closely behind by Snaps. Then, finally, they both saw Jess Comer ambling across the lot and looked at each other as if to say, "What kind of business could he have here?"

Jess took off his hat and stuck a small, brown bag under his arm. The preacher approached him and stuck out his hand. This man had been on his list for years, and this was the first time the minister had gotten him on his turf.

"Welcome to First Baptist," the young man said. He'd been a war chaplain and dealt with some demanding customers in the South Pacific.

"Thanks, I'm here to see the baby," Jess said. He'd combed his hair, but a thin cowlick stood at attention at the crown of his head.

Mary Lou started to say something, but Brother beat her to it. He eyed the man as he looked down on him from the second step of the church portico. He'd seen men prepared to fight, and he'd seen men who were searching for peace. Then, finally, Brother said, "Hey, Jess," he smiled and turned to Millie. "Come here, Mill. Let him see the baby."

Mary Lou fumed, but she held her tongue. Snaps stepped back as Millie nodded and brought the baby down the steps. She stood next to Jess and pulled back the baby's blanket.

The noon sun startled the boy, and he was about to start crying when Millie shielded his eyes with her hand. The baby instantly stopped and looked at Jess.

The old man smiled down at the baby. "He's a good-lookin' boy."

"His name is Stanley Frank Wright," Millie said.

"I didn't know that," Jess said. "I mean, I heard y'all had him, but I didn't know his name."

Snaps said, "We named him for our father and Stanley."

"Yes," Jess said, "your father was a fine man. I always liked him." He took a breath and touched the boy's forehead.

"I hoped y'all would be here at church today," Jess said.

"We'd love to have you join us next Sunday, Mr. Comer," the preacher piped up.

Jess glanced at him and smiled. "Anything can happen, preacher," he said, "anything can happen."

Jess pulled the sack from under his arm and gave it to Millie. Snaps took it and looked inside.

"Thanks for coming by," Millie said to the retreating old man.

Snaps pulled a pair of tiny Sunday go-to-meeting shoes out of the bag. The highly polished leather shone in the bright sunlight.

As Jess moved out of earshot, Mary Lou said, "Is that it? Do you think that's all he's ever gonna give you?"

"Anything is possible," Millie said, believing every word of that sentence. She smiled down at Stanley.

Snaps said, "Maybe that's all he's got left of the money."

The preacher wasn't entirely in on the joke, but he laughed along with the rest of them as they stood in God's holy and merciful light.

# Chapter 68

Mary Lou rocked back and forth in her favorite chair. It was one of the few that Frank had made for her so long ago. She touched the arm, making her believe it was his arm.

She thought about what had happened and wanted to add the next chapter to her journal. She liked poetry, but she loved her journal. So some entries went on for pages. The days the children were born. The days when the children graduated from high school. The days when the only thing she could report was that "it rained."

She would fill seventeen books worth of events before she passed away. Those pages would help her grandchildren and great-grandchildren answer the questions they would have as society progressed and generations ended. But her poetry was relegated to two single books.

There were only ninety-nine poems in the two books, with no torn-out pages and crossed-out words as the journal pages were transferred as a finished product to the poetry books.

Three poems topped her list of favorites, and the one she wrote on the day Snaps left for New York meant the most.

*The Faithful Few*
*Those who say nothing can be done,*
*Don't have their faith in the holy one.*
*Clouds that cover a rainbow due,*
*Will see the sun soon breaking through*
*When tempest roil and seafoam boils*
*The blessed ones are those who toil*
*The ones who till the rocky soil*

*My friends and family rejoice*
*The faithful few have made their choice*
*That life and love forever save*
*I call the survivors eternally brave*

# Chapter 69

They said their goodbyes on the front porch. It was a blustery January morning, but the temperature had moderated by the afternoon, and a bright, white sun filled the sky.

Snaps had packed all she thought she might need for the trip and ensured her cash was in separate places. So she put a third of her money in her pocket, a third in her purse, and the last third in her suitcase.

She looked around her room, glanced at the teddy bear sitting on the pillows at the head of the bed, and turned to see Brother in the doorway.

Snaps wore simple black pants, a white shirt, and black boots. She would put on a jacket downstairs.

"Do ya think you've got everything?" he asked.

"I'll just buy what I need if I've forgotten anything," Snaps said, looking up at him and smiling.

"You'll be fine," Brother said. He leaned against the door frame. He remembered how he'd shipped off to war from his room and what leaving felt like. Nevertheless, he believed Snaps would come back someday to live or visit. Either way, it was OK with him.

"I got scammed right as I stepped off the train," he said.

"How so?"

"There was a guy on the sidewalk with a table set up. It's a game called three-card monte. He'd take three playing cards and put them face down on the table. He showed the Queen and then shifted the cards around and over. You had to pick out of the three where the Queen was."

"I guess you had to pay to play," Snaps said. She sat her suitcase down next to the bed. She surmised it might take a while for this story to unfold.

"You'd bet a dollar and win the first three or four times. That felt good. And then you'd bet, maybe make it two dollars, and before you know'd it, you were losing."

"How much did you lose?"

"Ten dollars, I'll never forget it."

"So," Snaps said, smiling. "avoid the 'three-card monte.'"

"And anything else that looks kinda shady," Brother said, nodding. "We'd better get goin'. The bus to the train station is always on time."

They gathered up her belongings and made their way downstairs. Snaps' eyes widened, trying to take in as much as possible so she'd never forget her home.

Mary Lou, Millie, and Anne waited on the porch steps. Millie held Stanley Frank and tickled him under his chin so he'd be laughing when Snaps saw him.

She took him from Millie and hugged him. Then, Millie said, "There will be a time when you think of your baby, and you're gonna get a smile before you get a tear. I guarantee it."

"I know you're right," Snaps said as she touched the baby's cheek. He smiled at her.

Snaps turned and walked to the truck without looking back. Brother followed her, his keys jingling on his ring.

Snaps handed her suitcase and bags to the driver at the bus station. She turned and looked at Brother. She expected him to be sad, but he was smiling. "You take care," he said.

Snaps hugged him, and he put his arms around her waist. "I will. No 'three card monte' for me."

They both laughed, and she turned and put her foot on the bus's bottom step. She scanned the square of the little town, bustling now with shoppers, farmers, and professional people.

She took her seat near the window and waved to Brother as the bus pulled away from the station. A layover in Roanoke halved the over thirty hours on the trail.

Snaps read, slept, and ate as she watched the small towns and big cities pass by her window.

When she came out of Grand Central Station in mid-town Manhattan, she couldn't help but look at the buildings. She'd never seen anything so tall and with so many crammed together. She waved down a taxi and told the driver to take her to a hotel near Broadway. She still had the slip of paper Mrs. Northcutt had given her so long ago, even though she'd memorized every letter.

As the driver whizzed around the crowded streets, Snaps saw a crumpled paper on the taxi floor. She picked it up and read the masthead, *Backstage*. She flipped through the pages and saw lines of ads where actors could audition.

She checked into her room, put away her suitcase, and hid her money. Then, she rechecked the paper and walked downstairs. She was only a few blocks from the theater, and even though the temperature was colder than back home, it wasn't unbearable.

She found the backstage entrance and the stage manager. She said she wanted to audition, and the woman with flashing green eyes and jet-black hair handed her a clipboard. "Fill this out, honey," she said.

A line of other actresses was trying out, and Snaps fell in behind a thin, chain-smoking young woman with blonde hair and blue eyes. "I hope I get this," she said as she filled out the form.

Snaps filled in the hotel's name but not the address because she couldn't remember it. So instead, she listed the productions she'd performed in high school and some of her favorite songs. She'd read in *Backstage* that the part required singing and acting. She took a deep breath and smiled as she handed the papers back to the stage manager.

The manager was the mother to a single daughter. She looked at her list of actresses and realized this was the last audition, and she'd get home in time for dinner. How could someone named Ginger Wright from Tennessee have anything close to what the highly educated and trained actresses from Yale, The Old Vic, and California offer to this part? It was an open audition, and while the girl was a beauty in both face and figure, the manager didn't see any way she could compete with these highly trained and experienced actresses.

Snaps thought about all that had happened to her in the past two years and how she had matured into a woman and then a mother. She had felt anger, sadness, joy, hate, and love. She had thought of throwing herself off her rock stage in a fit of anguish and desperation.

She now understood the words, and her performance reflected that newly found insight. She took a deep breath and looked at the darkened theater with empty seats. A single row of five people sat in the middle of the auditorium. One man lit a cigarette and said, "Okay, Ginger, show us what you've got."

"I'm Snaps," she said.

"Oh, right, ginger snaps," the smoking man said. He took a deep breath and blew smoke from the side of his mouth. "Go right ahead."

He turned and started talking to another man seated two chairs over. The director nodded and turned his gaze back to the stage. He liked the way the girl looked and the way she stood there on the stage. She didn't have the hair coloring or skin tone he'd imagined for the character. Still, he knew it was essential to be flexible in casting. He had a weird gut feeling about this actress that had served him well in the past, and something told him to pay attention.

Snaps had a feeling, too. She imagined herself back home on her rock stage, looking out on the tree line as a beam of sunlight drifted behind the trees.

"To be," she began. Her voice was firm, steady, and filled with confidence, knowledge, and experience.

She stood in the center of the stage and felt the white, hot light of the spotlight on her face. She was home now.

Snaps said, "Or not to be."

## THE END

# Leave a Review

I hope you enjoyed this novel – if you did, I'd appreciate you writing a short review. Your ratings make a difference for authors; you're also helping other readers find books they might enjoy.

You can rate this book or leave a review at:

**Amazon**

**www.amazon.com**

**Goodreads**

**https://www.goodreads.com/#_=_**

**Barnes and Noble**

**https://www.barnesandnoble.com/**

Or your preferred retailer.

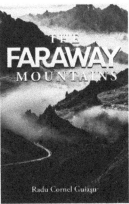

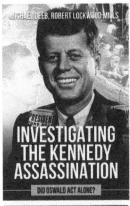
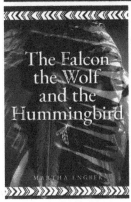
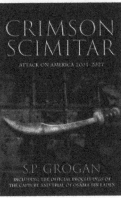